To. De

For all the good times, for our wonderful friendship over the years and a thank you for just being you.

Marion. 27-11-97.

Marion Clark, a miner's daughter, was born in the village of Cwmaman, Aberdare.

Married with one daughter, and two grandchildren, she is a Civil Servant by profession.

Already successful at having several poems published, 'Back to the Land' which has been reviewed on *Radio Wales'* literary programme 'Now Read On', is her first novel.

BACK TO THE LAND

by

MARION CLARK

Printed and bound by
Qualitex Printing Limited, Cardiff

Published by
Marion Clark

ISBN No. 0 9532110 0 2

Acknowledgement of thanks to

PETER FINCH
THE STATIONERY OFFICE
ORIEL BOOKSHOP
CARDIFF
FOR HIS INTEREST AND ADVICE

To Bryan

* * *

To Laura and Thomas
my grandchildren

* * *

And to all my family and friends
whose belief in me made the
dream come true

CHAPTER 1

A fine, damp mist hung low over the Preseli hills as Peter Malone the quiet Irishman was laid to rest in the tiny graveyard of Elim Chapel.

Anna his beautiful young widow glanced at the crowd of mourners around her, many of whom had come to pay homage to the gentle man who had left his native Ireland across the water, to seek a new life here on the Western Coast of Wales. A life which he had now lost, long before his time was due.

The silence of the day was broken only by the solemn voice of the Minister Goronwy Evans as he began to pray.

Anna soon became oblivious to his words as she began to cast her mind back to that eventful day when she had met the man she was to love and had now lost.

In her mind she heard Marged's voice calling out to her.

'Hurry along Anna, we'll be late for market!' Together they quickly gathered their baskets of eggs and their mother's newly baked scones ready to sell there, while their father gave them final instructions to return as soon as they could.

Owen and Huw their younger brothers had been envious of them as they set out on their journey as both boys were required to stay behind to help on the farm.

Soon the girls reached the market town which was already bustling with folk setting up their stalls in the hope of a good day's trading.

The smell of freshly baked bread wafted through the air causing their mouths to water. Anna raised her hand to wave to Susi Rees whose loaves of bread and Bara Brith were famed for miles around.

Further along stood Mrs Wil Edwards placing jars of home-made jams and pickled onions neatly on her stall, while stone jars of salt butter stood like a regiment of soldiers one behind the other. Large joints of smoked bacon hung from iron hooks ready to cut into succulent slices of meat to be sold.

Twm Rees' younger boy passed by, selling bunches of green mint which he held in his hand, while sprigs of sage hung from the belt of his breeches. These too were for sale.

Gwillym Williams, the boy who had never learned to speak, sat nearby whittling a piece of wood with a sharp knife. His hands moved quickly as he fashioned and modelled the shape taking place. Around his feet were displayed an assortment of wooden animals each one identical to the wild animals found in the nearby forests.

A voice called out to the two sisters. It was their friend Kate Harries, as she arranged row upon row of colourful silk ribbons on a wooden tray, which she began to fasten around her neck with strong twine of cord.

'Where are you going to stand?' she asked them. Marged and Anna looked around and saw a small open space nearby, and proceeded to it. There they began to sell what they had brought.

There were people everywhere and the air was filled with strange exciting sounds. Soon everything they had was sold except for a few scones. Then they saw the friendly face of Wil 'Cup of Tea' approaching them. He asked if their Mam had made scones. Anna nodded to him and he quickly bought the fruity buns.

'She has always had a light hand with scones, your Mam,' he said. 'These will do nicely with my cup of tea later on.'

The sisters smiled at each other as he paid for them. Wil had certainly lived up to the nickname that the villagers had given him.

Pleased now that all was sold, Marged and Anna decided to enjoy what little time they had left before returning home. This was the mid-week market, which was not usually as busy as the one held on Saturdays. However, today seemed busier than usual.

They wandered among the stalls stopping here and there to look at the various things for sale and soon found that the morning had passed by quickly.

Suddenly they came across an old woman who sat crocheting pieces of fine lace from pretty coloured silk threads. Her fingers moved deftly causing the lace to grow into many intricate patterns before their very eyes.

Anna became fascinated with her movements, and as the old lady saw the delight in the young girl's face she stopped what she was doing and placed the needle and silks at her side. She then delved her fingers into a basket nearby and took out a small piece of fine lace, which she held out to Anna.

Anna immediately shook her head and politely refused the offer, but the old lady then said,

'Take it my dear, it will bring you luck.'

Anna thanked her and placed the gift in her pocket, then quickly ran after Marged who had walked on ahead of her.

There was still so much for them to see before they headed for home.

As they turned the corner near the old Market Tavern, Anna came face to face with a tall young man who stood drinking from a large mug of ale.

He did not resemble any of the local lads she knew. His tousled hair was red in colour and as their eyes met she noticed the twinkle in them. He held her gaze for a moment and she suddenly felt embarrassed, and as she began to blush, the feeling caused her whole body to quiver.

'Come over here Anna,' called Marged in her native Welsh tongue.

'What is she saying?' asked the young man in a strange accent of his own.

Anna looked at him, wondering whether or not to reply to the stranger.

'My sister is calling me to join her. She wants me to see the shawls on display over there,' she replied.

As she began to walk away, the young man placed the mug down on a table nearby and began to walk after her to where Marged stood waiting.

'Excuse me,' he said politely, trying to introduce himself 'My name is Peter Malone and I've come from Ireland to look for work but so far I've not had much luck. Do you by any chance know where I might find a night's lodgings in these parts?'

Anna, however, felt sorry for the handsome young man as she said,

'We're pleased to meet you Mr. Malone. My name is Anna Lewis and this is my sister Marged. We live not too far from here, and there are a number of farms in the area who take on help during this time each year.' Looking at her sister she then added, 'What do you think Marged? Wasn't Twm Rees looking for extra help? I'm sure Da said that he was offering work and a bed in the barn to go along with it.'

'Now Anna, don't be hasty. I expect Mr. Malone is seeking something more worthwhile than the work of a farmhand with little wages,' said Marged sternly.

Anna's eyes searched those of the young man for an answer and he quickly replied.

'I'd be willing to take anything, that I will. I'm desperate to do any kind of work at present, with a view of bettering meeself in the future of course. So if you good ladies will direct me to this farm I'll not be troubling you further.' With that, he placed the cap he took from his pocket, on his head covering a mass of curly hair, and prepared to go on his way.

Anna hastily turned to Marged.

'It's on our way isn't it? We'd be only too happy to show you Mr Malone.'

The three of them walked away from the market. Anna and the stranger in front while Marged followed behind having little option to like it or not.

The way to Twm Rees' farm lay at the top end of the village. Anna cast her eyes toward the stranger now and then, as they walked along the peaceful leafy lanes.

He did not seem like most of the other Irishmen she'd heard her father speak of, men who although they worked hard on the land, were hard drinking men when the time came around. There were not many taverns to be found here and there in the countryside, but the few that were had made sure the Irishmen were welcome when payday came around. This of course did not sit well with local folk who although they were hard working people they sought their enjoyment in their Chapel services along with their families.

Peter Malone broke the silence between them as he began to tell them of his journey by boat to nearby Fishguard.

As he spoke in his soft lilting voice, something told Anna that this would not be the last time their paths would cross.

Soon they reached the crossroads where one road led to Llanboidy and the other to Login. Marged by now was quite determined to break up their cosy chat and quickly gave directions to the farm in the distance.

Then speaking sharply to Anna she said, 'Now then Anna, it's time we were getting back. You know what Da has said.'

On hearing this, Peter Malone looked directly at Anna with a grateful look in his eyes and said, 'I'm much obliged to you for your help.' Then turning to Marged he added 'I hope to be seeing more of you both if I am lucky enough to stay.'

He lifted his hand; touched his cap lightly to them then began to climb over the stile and proceeded across the field toward the farm.

'Remove that silly look from your face Anna before we reach home,' said Marged.

'What do you mean?' replied Anna smiling innocently, but Marged had already turned away proceeding up the lane at a fast pace.

Anna followed meekly behind; her thoughts still with the stranger. She hoped fervently that he would get the work he sought, for she had already decided that she wanted to see him again.

CHAPTER 2

Cefn Glas was a small, thriving farm as good as many a farm to be found in the surrounding Welsh countryside.

Wil Lewis had inherited it from his father and grandfather before him and he was proud of the land, which gave him his livelihood, and of the family who shared it with him.

Although times were hard, he was grateful of the family now grown who helped him in the duties of the farm. However, he ruled them with an iron hand as he, himself had been ruled by a strict father.

Owen and Huw, his two young sons, already knew what was expected of them and the roles they had to play to keep the good name of Cefn Glas, their home.

Wil looked up from the fence he was mending and stopped to wipe the sweat, which trickled from his forehead downward to his chin. He surveyed the land around as the sun shadowed the surrounding fields each one resembling pieces of a patchwork quilt. God, but it was good to be alive on such a day as this he thought to himself. He returned to what he was doing, wishing he had brought one of the boys up to the top field with him. He could have finished the fence so much sooner.

'Da, I've brought your lunch.'

He looked up to see Anna walking along the path toward him. In her hand she carried a basket with a muslin cloth over the top of it.

'I've brought you bread and cheese,' she said.

'It's thirsty I am merchi,' was his reply.

Her father wiped the sweat from his hands against his breeches and sat down on the green grass where he proceeded to guzzle the water from a bottle, which she held out to him.

Anna did not join him as she stood and said,

'Mam is asking if you'll be much longer up here. Don't forget we have the Chapel Meeting this evening.'

'Tell her I've not forgotten,' he replied munching now at the rather large fresh slice of bread while holding a wedge of strong smelling golden cheese in his other hand.

'I'll not be long,' he said in between another mouthful of food. 'Tell her to warm the water for me to wash by the time I come down in another hour or so. Will you?'

'I'll be going, then Da,' said Anna, 'I've other things to get on with.'

'Why didn't you have one of the boys to bring my food?' he asked, 'It's quite a climb up here on a hot day merchi.'

'I wanted to come myself,' said Anna laughing as she turned away to walk back down to the lower field. 'I just had to have an excuse to get a way from the farm on such a lovely day', she called, waving her hand in farewell to him.

Wil Lewis turned back again to his work. Even though he had no favourites among his children, it was always Anna that could please him the most with her kind, thoughtful ways. He knew that sooner or later both his girls would take their turns in becoming fine wives but he secretly hoped that the time would not come for some time yet.

Now he really had to stop daydreaming if he was to finish in the top field today, and so he proceeded once more to carry on with the tedious task before him.

The Chapel Meeting was the highlight of the week and it would be there, she might hear whether he had found work and was still here in the village. She could hardly wait as he had been on her mind constantly since they had met.

The bright orange sun had begun to set over the brow of the hill as the Lewis family walked together to their Chapel. Beti and Wil, his Bible tucked beneath his arm, walked in front. Owen and Huw followed, while Marged and Anna brought up the rear.

Wil Lewis had the honour of being a Chapel Deacon and was held in high esteem.

Anna was very proud of her father, especially when his deep baritone voice rang out in Chapel while he sang his favourite hymns.

She understood how her mother had chosen such a strong character of a man, and prayed that she too would meet that kind of person one day.

Her heart leaped as she saw Twm Rees and his family enter the Chapel and wondered if the young man had found work with them.

The service seemed endless as the Minister's voice droned on and on. The seat beneath her had become so hard she began to fidget until Marged began to nudge her arm to be still.

At last it was over, the service had come to an end and the congregation began to file out of the building one by one.

As Anna came out through the large oak door she noticed her father was already in conversation with Twm Rees and so she calmly walked over to join them.

'A good day's work today, then Wil?' asked Twm. 'Have you finished in the top field yet?'

'No,' replied her father 'I hope to finish tomorrow or the day after.'

'I've done very well,' Twm contrived, 'I've hired a hand. A willing lad at that, which makes the work so much easier. He's an Irish boy and although I've not had much to do with his kind, I am very satisfied with him. It looks as if I'm going to finish a lot sooner than I thought. What about you, Wil? Are you needing help as I know the lad is desperate for work?'

'We shall see,' replied Wil. 'I may need someone after all as there are jobs my boys can't handle, and if the lad is as good as you say he is, he might well come in handy.'

On hearing her father's words Anna's heart began to race and she could feel a warm flush entering her face at the thought of meeting the stranger once more.

'Anna, what's the matter?' asked Beti who had noticed how flushed her daughter had become. 'Are you feeling alright?' she asked again.

It was young Huw who spoke up, 'I expect it's because Ifor Evans has asked to walk her home Mam.'

'Shut up,' said Anna angrily to her brother. 'Ifor must be tired of me refusing to walk with him each week. Just because he's the Minister's son am I supposed to say yes,' she said.

She quickly tried to hide her embarrassment but Marged had caught the look in Anna's eyes, which tried to hide her true feelings.

Later when they were alone Marged asked her, 'You're not going to put your mind on the stranger coming to work here are you? It would not be good for you Anna, you are asking for trouble.'

Anna did not reply, but shook her dark brown curly hair in a 'devil may care' attitude. Marged could think what she liked, she would hope and pray that Peter Malone's next job would be here at Cefn Glas.

After supper she excused herself and went upstairs to the room she shared with Marged as she wished to be left alone.

As she lay on the bed breathing in the night scented air, she began to whisper her prayers softly and ended in saying,

'Dear Lord, please let the stranger's path lead here so we may meet again. Amen.' Gradually after much tossing and turning in her bed she finally fell asleep.

The early morning sun shone brightly through chintz curtains, heralding yet another warm day.

She looked toward Marged who was still asleep, then stretched out her arms and began to move quietly so as not to wake her sister.

She put her head back on the pillow for a second or two trying to remember her thoughts of the previous night.

What on earth had come over her?

She felt ashamed that she, Anna Lewis had actually prayed to the Almighty to bring Peter Malone to her. He would probably have no time for the likes of a farmer's daughter. Didn't he say he was only here until something better came along? Well then, she would waste no further romantic notions on him. With that thought she pushed back the covers and called to Marged to wake up. There was a good deal of chores to get through today.

Beti Lewis looked at her youngest daughter with pride. Anna had grown from the tomboy of yesterday into a beautiful young girl. Many a lad in the village was ready to come calling on her if Wil would give them half a chance.

Wil however, chose not to remember how his own heart led him to court his beloved Beti and he had decided for the present that no one would be good enough for either of his daughters. Not just yet, at any rate!'

'A penny for your thoughts Mam,' said Anna. 'Did you hear what I said about the washing?' she asked her mother.

'They are worth more than a penny merchi,' answered Beti. 'I've gathered all the clothes together and there's plenty of rainwater to be boiled. But first have your breakfast.'

Marged then entered the room.

'Call the boys will you?' asked Beti. 'There's plenty of warm porridge in the pan. Enough for everyone.'

Marged nodded, went to the foot of the stairs and called to the two brothers in a loud voice. She was answered by several grunts and groans but soon the three women could hear them moving about above them in an attempt to get up.

'Finish your breakfast while I get some more wood for the fire, then the water will soon be ready', said Beti wiping her hands on her apron.

She gathered the wood outside and in hardly any time at all the water had boiled, the washing was done by the three women working in unison, and soon the sheets were billowing in the breeze as the garden line groaned with the weight of them.

Anna helped her sister as she was told, while Marged said,

'Mam, has decided to bake bread for Twm Rees, she's asked me to take some to him when I've finished here.'

'It's alright, Marged, I can go now if you like', said Anna.

'I know your little game,' answered Marged 'you're hoping the Irishman will be there don't you?'

'Mind your business,' said Anna curtly, 'I know what I'm doing.'

'Be it on your own head then', snapped Marged pegging the remainder of the washing on a smaller line nearby.

Anna was soon on her way with a basket of small loaves of freshly baked bread, which Twm would welcome, seeing that he had very little home cooking done since Olwen his wife had recently died.

She opened the gate and stepped lightly through a field filled with golden buttercups. The air was fresh and as she listened to the birds in the nearby trees, her heart sang in tune with them.

As she reached Twm's farm she called out, but as there was no reply she decided to take a look in the field at the back of the house. She lifted her hand to shade her eyes from the sunlight and as she did so she began to see Twm in the distance. Alongside him stood Blackie his dog while old Sam his horse stood nearby. And there, wielding bales of hay as if they were as light as a feather stood Peter Malone, tall and handsome in the sunlight.

Anna called out once more, 'Hello there.'

'I've some fresh bread,' she said 'Mam baked it for you.'

'Beti's a good sort, that she is. She knows how we loved my Olwen's bread. God rest her soul. The children will enjoy this, they don't get much home cooking since their Mam has gone,' said Twm wistfully.

All the time the farmer had spoken to her, Anna was aware that Peter Malone had not ceased to take his eyes from her.

'I'll do some baking for you Twm. I'll bring it over tomorrow,' she offered.

'Thank you again merchi but you have enough to do. This will be plenty for now,' he said gratefully.

'Now come on lad, let's get on with the work before the daylight fails or we'll not be finished,' said Twm.

As he turned away, Peter took his chance to speak to her.

'It's a pleasure to see you again Miss Lewis', he said politely.

'My name is Anna,' she replied. 'Will you be at the picnic on Saturday? Everyone will be there. It's the Chapel picnic you know.'

'You'll be there?' he asked.

'Yes,' she replied shyly.

'Then if the work is finished, I'll look forward to seeing you.'

'Well boy,' shouted Twm 'It won't be finished while you carry on swooning over young ladies!'

Peter laughed as he ran to catch up with the farmer.

'Leave the bread on the kitchen table,' shouted Twm again as Anna made her way back toward the farmhouse.

She looked back and finally waved her hand to the two men as they led the horse further up the pasture.

Her heart was happy in the knowledge that her journey here had certainly proved worth while.

The next few days that passed were slow and uneventful for Anna.

Then, as Saturday arrived she became full of anticipation. Would he come to the chapel picnic or not?

Her father and the boys laughed together in the yard as they got cleaned up and washed in readiness to go to the picnic. Anna had decorated her bonnet with fresh flowers from the garden, and was putting the finishing touches to it as her mother asked,

'What's this? Expecting to meet someone special is it?'

'Who knows Mam? Maybe one of these days I'll find a husband but for now I'll settle just to look pretty,' was the answer.

Wil entered the kitchen and on hearing this he laughed as he said, 'Now then merchi. I'm not ready to part with you yet!'

He quickly planted a kiss on her forehead, which was most unusual for Wil.

'Wil Lewis!' said Beti astonished at his actions. 'When will you realise our girls are grown women now. You cannot keep them forever. They will soon have their own lives to live.'

Wil groaned at her words. He was never ready to accept this way of thinking. However, there was a certain pride in his heart as he acknowledged how beautiful his younger daughter had become.

Now it was time to leave for the picnic. Owen and Huw in their best clothes had been warned that they were to remain clean and tidy. Marged dressed in blue wore a straw bonnet trimmed with ribbons. She had not found it necessary to decorate it with flowers, or so she said.

Anna wore a dress of yellow, printed with small white flowers, and as she tied her colourful bonnet on her head with an air of expectancy she knew this was going to be a good day in her life.

Taking her sister by the arm she said, 'Come then Marged, let's go and find out what the day holds for us.'

Marged could never be cross with her younger sister for long, and so the two of them gathered their baskets of food which Mam had prepared earlier and set off laughing as they walked together down the lane.

The picnic was to be held in the grounds of the chapel. Then, if the weather turned unkind, tea could be held in the vestry. However, today was such a glorious one that there would be little fear of the weather changing and everyone could look forward to the games and races being held later in the afternoon.

Anna looked eagerly around her. Would he be here she asked herself? Like it or not, she was determined to enjoy herself. Her mother had already given orders for the baskets to be emptied of the delicious food they had brought. Tables were already being filled with every kind of cakes, scones, tarts and fresh cream with lots of meats, cheeses and fresh produce fit for a King's banquet. Each member of the congregation had carried their own food to add to the long tables set up on the grass.

A loud voice called out above the chatter and din that everyone was making.

'May I have your attention please?' It was the Minister, Goronwy Evans as he bowed his head in prayer he said,

'Lets us thank the Lord in prayer for the bounty of food before us so that our festivities may begin.'

There was silence, each member stood with heads bowed as they listened to the Minister about to pray.

A few seconds later, the prayer was over and everyone began to tuck into the food provided. All kinds of fruit and home-made jams along with everything else were soon beginning to be devoured. The food was washed down with lots of home-made lemonade and bottles of stone ginger. There would be no alcoholic beverages to be found there today.

Anna had not felt at all hungry. All that was in her mind was whether Peter Malone would finally turn up at this event.

It was not until she saw her brothers preparing to enter the egg and spoon race that she noticed him standing watching her from the shade of the big oak tree.

She walked toward him.

'You came then?' she said.

Before he could answer, she continued, 'Will you join us, surely you'll have something to eat Mr. Malone?'

'Must you be so formal Anna? I told you my name is Peter,' he replied laughing at her. Why did these Welsh people always think you were hungry and ready for food? He had learned by now however; it was only their way of showing their hospitality.

'Well then Peter. Will you join us?' she asked again.

He hesitated, then spoke softly,' I'm afraid I'd only feel out of place. The reason I came was to see you again, as I know I should have to keep my distance should I be lucky to come to work for your father at the farm.'

Never had anyone spoken to her like this. Anna became aware of his frankness and immediately began to realise how they felt toward each other.

'Come now, you must change your mind. I'll not take no for an answer. Come and meet my Mam, you'll like her,' she said still trying to persuade him.

How could he refuse such an offer? The two made their way across the grass to where Beti stood handing out cups of tea. Before they reached her however, Goronwy Evans, the Minister stepped in front of them.

'Well young lady, aren't you going to introduce this young man to me?' he asked.

'Sorry Mr. Evans,' she said holding tightly on to Peter's arm. 'This is Peter Malone who has come from Ireland.'

Then he asked,

'You're not of the Catholic faith are you my boy? You being Irish and all?'

Peter became surprised at this question but replied,

'No sir, I'm not a Catholic.'

'Very good then,' smiled the minister. 'Now enjoy yourself there's plenty for all here.' Then he walked away to join the other members of his congregation.

Anna by now had begun to apologise for the minister's rude behaviour, however Peter was rather amused at what had taken place.

'I don't mind his questions,' he said. 'But I do find that some of your countrymen are so inquisitive.'

Seconds later he stood to shake hands with Beti Lewis.

'I can see where your daughters have inherited their good looks from,' he complimented her.

Beti eyed this tall young stranger whom her daughter was obviously interested in. He seemed quiet spoken and well mannered. If his work was as good as Twm made out, then he would indeed be an asset to Wil as the boys were still too young to help their father with the heavy manual work on the farm.

It was then Wil joined them, again offering refreshments which Peter politely refused.

'Now then, if you're coming to work for me lad, you'll need every ounce of strength and as my Beti is renowned for her cooking let's get and eat,' said Wil slapping the boy's shoulder in friendship.

Peter marvelled at the friendliness of the people around him. He had not felt as good as this in a long time. He looked at Anna and as their eyes met she smiled at him.

If only he had read her thoughts he would have known how happy she was to be near him.

In a few days time he would be at Cefn Glas and the future looked brighter than he had dared to hope.

CHAPTER 3

After the meeting at the picnic, Peter went from farm to farm his good name preceding him. No task was too large and he was fortunate that work was plenty.

The summer days hot and long were coming to an end, and with the harvesting now done he felt it was time for him to move on.

He loved the young Welsh girl with her beautiful dark eyes and hair and the soft lilt in her voice, but how could he offer his love to her with no future prospects of work in store?

They had arranged to meet that evening, and so he'd decided to tell her of his plans to leave. As he walked down the lane he saw Anna standing in the moonlight.

God! She was lovely. He was sure she felt something toward him and although their friendship had blossomed, he had never dared to approach her in the way he so badly wanted to.

'There you are,' she said, greeting him. 'It's a lovely evening Peter. Look at the moon, a true harvest moon if every I saw one.'

He did not reply but gathered enough courage to say,

'Anna, there's something important I have to tell you.'

'Let me speak first,' she replied eagerly.

He let her continue.

'My father asked me to give you a message. It seems a drover is needed up at the Big House. Carwyn Thomas the owner is also offering a small cottage along with the job, and should you be interested, my Da is willing to speak up for you.' Then she added, 'That is if you intend to remain in these parts.'

As she finished the last sentence she cast her eyes down, afraid to see what his answer might be, as she tried so hard to hide the hope she felt within her.

He hesitated a second then replied, 'Would it matter to you if I stayed Anna?'

She looked up at him.

'More than you know Peter,' was her reply.

He moved closer to her, their bodies almost touching, then he took her in his arms and he began to kiss her tenderly.

Anna wrapped her arms around him to return his kisses, which came more fiercely this time. By the time he released her she was breathless from his embrace. He wanted to hold her for much longer but common sense told him to let her go.

'You'll stay then?' she asked.

He nodded and taking her hand in his he said,

"It's time to get you home. If your father is willing to speak for me then I'll not incur his wrath by arriving later with you.'

They walked hand in hand together in the moonlight. The uncertainty of the day had now disappeared and again his future looked brighter than he had ever hoped for.

Peter's luck had changed for the better. He began to feel a sense of belonging at last.

Soon his journeys as a drover for Carwyn Thomas at Bryn Cethin Farm took him far and wide over the Welsh countryside, and he began to learn more of the Welsh people with their down and out friendliness, their love of music and sense of fair play.

He enjoyed the freedom his journeys brought him, but each time he looked forward to coming home to his little cottage which he now counted as his own.

Anna had helped him there, adding little feminine touches here and there, while Beti and her husband could not fail to notice the love in Peter and Anna's eyes as they fondly spoke of each other.

Marged on the other hand still held some reservation toward Peter, or so he felt. Was it because she had felt so close to her sister? Could it be that she was more than a little jealous of him?

This time, as Peter journeyed home, he had decided the time had come to approach Wil Lewis and ask him for permission to marry his daughter, for he could wait no longer.

That very evening after putting on his best shirt and waistcoat he began to feel slightly nervous as he slicked his hair down into place with tap water. He proceeded to tie a coloured neckerchief around his neck and finally wiping his boots as clean as he could he then walked sprightly down the lane to Cefn Glas.

Peter arrived to find Wil Lewis sitting on the doorstep of the farmhouse smoking his pipe in the cool evening air.

On hearing the approach of footsteps Wil looked up.

'Well boy! Home again is it?' he said taking his pipe from his mouth and giving the bowl a slight tap in his hand to clear it.

'What brings you up here this time of night? Nothing wrong is there?' he asked.

Peter coughed nervously before he replied, 'I've come to have a word with your good self Mr Lewis.'

On hearing the men's voices, Anna arrived in the doorway, but as soon as she noticed Peter who was dressed in his best clothes she quickly retreated back into the house as she partly guessed what his intentions were, since they had spoken of this moment often enough.

'Speak up then boy. What can I do for you?' asked Wil.

For a moment there was silence, as Anna and Beti stood pressed up against the front door waiting for Peter to begin. One woman, in fear of what her father may say, the other listening intently to the tone of her husband's voice.

Peter's voice became strong as he said, 'As you know, I've begun to rebuild my life again thanks to you Mr Lewis, and now I feel the future would be a better one if you will allow me to share it with your Anna. I should like to take her for my wife if she'll have me, and if you are willing to give us your consent.'

There! He had said it, now what would be Wil Lewis' reaction? 'Do you love her?' Wil asked quietly.

'More than life itself,' was the boy's reply.

Anna held her breath. Only the tick of the kitchen clock could be heard in the silence that followed.

Wil finally broke the silence,

'Well my boy, it's plain to see Anna feels as you do, but if I ever find out you've been hard on her you'll have me to reckon with. Now go and find her with my blessing.'

He held out his hand to Peter who shook it again and again.

Anna meanwhile hugged her mother behind the partly closed door, and as Peter stepped up to knock on it she came bursting through, eyes shining brightly as she said, flinging herself into his arms,

'Oh yes Peter. I will marry you!'

With a twinkle in his eye the handsome young Irishman replied. 'Wait now, I haven't asked you yet!'

As he saw the surprised look on her face he added hastily,

'Miss Anna Lewis, will you marry me?'

She laughed heartily, 'Yes, Peter Malone, but you'd better not keep me waiting long or I'll change my mind.'

Beti and Wil congratulated the young couple, then Wil suggested Beti bring out the parsnip wine from the larder and soon they were toasted in fine style.

Marged and the boys joined in the celebration, but in the midst of it all. Anna and Peter only had eyes for each other.

Later that evening, as they prepared to go to bed, Beti who sat brushing her hair asked Wil,

'I must know. Why did you give in so easily to this marriage, knowing you did not take easy to the thought of losing either of our girls?'

Wil yawned, then replied,

'Peter's a good lad. Our Anna could have done a lot worse than marry him. He loves her and I believe he'll always look after her. And we still have Marged, merchi. Now go to sleep Beti fach, I'm tired.'

'But Wil,' she protested, wanting to speak longer with him.

Wil grunted, kissed her goodnight and turned over to go to sleep.

Peter Malone's attention turned toward the rear of the chapel as the strains of the organ music announced the arrival of his bride to be.

Anna Lewis entered on the arm of her father with Marged her sister walking in attendance behind them.

The chapel was full to capacity, but Peter only had eyes for his Anna. As she walked down the aisle toward him a shaft of sunlight shone through one of the nearby windows lighting up her dark brown hair and causing her to smile while her eyes twinkled in anticipation as she reached his side.

Suddenly as she stood there, all the previous nervousness within him began to disappear. There was a silent hush as the minister stood before them to perform the marriage of Anna Lewis to Peter Malone, speaking sometimes in both the Welsh and English language.

Peter stole a silent glance toward her but Anna kept her eyes in front of her as she concentrated on the all important words, which were to make her his wife.

As the Minister nodded to Peter to place the ring on her finger, Anna proudly held out her left hand and so it was that her dream of becoming Mrs. Peter Malone was finally fulfilled.

Then it was, into the tiny adjoining room, where the big black Chapel Register was to be signed and witnessed. And finally to the strains of organ music once more, they were then greeted by the congregation, as they walked out of the Chapel into the fine spring morning.

All around them daffodils sprang up through the earth, giving a delightful golden glow to the countryside as they began their journey by buggy to Cefn Glas.

'Happy Anna?' he asked.

'I have longed for this moment,' was her reply. He pulled the warm woollen rug around her, thankful to Beti for leaving it in the buggy to keep them warm. Although the sun shone brightly there was a keen wind in the air and as Anna began to shiver he put his strong arms around her.

Soon they arrived at the farm where more well wishers waited to greet them. There was food and drink for everyone as Beti and the women had spent days preparing for the celebration.

Joseph, one of the drovers began to speak on Peter's behalf while Wil thanked everyone for coming. Then the dancing began until finally the celebrations lasted well into the evening and Peter felt it was time to leave.

'Do you think we can slip away now?' he asked his new bride.

Anna blushed slightly at his remark.

'I'll go to tell Mam, then we can leave quietly by the back door so no one will notice,' she whispered.

When all was arranged, the two reached the door and stepped into the semi darkness. Immediately a huge shower of rice engulfed them and shouts and high pitched voices of good luck wishes surrounded them.

All this was the result of two very wicked young boys who had been waiting for this moment all evening. Owen and Huw ran off laughing before their father could reprimand either of them.

The happy bride and groom ran down the lane laughing until soon they reached their own safe haven.

Peter unlocked the door to the cottage, then lifting Anna in his arms he began to carry her over the threshold. He began to set her down gently but held her tightly in his arms as they kissed. Immediately their kisses became hot and fierce but Peter not wishing to rush her let her body go as he made an excuse to light the nearby lamp.

On entering the room they had felt a chill in the air, but to their surprise they found a log fire had already been lit in the grate.

'My father, I expect,' said Anna warming her hands by its glow.

She shivered slightly.

'You're cold Anna,' he said.

She nodded nervously as he took her in his arms again.

'Why don't you go up to bed, it will be warmer there. I'll follow soon,' he suggested, feeling a slight tension within her body.

Grateful of his suggestion Anna waited while he lit another lamp, then taking it from him she climbed the stairs alone. She knew what was expected of her but she was as nervous as could be.

She quickly undressed, got into bed pulling the warm quilt around her so that it almost covered her face and waited.

Downstairs Peter also sat waiting. How much time would she need he wondered?

God how he loved her. He had long waited for this night. Did she feel the same? Would everything be alright? He could wait no more. He began to climb the stairs and as he reached the door he noticed the room was in darkness. Had she fallen asleep already?

He turned the lamp down low as he began to quietly undress so as not to disturb her, after all it had been a long day for both of them.

Turning out the light, he got into bed pulling the clothes over him.

Her body felt warm. The need beginning to rise within him he reached out to touch her. Anna gently turned toward him her arms outstretched to him.

As he began to kiss her he gasped,

'Anna I need you so badly, I promise I'll not hurt you.'

'Peter, I love you so much,' was her reply. Soon all the passion previously withheld by both of them suddenly burst until their bodies came together again and again until finally exhaustion overtook them and sleep prevailed.

Several times during the night they awoke only to find each other again and again.

As the new day dawned and they lay in each other's arms, words were of no importance. Their love was enough.

CHAPTER 4

The season turned from spring to summer and life had become good for Peter and his Anna.

Their cottage became full of love and laughter. Peter began to settle to his new life, most of the time driving Carwyn Thomas' cattle to the surrounding market places for sale but sometimes he was needed to work on the land.

Anna saved what little money she could by selling the vegetables she herself had planted and nurtured in their small garden. She stowed the coins safely away in an old tin box, which stood on the stone shelf in the pantry, where it was only to be opened in case of an emergency.

Somehow she never quite accepted his having to work away from home, but Peter loved the outdoor life while at the same time longing to return home to Anna at the end of each journey.

Anna kept busy, still helping at Cefn Glas while her brothers and Marged were regular visitors at the cottage.

Soon a whole year had passed, and as Anna sat in the rocking chair, she could hardly wait for Peter's return home so excited was she.

'I'm home Anna,' his voice called out to her as he paused to take off his muddy boots, leaving them outside the door.

She darted from the chair to greet him.

'I didn't expect you so soon Peter,' she cried flinging herself into his strong arms.

'Steady on now,' he said laughing at her 'What's all this? Have you missed me more than usual then gel?' he asked.

Anna lifted her face to his as he kissed her gently then she said,

'Don't be silly, I'm always missing you. Now get and wash while I'll get supper ready. It's good to have you home again Peter.'

She tore herself free from his grasp while he turned to leave the house in search for the barrel of rainwater in which to wash the dirt and grime from his body.

All the time he scrubbed himself he thought how good it would be when they would at last settle beneath the sheets to fulfil their love once more. In the beginning she felt shy of their lovemaking, but as time passed Anna had begun to show that she too had begun to enjoy the love and satisfaction their nights together had brought them and for that Peter loved her even more.

Catching sight of him through the window, seeing his strong body stripped to the waist as he washed himself vigorously sent shivers down her spine as she then called out.

'Hurry along Peter, supper's nearly ready. Are you hungry?'

Seeing her face at the window he called back,

'Hungry for you I am girl.'

'Behave yourself Peter Malone, or you'll get no supper,' she shouted back to him.

'Suits me fine Anna. I can always live on love gel!'

'You're impossible!' she gave in, laughing to herself as she carried on preparing the meal.

Immediately Peter entered the kitchen he noticed the table laid with the best lace tablecloth and in its centre stood a vase of flowers which would have brightened even the dullest of rooms. There was a large plate of succulent home cooked ham and a glass dish, which held ripe red tomatoes, and alongside it stood a jar of his favourite pickled onions. As a final touch, Anna added a large chunk of strong smelling cheese to the plate. Then she invited him to sit down opposite her, while she began to slice a loaf of bread spreading the slices with thick salt butter.

Peter sat back in the chair; he could eat no more. As Anna poured another mug of elderberry wine she said.

'Sit yourself by the fire while I clear away these dishes.'

Peter moved toward the rocking chair his eyes following her as she walked around the room.

'Sit by me Anna,' he said as she finished what she was doing.

She sat down on the floor at his feet, folding her long skirts around her knees.

Placing her head in his lap he began to stroke her long black hair.

'You're very quiet,' he said. 'Is everything well at Cefn Glas?'

How was she to tell him she wondered? What would be his reaction to her news? She could contain herself no longer and so she finally blurted out.

'Yes everything's fine there except Owen fell from the old apple tree and Doctor Pugh had to be sent for. It's alright, nothing broken, just a few bruises.

Twm has come to his senses at last and taken a housekeeper to help him. Oh! There's one more thing.'

'What's that?' he asked continuing to stroke the soft curls back from her forehead.

Without looking at him Anna began slowly 'I've been to see Doctor Pugh myself and it seems we shall be having our baby early next Spring.'

There was silence. Had her words registered in his mind?

'Peter, did you hear what I said?' she asked looking up at him.

'A baby?' he asked. 'Our baby?' She nodded, not knowing whether he was pleased or not.

He took her in his arms and held her tenderly as he spoke softly.

'Anna, you have made me so happy. At last! A family of my own.'

All of a sudden, the full impact of her news hit him hard as he swept her up in his arms shouting out loud so as to let the whole world know.

He swung her body up in the air.

'Put me down,' she laughed.

Suddenly as if now realising his full strength and rough handling of her. He set her down gently apologising all the time. He would have to be more careful with her in the future, he thought to himself.

'Have you told anyone else?' he enquired.

'Only Mam,' she answered, 'I wanted to be sure before I told you.'

Peter led her to the rocking chair and placed her gently on it, this time it was his turn to sit on the floor near her feet.

They talked long into the night, he wishing that he had his mother to tell the good news to. But she lay buried across the water never to know the joy in his heart that night.

Later as they lay together, Anna reached out to him.

'Is it alright?' he asked, not knowing whether it was the correct thing to be making love to her now.

'No harm will come to me Peter,' she assured him gently. 'It will be time enough to cease.'

The love that followed was both tender and fulfilling until they drifted to sleep in each other's arms.

CHAPTER 5

While Anna's life continued happily, it had not been so for Marged who although satisfied that her sister was settled at her little cottage, missed her each day until she had to admit to herself how lonely she had become.

They visited each other of course but it could never be the same.

Beti, noticing how quiet her elder daughter had become suggested that Marged apply for the post of parlour maid at Bryn Cethin.

Maybe that would bring the girl out, and knowing Leah Thomas as she did, she was sure that Marged would be treated well.

On hearing this, Wil became adamant. No daughter of his was going into service! A skivvy for Carwyn Thomas at the Big House? Not if he had anything to do with it!

However, with Beti, Anna and Marged working on him he finally relented, on one condition, and that was that Marged return home each evening to her own bed there at Cefn Glas.

Leah Thomas had been well pleased to receive Marged Lewis in her home believing her to be a steady, reliable young girl, so different to some of the flighty girls she'd previously had to dismiss.

So for several weeks now Marged had begun to enjoy herself at Bryn Cethin although even Beti had become fed up on hearing what a lovely home it was and what beautiful, expensive possessions the Thomas family owned.

Then came the day when Leah Thomas asked Marged whether she could stay overnight to help with guests arriving for the annual Fox Hunt.

'I shall need your help Marged,' said Leah Thomas fussing over her guest list.

'I shall have to ask my father's permission first,' said Marged, knowing full well that Wil would most certainly not grant it.

'If there's a problem then perhaps my husband could have a word with him?'

'No, thank you, I'm sure it will be alright,' said Marged not wanting the Master to get involved, as she was sure it would add to her troubles.

'Very good then. I'll expect you early on Friday morning as usual, and a room will be prepared for you to stay', said Leah Thomas.

Marged broke the news to her mother saying, 'He'll never agree for me to stay the night there Mam. What shall I do?'

Beti, quite proud of the fact that her daughter had been chosen to help out replied,

'Don't worry about him. I can handle your father, just you wait and see.'

Marged wished she felt as confident as her mother but only time would tell. The Thomas family was considered to be quite wealthy in those parts, owning the large working farm, Bryn Cethin, the Big House, and many acres of the surrounding countryside. Beti could see the improvement in Marged since she went to work for Leah Thomas, the mistress. She was not about to see her daughter lose such an opportunity on such a special occasion.

After much arguing Wil finally gave into her once more.

'Very well woman, but only this once,' he retorted.

Marged packed her nightgown and cap and walked happily over the fields to the Big House in anticipation of what duties would be required of her. She was shown to her room where she laid her night things out on the bed, which stood in the corner of a small room on the second floor of the house where the servants slept.

By the side of the bed stood a cupboard and on it was a large jug and basin where she could wash herself. As she sat on the bed she felt grateful for her newly found independence. Then it was time to report to the mistress.

Marged found Leah Thomas in the kitchen issuing orders to the cook and one or two other maids who smiled in welcome to her.

'You shall serve in the breakfast room Marged,' announced Mrs Thomas.

'Yes, Ma'am,' she curtsied as she replied.

'Very well then, you may start by taking the teapot in with you. I daresay my husband is already waiting there,' said the mistress.

Marged entered the room but to her surprise found only a younger man sitting at the large table.

This must be Mr Rhys, the son, she thought to herself and from what she could see he looked as pleasant as each of his parents. It was said he had important work with a shipping office at Swansea. Well, it was none of her concern, she was here to do her own job and so she said politely,

'Would you like some tea sir?'

He did not raise his head as she stood near him holding the heavy silver teapot in her hands. She stood there waiting patiently, then she heard his reply,

'Not now, thank you.'

Marged curtsied and turned away to place the teapot on its stand on the polished sideboard nearby.

Then a much deeper voice said,

'Wait girl, I'll have one.' It was Carwyn Thomas, the Master, as he entered the room and pulled up a chair at the table opposite his son.

Marged quickly picked up the teapot, walked to his side and carefully began to pour the tea into his cup. As she turned away however, she accidentally knocked a small silver spoon from its saucer and it fell to the floor.

Feeling slightly embarrassed she bent down to pick it up saying,

'I'm sorry sir, I'll fetch a clean one straight away.'

The spoon however had fallen near Rhys Thomas' foot and he too bent to retrieve it at the same time. Then their eyes met, and for the first time he began to notice this quiet, attractive young girl standing in front of him.

Marged blushed and quickly picked up the spoon and hurried back to the sideboard where she obtained another, which she quickly gave to the Master. She knew the young man's eyes followed her, she could feel them almost burning a hole in her body.

'What do you intend to do this morning Rhys?' asked his father. Turning his gaze from the maid he replied, 'I thought I'd go for a ride father. I'd like to try out that roan you have in the stables.'

'Don't forget the guests are arriving early and I shall expect you here to greet them,' said his father.

'Very well,' he replied politely. It would not do to cross his father and so both men carried on eating their breakfast. Marged left and returned a while later to clear the table. However the young master still remained seated there.

'Sorry sir,' she said, 'I'll come back later.' As she passed his chair, his hand reached out and caught her by the wrist.

'Pretty little thing aren't you?' he said.

'Why haven't I seen you before?'

'I'm new here sir,' she replied shyly.

He could see how embarrassed she'd become and began to laugh at her.

Marged tried to pull her hand away and he could see she was not amused. So this one has spirit as well he thought.

Releasing her he sat back in his chair and smiled. He would have to remember this one, could she be fair sport? He dismissed the thought. Why waste his time when there would be fair game among the guests soon to arrive.

Marged in the meanwhile had returned to the kitchen with face flushed, no one had ever spoken to her in that way and she would not make up her mind as to whether she liked it or not.

The remainder of the busy day passed quickly for her, and soon with her duties ended she retired to bed. As she lay down on the clean cotton sheets she let her mind wander back to the events of the evening as she stood waiting in attendance to the Master and Mistress and their dinner guests.

She had watched Rhys Thomas charming the ladies with tales of the big ships and the Sea Captains he'd dealt with, and of the place where he both lived and worked. Try hard as she may to deny it, she felt that some of his charm had rubbed off on her and she found herself liking him more and more.

Realising the impossibility of it she turned over to sleep. It would soon be five o'clock in the morning and she'd have to wake early to serve breakfast to the folk arriving for the hunt.

The smell of freshly baked bread and home cured smoked bacon filled the air. Dishes filled with devilled kidneys and fried mushrooms gathered early from the fields; plates of eggs and fried tomatoes were quickly consumed. Hot scones and griddle cakes oozing with butter and a variety of jams left guests so full it was debatable whether some of them could later sit astride a horse let alone join in the hunt.

Marged and Sally the other maid darted to and from the kitchen and soon breakfast was over. The sound of a hunting horn echoed in the air and there was laughter and merriment as each person left the room to assemble in the courtyard.

There were men dressed in riding jackets, some red, some black; each wearing riding hats and carrying small leather whips in their hands.

Women in their long black riding habits, white lace frills at their throats sat side-saddle on their horses ready for the 'off.'

Hounds barked and yelped in the excitement. Although Marged had seen all this before it had never quite been so exciting for her.

As she looked out of the window, she saw Rhys Thomas sitting on the back of a beautiful black horse, a fine figure of a man who knew exactly what he was about.

The Master of the Hunt gave the signal, the horn sounded again and the dogs were released. As they ran out through the front wrought iron gates of the farm they were followed by the riders and soon the sounds of the dogs disappeared into the distance.

'Run Mister Fox as fast as you can,' said Sally standing beside her, as she and Marged watched them leave.

'Sally! Marged! Come now! Stop wasting my time. There's much to do. They'll be back soon, wanting more attention again.'

Cassie Evans stood in the doorway shouting orders at the two girls who quickly carried on with their work. It would do them no good to ignore Cassie who had been put in charge of the maids for the day.

'Stuck up bitch!' muttered Sally as they hurried along. Marged on the other hand decided to remain silent.

Later when the mistress had returned she sent for Marged saying,

'I hope you don't mind but I've sent a message to Cefn Glas to ask whether you may stay one more night Marged. I cannot do without your help. I'm sure it will be alright.'

Leah Thomas was used to getting what she wanted but Marged was none to sure of her father's reaction.

Sally then entered the room.

'Sorry to trouble you Ma'am but there's a young lad at the back door asking to speak with Marged here. I thought you should know.' She curtsied and left.

'I expect it's one of the boys Ma'am. Come to let me know my Da's answer to whether I can stay or not,' said Marged almost too afraid to go and see who was there.

'Then call the lad into the kitchen, girl and we'll soon know,' said Leah Thomas.

It was Owen who stood there, looking around the large kitchen in amazement.

'Posh place this, our Marged,' he said loudly.

'Hush now,' she replied trying to quieten him.

'What have you to say?' she asked eagerly.

'You may stay, but home early in the morning it is Da said. He was 'off top' Marged, but Mam swayed him by saying how important it was for you to stay.'

'Thank you for coming Owen, now you must go,' said Marged watching his eager eyes as they looked at all the food being prepared for dinner. Cook also saw the boy's look and immediately began to cut a huge slice of bread, which she spread thickly with beef dripping. Adding a little salt to it, she handed it to the boy whose face began to light up at the thought of getting his teeth into this chunk of bread. Then he was gone!

Everything had to be perfect for the small dinner party. Marged stood to attention at one corner of the dining room, Sally at the other. Both were dressed in black, their hair combed neatly in place under white starched caps and their hands folded over neatly starched white aprons. Rhys Thomas sat next to an attractive young lady, a friend of the family. Marged noticed how loud his voice was as he tried to impress her while helping himself to yet another glass of port.

His companion however, was trying hard to ignore him but he failed to see what a nuisance he was making of himself

What I would give to be sitting there right next to him thought Marged.

Suddenly he stopped talking as he took a sip from his glass and looked across the room toward her. Their eyes met, and as she turned away she noticed his companion leaning toward him whispering in his ear and knew then that they were talking about her.

He began to laugh loudly and she immediately made an excuse to leave the room promising herself that when the meal had ended she would be free to retire to bed and would leave as early as she could the following morning.

As she lay in bed Marged reflected on how life was different to that of the rich people she had served at dinner, and decided then that she would not change her own life for anything.

Meanwhile Rhys Thomas had become so drunk his beautiful companion had tired of his company and retired to bed leaving him feeling alone and rejected.

His pride had been hurt, women usually let him have his own way and his inside boiled with disappointment and rejection.

Wait a moment, he thought as he remembered that little maid who had taken his fancy. What was her name? Margaret? No, Marged! That was it!

He knew where to find her. She would not turn him away and so climbing the stairs he went in search of her.

Swaying here and there in the shadows he reached the second landing to the servants' quarters.

He could find his way perfectly in the darkness and so he turned the doorknob quietly as he entered the bedroom.

Marged lay there still awake. 'Who is there?' she asked as she turned to light the candle.

'It's me, Rhys Thomas,' he answered quietly. 'I have a message from my mother.'

'Tell her I'll get dressed now,' she said rising from the bed in the darkness where she could now make out the shape of his body.

'No, don't do that,' he whispered as he began to reach out to her.

The moon previously hidden behind some clouds now suddenly shone its light into the room lighting up the darkness. Marged could see his silhouette as he sat on the edge of the bed near her. He reached out to touch her saying,

'All day I've imagined how you would look like this, you are so pretty.'

Marged pulled the blankets up to cover her bare shoulders while her heart beat uncontrollably. Why had he come to her, of all people?

'Don't be afraid,' he said, taking the edge of the blanket between his fingers, gently pulling it down to reveal her shoulders once more.

Marged could not believe what was happening to her as his hand reached out to stroke her hair while his fingers moved gently over her lips.

He leaned forward to kiss her but she held herself back from him. Before she realised what was happening, he stood up quickly releasing her while he shed his clothes and roughly pushed her to one side of the bed as he jumped in naked beside her.

'Don't! Please don't,' she cried out as her heart beat wildly in fright.

'For God's sake be quiet will you,' he demanded. 'You'll wake everyone up. Don't come the innocent with me and don't say you've not thought of this moment. I've been watching you all evening and I've seen it in your eyes when you've been watching me.'

'My God! What have I done?' she cried. 'Please, go now. I won't tell anyone you've been here. You are mistaken, please leave me alone.'

He did not hear her as she begged and struggled to free her body, which had now become wedged between his and that of the cold bedroom wall. He placed his large hand over her tiny mouth while his other hand struggled to lift her nightgown over her body. She felt she was being suffocated, and try as she may to cover her nakedness she could not fight him off for much longer.

Within seconds he had overpowered her and her strength had failed. She tried to scream but no sound came from within her.

His face was now so close to hers, his breath stale from the smell of alcohol!

Then he began to thrust himself inside her body again and again until finally his drunken passion was spent, and he fell exhausted against the pillow beside her.

She lay there sobbing quietly, not an ounce of strength left within her.

They lay there for she knew not how long until he got up to dress himself. Then whispering to her he said,

'You'll say nothing of this to anyone, you understand? After all, who'd believe your story? It's your word against mine. Why should I have wanted a simple maid when I could have my pick of any young lady here this evening?'

With that statement he left the room to disappear into the darkness leaving her alone to be consumed by guilt and shame.

Her body ached all over; she would never feel clean again. One thing was certain, he was right. Who would believe her? Had she really been to blame?

Marged Lewis coupled both arms around her knees and rocked backward and forward sobbing quietly into the night, robbed of a sleep that might never come to her again.

CHAPTER 6

A gentle breeze lifted the warm air as Anna began to peg the washing on the line. Her back ached as she stood on the tip of her toes finding difficulty this time to reach and bend to the washing basket. She was now very heavy with the child she carried and she prayed that Peter would return from his journey in time for the birth.

'Anna, where are you?' a voice called. It was Marged.

'I'm in the garden,' she called back. 'Put the kettle on, will you? I've nearly finished here.'

Marged however joined her in the garden and began to help her with the remainder of the clothes to be pegged on the line.

'You shouldn't be doing this Anna. What if you fell out here?' she said.

'Hush now' was the reply.' I'm alright. It's nice to see you, we'll have a cup of tea and a chat and you can tell me all about your work at the Big House. Mam and Da alright, and the boys?' continued Anna as she finally lifted the empty basket to walk back down the path toward the cottage.

Marged followed quietly behind as her sister continued to chat with her.

'Can you stay for a while?' asked Anna. 'We've not had much time together lately. Mam said you've been busy up at Bryn Cethin. You must be one of Mrs Thomas' favourites then.'

Marged immediately broke into tears.

'What's all this?' asked Anna surprised at her sister's outburst as she led her inside where they sat down together at the table.

'I'm in terrible trouble Anna. I have to tell someone, I'm so ashamed,' said Marged continuing to sob.

'Now then, it can't be as bad as all that. Whatever it is we shall work it out together' replied Anna, concerned by now at her sister's statement.

Marged lifted her head and began to wipe the tears from her eyes.

'I don't know where to begin except to say that I have brought shame on the family and I don't know which way to turn to. How am I going to live with it?'

She hesitated for a moment then blurted out.

'Anna, I think I'm going to have a baby.'

'Are you sure?' Anna asked. At the same time, the news had astonished her, as she looked at the sister who had grown up by her side so gentle and quiet by nature. How or why had this happened?

Marged nodded silently then began to sob once more.

'Calm down now. Start at the beginning. Who is the father and have you told him yet?' asked Anna taking Marged's hand in hers and gently pressing it to her own.

Shaking her head Marged whispered, 'I cannot tell him Anna.'

Finally the whole story was told and as it became clear, Anna listened in silence her anger swelling up inside her, while her compassion for her sister's innocence overwhelmed her.

Marged ended by saying,

'Was it my fault Anna? How am I going to tell Mam and I dread to think what Da will say?'

'You must never blame yourself, Rhys Thomas will have to pay for what he's done', said Anna.

'No!' shouted Marged rising from the table as she began to pace backward and forward. 'You must promise me that you'll not tell. It has to be our secret, no-one must ever know he is the father.'

'I cannot promise that Marged,' said Anna knowing in her heart that the man who had ruined her sister's life must now be made to pay for what he had done.

Marged sat down, looked at Anna as she said,

'You have no choice. Have you forgotten this cottage is owned by his family? He could make trouble for yourself and Peter. I cannot risk that, besides, he said he will deny it, and as he intends to return to Swansea soon, my secret must be kept.'

Anna paused. Marged was right but the thought that this evil man would not be punished angered her even more.

'I shall have to tell Peter, it would not be fair to keep this from him. Will you allow me to do that?' asked Anna.

Marged nodded.

'Then, when you are ready, we shall go together to break the news to Mam and Da. You'll not be alone in this Marged,' Anna assured her.

'I thank God for you,' said Marged hugging her tightly.

Anna fought back the tears which began to swell in her eyes thinking only of the shock this news would bring to both parents who had recently been so joyful at the news of her own child soon to be born. There would be difficult times ahead of them but the promise had been made. She would have to abide by Marged's decision in not naming the father of the child, and come what may, she would stand by her sister to the bitter end.

Peter returned home a few days later and he too became furious on hearing Marged's news. The Thomas' boy deserved a good hiding but Marged was right in what she had to say. The arrival of their new baby and the possible risk of losing the cottage convinced Peter that no action could be taken by either himself or Anna. Despite all this he vowed he too would stand by Marged and do all he could to help her through her trouble.

At the same time that Peter again departed on another cattle drive, Rhys Thomas decided it was time to leave Bryn Cethin. He had stayed too long.

That very evening, Anna arrived at Cefn Glas. She had arranged with Marged that the time had come to break the news to their parents.

'Come in merchi,' called Wil. 'Peter's gone again I see. Well, not to worry as I shall walk you back home, we can't have you falling in the dark not with your time so near.'

Anna kissed him on the forehead as she took off her shawl placing it on the back of his chair.

'Here, come and sit down while I make us some tea,' said Beti pulling up a chair alongside Wil.

Anna sat on it but could not make herself feel comfortable. Seeing this, Wil got up from the easy fireside chair and offered it to her.

Gratefully Anna sat herself down again; this time all felt well.

Beti filled the kettle with water and leaned forward to place it on the open fire saying,

'Just think Wil. Our first grandchild. Won't it be wonderful?'

Marged, who was sitting the other side of the table sewing buttons on some shirts suddenly, stopped what she was doing. This was her opportunity, and without a second thought said, 'It's not the only grandchild you' ll be getting Mam.'

Anna's heart started to thump, its beat seemed out of control. What had possessed Marged to break the news this way? It was not at all as they arranged. She looked at her mother then her eyes turned in the direction of her father.

Neither of them spoke. Surely they had heard what Marged had just said?

Beti looked at her daughter and as Marged cast her eyes downward she said,

'Yes Mam, it's true. It's having a baby I am.'

It was Wil who jumped up from the chair. 'Good God girl. What are you saying?'

Marged immediately began to cry, she knew by the look on her father's face that she should have waited for Anna to put their plan into action. The damage was done and now she would have to take the consequences.

Her mother sat down speechless. Her father however, bellowed in his temper.

'Who is the boy and when did this happen? How long have you known?' Before Marged could reply. Wil continued, 'To think a daughter of mine should bring such shame to this family. Well whoever he is he'll have to marry you. I'll see to that. Well, what do you have to say for yourself? Who is he, I demand to know?'

Marged looked up and her eyes caught those of Anna's across the room, which seemed to say 'I cannot help you!'

Then as she looked at her father still standing there in this terrible rage she said, 'I'm sorry Da, I cannot say his name. It would be of no use.'

'I don't suppose you know his name. How many boys have you been with then? A fine upbringing you've had and look how you have betrayed you mother and myself I can't bear to be in the same room as you.' He left, slamming the door behind him.

Marged collapsed into tears as she began to rock backwards and forwards in the chair while Anna got up to comfort her. Beti sat in the chair, unable to move or do anything. Marged looked at her sadly.

'I would give anything it this were not true Mam. Believe me I never meant it to happen. I cannot marry the child's father. What am I to do?'

'Come here,' said Beti holding out her arms knowing then that her daughter would need all the help she could get. Whatever the reasons were she could not abandon her and as they held each other tightly she whispered, 'It's such a shock to us Marged. I cannot understand how you let this happen, maybe I shall never know, but as for your father, don't expect too much from him. He's hurt because he loves you and feels you've let us down and he may never understand that you are hurting also.'

Marged clung to her mother as tears once more began to fall, then it was Anna's turn to speak.

'Leave her to me Mam. Go to him and try to reason with him, will you?'

Beti turned to her. 'You knew didn't you?' she asked.

Anna quietly nodded and at that moment Beti felt betrayed. She had always been so close to both her daughters, but neither had felt it necessary to include her into this problem they had both shared. As she went in search of Wil, she prayed that somehow she could reason with him but something told her it would be one of the hardest tasks she would ever have to do. She walked toward the barn where she found him sitting in silence. He did not look up as she approached him.

'We have to talk Wil,' she said, placing her arm gently on his.

'There is nothing to say,' he replied sadly. Beti sat beside him waiting patiently until he said,

'Our Marged, who'd have believed it? Where did we go wrong? It will be the talk of the village and as for the Chapel, the deacons will have to be told. The shame is hers, she's to blame, and as for the father of the child, why doesn't she name him? At least then I would have had the satisfaction of facing him with my anger.'

'What's done is done Wil. She has her reasons, God only knows what they are but she has been a good and faithful daughter to us and we cannot let her stand alone in this. Please come back inside and talk with her,' Beti pleaded.

Wil shook his head and refused to move. 'Come now, think of Anna, she is upset also and so near her time. Think what this is doing to her.' Beti continued.

'Anna? At least she is happy. I wanted the same for Marged. Was that wrong? How do you think I feel now? I love my family, you know that Beti!' he almost cried out in pain.

'Then it's time you showed it Wil Lewis. Now come back with me,' Beti said as she stood up.

'Very well, but it will be on my terms,' he said.

Beti knew then, that it was all she could settle for.

Back inside the house the two sisters comforted each other. Never in their lives had they witnessed their father in such a rage.

'I'm so grateful to you Anna. Thank you for being here with me,' said Marged.

'Don't thank me, I said little in your defence. Maybe if you'd broken it to them a little easier? You are sure that you'll not tell them the truth? They would accept your innocence Marged,' said Anna hoping her sister would come to her senses.

Marged's eyes flashed with anger as she replied, 'No! I cannot let them know the truth. Hush now, I think they are coming back!'

Beti entered the room followed by Wil who went to his chair without saying so much as a word. Marged fixed her eyes on her father, waiting for him to speak. It was Beti however who said,

'Your father has something to say to you.' For a moment there remained a deathly silence and without looking toward them Wil said calmly,

'Marged, you have let us down badly. We have always tried to do our best for you. I don't know how this has happened and as you are determined not to name the boy, maybe I shall never know or understand it.'

Marged clasped her hands tightly, dreading to hear the words her father had to say. Would he stand by her? Many a young girl in her condition had been forced to leave their homes for the shame they had brought on their families.

'So I have thought this over carefully and with God's help we shall stand by you.'

'Thank you Da,' said Marged interrupting him for a second.

'Let me finish.' he bellowed. Marged stood rigid to the spot and allowed her father to continue.

'We shall endeavour to work this out together, for the good of all concerned. More than that I cannot say. The boys shall have to be told, as they are now old enough to understand.'

Marged nodded in silence, grateful at last to her father for his decision.

'One more thing,' said Wil. 'I shall have to speak with the Chapel Deacons. You realise that don't you?'

Marged nodded again, this time holding her head bowed low to the ground.

'As for the boy,' said Wil, 'He's lucky not to be getting a good hiding from me, and as for you Anna, I'm disappointed that you were a party to this deceit.'

'Now then Wil, there's no need to go on to Anna, you can see how flushed she is looking,' said Beti trying to draw the attention away from Marged to where Anna sat in the corner.

Attempting to rise from the chair Anna said, 'I must be getting back. All this has been too much for me.'

Quickly Marged stepped in, 'I'll come with you. It's getting quite dark.'

'I'll be the one to walk Anna home,' said Wil gruffly. 'I'd welcome some time to myself on the walk back.'

Marged handed Anna her shawl, which she placed over her shoulders, as the evening air felt cold. Then she squeezed Marged's hand as she whispered, 'Don't worry, it will all work out.'

As Wil opened the door, he took her by the arm.

'Mind the step Anna. We don't want you falling. There have been enough shocks in this house for one night.'

As father and daughter walked together, they had few words to say to each other until they reached the door to the cottage.

'Are you coming in?' she asked.

'No merchi,' he replied. 'Are you sure you'll be alright now? I'll be getting back, there's a great deal on my mind and I have to think things out for myself.'

As Wil turned away, Anna stopped him saying, 'Don't blame her too much Da. She has told me that the boy was not from the village. It is hard for all of us to accept but Marged will have to live with this for the rest of her life.'

Wil looked at her and said, 'I have a feeling Anna that you know a lot more about this business than you are prepared to say.'

She did not answer him except to wish him goodnight as he walked away into the darkness.

A week later Beti called at the cottage to tell Anna that arrangements had been made for Marged and Wil to attend a meeting with the Deacons of the Chapel that very evening. There, they would be informed of Marged's condition and due to the sin she had committed it would be decided whether she would be allowed to continue to worship at Elim Chapel.

As Wil was also a Deacon there, it would be his shame as well as hers. Anna knew in her heart that it would take courage for Marged to face the elders, as she said, 'Tell her my thoughts go with her Mam and I pray that everything will go well for her. It will be quite an ordeal.'

'Is there anything you wish to say to your father?' asked Beti.

'No,' said Anna. 'It's so unfair to do this to her Mam. Believe me, Marged is innocent.'

'Your father has no choice in this matter Anna, you know that only too well,' said her mother sadly knowing that the rules of their Chapel had to be adhered to.

'Then tell her to call to let me know what happened, as I'll not be coming down to Cefn Glas now. It's my feet, they are so swollen today,' said Anna.

'I'll see myself to the door, you must rest Anna,' said Beti as she prepared to leave.

As she watched her mother depart, Anna burst into tears. She longed for Peter to return when she would again feel his comforting arms around her.

Marged arrived the next morning and before she could remove her shawl and bonnet Anna began to bombard her with questions as to what had happened at the Chapel the previous evening.

'I was so nervous Anna. Da did not speak to me on the way and when we arrived there the Deacons were already assembled in the big seat waiting for us. We stood before them and as he began to speak to them I felt a terrible shame come over me until finally I raised my eyes only to find such a look of disgust on Justin Williams' face that I looked away again. When I told Mam of this, she said. that him of all people had no right to condemn me since he's been carrying on with Mary Ann Roberts and was probably the father of two of her children at least!'

'Oh! Get on with you Marged,' said Anna impatiently, 'Tell me what happened to you!'

'Well, they read from the Bible condemning me for my sin and then retired to the Vestry to make their decision. It is that I am not to attend Chapel and Da is to see to it that I read the scriptures every day. And only when they decide I am cleansed of my sin will I be considered to go there again, which will probably be after the baby is born. I was condemned for not naming the father and now the whole village will know by this evening. What shall I do? Da has not spoken to me since.' With that, Marged broke into tears sobbing.

'Come now, don't get upset,' said Anna softly. 'You know people are about to talk but you'll get through this. You are innocent, and now that Rhys Thomas has left, there is no one to connect him to you and it will be easier for you to carry, on.'

'I wish I could believe you Anna. I've told Mrs. Thomas I can no longer continue to work there and I daresay by now she will have heard in the village and know what my reasons are. This will leave me with time to come and help you all I can, if you'll let me,' said Marged.

'I'll be glad of it', said Anna trying to reassure her and at the same time wanting so badly to give her sister the love and attention she would now need.

Peter came home with news that for the next few weeks he would be working on Carwyn Thomas' land nearby, which delighted Anna who had wanted him to be there when the baby arrived. In the evening they would sit together by the fireside, happy with what little they had. Anna never questioned him about his life in Ireland and the family he had left behind. But now and then she would sit and listen when he chose to speak of his homeland and she knew in her heart how much he looked forward to having a family of his own again.

Earlier in the day, Owen arrived, bringing with him bundles of wood, which he had cut, for the fire. The boy had seemed upset so Peter had suggested he helped him in the garden, and as they began to talk he soon found out what was bothering him.

It appeared he'd had an argument on his way home from Bible class. Some of the boys had shouted nasty things to him about Marged.

'Wanted to fight them, I did Peter, and I'd have beaten them too, but I had my best suit on and I knew that Da would tan my hide when I got home,' he said defiantly.

'It takes a wise man to make a decision like that, Owen,' said Peter looking at the lad who was now turning into a fine young man.

'Well, I don't know about that Peter, because my blood still boils when I think of them. Terrible things they said about her. Why did our Marged allow this to happen? If I knew the boy who was responsible for it I don't think I could hold my temper because I'd have to fight him, that I would!' said Owen.

The two sat together on the low garden wall while Peter tried to explain that Marged would now need all the help and understanding they as a family would have to give her.

'It is not for us to judge her Owen but to support her. It will not be easy, but you have made a start today by walking away from a nasty situation.'

The young boy nodded glad now that he had confided in Peter. As Anna watched them from the window, seeing Peter's hand as it rested on her brother's shoulder, and the look on Owen's face as he listened intently to what the older man was saying, she felt grateful to him. How lucky she was to be married to such a man.

Marged became a regular visitor to the cottage as she rarely ventured near the village since her school friend Carys Jenkins had ignored her as she stopped to chat with her.

It had hurt her deeply as did the looks and stares given by most of the community, but it made her more determined than ever to do right by the child. After the initial shock both Beti and Wil tried to support her and her brothers Owen and Huw would jump in defence of her but the shame was hers alone to bear. It was such a happy time for Anna and Peter and she envied them.

It was quite early in the morning, dawn was just about to break when Anna felt a sharp pain, which immediately woke her. She shook Peter's arm gently trying to wake him and as he opened his eyes she whispered to him.

'You'd better get up, I think I'll be needing Mam and Marged soon.'

Peter flung off the bedclothes and jumped from the bed, then fumbled to find his clothes and boots in the semi darkness. God! Had the time come at last he thought?

The early morning air felt crisp as he struggled to put on his trousers and he began to shiver.

'Will you be alright?' he asked as he reached the door.

'Yes,' she said feeling another sharp pain, which caused her to gasp. 'And Peter, call on the way and ask Shona Jones if she'll come!'

Shona had safely delivered half the population of the village and had been readily standing by for Anna Malone whose time had now come.

As Peter hurried from the cottage, Anna got herself out of the bed and amidst several sharp pains, managed to get down the stairs where she tried to light the fire. They were coming more often now, and she felt herself beginning to vomit but nothing came from inside her. She lit the fire but had to give in as she collapsed in the nearby chair. She was exhausted and relieved to hear voices coming up the garden path.

Beti rushed through the door and as soon as she saw her she said, 'What on earth are you doing Anna? You should be in bed.'

'I had to light the fire Mam in case we'll be needing hot water,' she answered as her body doubled up once again in a painful spasm.

Marged came to help her out of the chair and up the stairs to the bedroom.

'I'm afraid Marged,' she said.

'Hush now, we are here with you,' answered Marged trying to reassure her as she settled Anna beneath the sheets holding her hand tightly.

Minutes later Peter arrived with Shona Jones the midwife who immediately gave everyone orders.

'What can I do?' asked Peter looking at her.

'You can keep out of my way, that's what you can do,' said Shona Jones busying herself around in the kitchen after she had been upstairs to see Anna.

Seeing Peter looking so bewildered, Beti told him to go to find Wil who had already left to work in one of the fields.

'This is going to take some time my boy so be off with you. You can tell him that likely or not he'll be a grandfather by the end of the day,' she said.

Peter did as he was told but first he climbed the stairs to spend a few moments with his Anna. Marged stood outside the bedroom door leaving the two of them in each other's arms.

'I'll not be far away Anna, I feel so helpless' he said holding her close to him.

'Everything will be fine, you'll see,' she replied, ' Now go and find Da and come back later.'

He nodded, looking at Marged on his way out.

'You'll not leave her, will you?'

Marged squeezed his arm gently then reassured, he left.

It was hours later that the men returned to the cottage, as Wil who had been through this four times in all knew that there was no rushing to bring a baby into the world. He had tried to tell Peter how nervous he had been when Marged was born, then followed Anna and finally when Owen and Huw had arrived, his life had been made complete.

Will had begun to mend the garden fence while Peter continued to chop firewood unable any longer to listen to Anna's cries from the bedroom as Shona Jones came and went time and time again.

It was then that he heard a small crying noise, then silence. Surely there was something wrong? Then he heard a loud smack and another cry pierced the air, bringing Marged out to the garden crying with tears of joy.

'Peter, come quickly. You have a little girl.'

Peter laughed out loud as he began to hug her.

'And Anna?' he asked.

'She's fine. She's waiting for you,' said Marged but he'd already started to run up the path and into the cottage where his wife and baby daughter waited for him.

Marged turned to face her father who had sat down on the bench nearby.

'You have a lovely little granddaughter Da,' she said softly.

Wil nodded his head. 'Thank God,' was all he could say.

Marged walked slowly back into the cottage hoping and praying that when her time came he would welcome her little one also.

So it was that Elizabeth Lewis Malone, named after her grandmother Beti, was baptized in Elim Chapel where her name was recorded in the huge, black Chapel Register. As the days passed, she came to be loved by everyone especially by her father, who for him, the dream had come true. A dream where he could at last rebuild a family that he'd lost.

Then it became Marged's time. A little boy was born to her at Cefn Glas, a beautiful child with dark, curly hair and dark eyes. From the moment she held him in her arms Marged worshipped him. Thanks were given for the safe deliverance of mother and child but there was not the rejoicing that had been at Anna's little cottage.

Tongues wagged again in the village but this time they did not upset Marged. This child was hers and no one would ever come between them. Her father never mentioned the father of her child again and soon he and Beti her mother helped in every way they could to raise the child with her.

Mrs Thomas had offered her work at the Big House but Marged declined the offer knowing she would never go there again. She named the child John William Lewis. The baby did not have his father's features and for that she was grateful. The time came when she was allowed to return to her Chapel and this she did knowing it would please her father once more, but there were still those who shunned her presence there. However, she ignored them as she comforted herself by continuing to attend the meetings. She took her son to play with little Elizabeth, as often as she could and as the two babies grew together both she and Anna became closer than ever before and gradually Marged began to accept her life such as it was.

Elizabeth was a bonny child with fair, sandy curls, which sometimes looked as if they were tinged in gold. She reminded Peter of his sister Kathleen and many times he would sit looking at her wishing his own family could share in his joy. His thoughts often returned to Ireland now, but he knew he could never recapture his boyhood days. He was glad to be working nearer home but now and then he would still journey to the surrounding markets with cattle and livestock for Carwyn Thomas. Peter returned from one of these journeys bringing home with him another drover by the name of Morgan Harries.

Marged who was visiting with them at the time was conscious of the stranger's eyes on her as she laid the table for supper.

'I hope I'm not putting you out Mrs Malone?' Morgan asked as he saw Anna preparing a bed for him by the fire.

'Not at all, I'm glad Peter persuaded you to stay. After all, I'm always grateful when Peter tells me that he's lucky to find a bed for the night when he's away. I worry so much about him. Does you wife worry about you?' Anna asked.

'I'm not married, but as for my mother, she worries about the four of us boys at home although I'm the only one who has to go away on times,' he replied.

Morgan could not take his eyes off the quiet girl as she began to place the dishes on the table. Peter had told him about her and that she had a son, and he wondered how any man could abandon her and the child.

'There now, I've finished Anna,' said Marged laying a jug of milk down in front of her. 'I'll not stay to supper as I've promised to be back to put John to bed,' she added.

Morgan Harries stood up and holding his hand out to her he said politely, 'I'm pleased to have met you Miss Lewis, I hope we meet again sometime.' Marged shook his hand, 'I'd like that,' she said quietly.

Peter sat in the corner lighting his pipe and seeing the two together laughed as he said,

'Look out Anna. I think Morgan Harries has been smitten with our Marged.'

The couple immediately released hands feeling very embarrassed as Marged then bid goodnight to them and Morgan sat down at the table to devour the meal in front of him.

In the months that passed, Morgan Harries became a regular visitor to both the cottage and Cefn Glas Farm. He paid court to Marged having no concern as to what people had said about her and the child. He knew that both Beti and Wil were wary of him, as to what his intentions might be toward their daughter, but as time went by he proved to both of them that his feelings were genuine as he came to love Marged and the baby, John, and eventually he was accepted by everyone.

His mother and brothers were delighted at his newly found happiness as they were convinced he was becoming a confirmed bachelor and they welcomed Marged and the baby with open arms.

Marged and Morgan were married quietly in a small Chapel near Morgan's home but came to live at Cefn Glas until such time as they would have a place of their own.

Marged was happy at last; moreover John needed a father. Although the child was deeply attached to his grandfather Wil, he had now begun to follow Morgan around like a shadow.

Beti was in her element, delighted at last to have a large family to look after once more. She intended to make the most of it. Soon it would be Owen and Huw's turn to find partners for themselves. Owen had now passed eighteen and had an eye for the girls, while Huw just sixteen years old was shy and retiring by nature.

The two boys often went to visit Anna and Peter at the cottage. Anna was heavy with her second child and was glad to see them as they called by, ready to give a hand with the chores if Peter was away. She had encouraged them to talk to her about their friends but one evening as she sat with Peter she said,

'I think you should have a word with Owen and Huw.'

'What about?' he asked.

'Their courting of course,' she said in a 'matter of fact voice.' 'I doubt if Da has told them anything and God forbid they'll bring trouble home. He'd kill either one, you know how strict he can be.'

Peter laughed. ' No one warned me when I courted you my girl. I had to find out on my own, that I did.'

Anna blushed as he pulled her toward him trying to place his hands around her full body. She struggled to get free as he laughed again.

'Will this one be a boy Anna?' he asked.

'Time will tell. It's a boy you'll be wanting is it?' said Anna. He did not reply but she could see by his face that is what he hoped for.

Peter loved Elizabeth his little daughter and he made every minute with her count while he was at home, telling her stories and singing to her as they climbed the stairs to bed. However, he longed for a little boy. If it were to happen, their life then would be complete.

Peter's wish however was not to be granted for another little girl was born to Anna while he was away.

'You're not disappointed?' Anna asked as he sat at the side of the bed looking at this tiny baby whose black hair and eyes were dark, Welsh eyes that had bewitched him from the first time they had met.

'Of course not,' he replied honestly. 'She's as beautiful as you Anna.'

'I've not named her yet but I thought we would call her Kate after your sister Kathleen,' she suggested.

'Yes it's just right for her and I thank you for thinking of it.'

Peter lifted little Elizabeth up on his knee and as he cuddled her to him he thanked God for the gift of his two precious little girls.

CHAPTER 7

A full year passed and although Peter disliked having to be away so often he knew he was lucky to get work at all. Times were hard; Anna grew vegetables to sell at Market and sometimes took in sewing. Wil and Beti helped when they could but Peter did not wish to be in debt to them. Marged and Morgan who had not yet been blessed with children of their own called to see Anna regularly, spoiling the two little girls with love and affection.

One morning Beti made an unexpected visit as Anna was pouring herself a cup of tea. Noticing the worried look on her mother's face Anna said,

'You're just in time Mam. Sit down and join me, we can have a chat. Is this a social call or is something worrying you?'

Beti hesitated for a second, then began,

'It's Owen, I saw him at the market. I thought he was supposed to be helping your father but there he was, large as life, talking to a pretty young lady. Dressed in blue she was with an expensive looking shawl on her shoulders. I think he saw me but then he hurried away with her and when I asked if he was there he said I'd made a mistake.'

Anna listened patiently, trying to understand why her brother had behaved in such a way.

Her mother continued.

'Mrs Richards, the shop, told me she'd seen Owen earlier with Miss Medi Preece of Bryn Cethin. She's come to live with her grandparents since her mother Rowena died recently. Marged must have known also, because when she called they went out into the garden and after they had a terrible argument Owen then came to tell me the truth. He's meeting her regularly and now he wishes to bring her to meet us. I've not told your father of this and I am so worried Anna. I don't know why Marged lost her temper with him. It appears she's upset Owen by saying Medi Preece was so high and mighty, and that she was only toying with his affections, him being a farm boy and all. He told her to mind her own business then she went off in a temper. We've not seen her since. It's not like Marged to act in this way.'

'I'll speak to Marged, now don't you worry Mam,' reassured Anna. 'As for Owen, you can tell him to bring the young lady here to tea on Sunday and I'll talk with him also, and I would avoid saying anything to Da about it yet. Peter is home so I'll have plenty of help.'

After her mother had left, Anna poured herself another cup of tea and began to ponder over what her mother had told her. It was obvious to her why Marged had acted in such a way. She did not want her brother to associate with any one from Bryn Cethin, but Anna knew if Owen had made up his mind to befriend Medi Preece there was nothing she could do to prevent it.

Now that her mother had gone, so distressed was she that Anna had forgotten to tell her the news, she was pregnant once more!

On Sunday afternoon, after Chapel, Owen brought Medi Preece to the cottage and after all the necessary introduction; they then sat down to tea.

'You have a cosy little place here Mrs Malone,' said the girl politely as she tried to make conversation.

'Yes we are happy here,' replied Anna, 'but it is a far cry from the Big House. I expect you are finding it strange after living in a busy place like Swansea?'

'It was strange at first, waking up to the sounds and smells of the countryside. My grandparents are wonderful to me but I miss my mother and father dreadfully,' Medi said.

'I was sorry to hear of your trouble, your mother was so young. Now that you are here, do you see your father often?' asked Anna.

'He's very busy as he works in partnership with my Uncle Rhys, and as he travels a great deal he thought it appropriate for me to live with my grandparents at Bryn Cethin. However, he tries to see me as often as possible.'

All the time the girl spoke, Owen could not take his eyes from her and it became obvious to Anna that he was besotted with her.

'How did you both meet?' asked Anna.

Peter looked toward his wife; it was so unlike Anna to pry into people's affairs. What indeed was she up to?

Medi gazed at Owen then held her hand out toward him.

'We met at Bible Class,' she said. 'I've walked Medi home several times since then,' added Owen, 'but not to the front door of course.'

'I've told him he's being silly, but he feels that Grandfather would object. I can make up my mind to choose my own friends,' she said.

Anna looked at Medi and saw a girl who knew what she wanted and would set out to get it.

Elizabeth and Kate who had been on their best behaviour throughout, were now becoming bored and Owen immediately offered to take them out into the garden to play while Medi offered to help Anna clear the dishes from the table.

Later when Owen managed to get her on her own he eagerly asked, 'What do you think of her Anna? Isn't she lovely?'

'Yes, she is,' replied Anna,' but I shouldn't want you to get hurt. Mr Thomas may have big plans for her, she comes from a rich family Owen.'

'Are you saying that I am not good enough for her Anna? Marged tried that approach and I shouldn't want to fall out with you over it as I did with Marged,' he said sternly.

'Now calm down. She's a very nice young lady and it's obvious she likes having her own way,' said Anna.

'Despite what everyone may say, my mind's made up. One day Medi will be mine, whatever it takes,' he said kissing Anna tenderly on her forehead.

'Get away with you now,' she laughed, she could never stay angry with Owen for long, and as she watched him carry the cool drinks for them out to the garden she knew nothing would make him change his mind.

After the young couple had taken their leave Anna asked Peter what impression he had of the young Miss Preece.

'I've seen her up at the Big House and she always seems so alone. It's obvious Owen is deeply in love with her but he'll need to watch his step. The Thomas' think the world of her and they may plan for her to marry into a wealthy family.' Then Peter asked,

'Have you told your mother the news yet?'

'No, she had so much on her mind when she called that I had no chance to tell her about the baby. This time I feel sure it's going to be a boy Peter.'

'Let's hope so Anna. Carwyn Thomas has said there'll be some work on the land and we could do with the money so I'll not be away for some time, I'll be near at hand to help you.'

'Oh! That's good news, Peter. I do hate being here without you,' said Anna.

'By the way, where was Huw today? I thought he was coming to tea also?' asked Peter.

'I think he felt shy, knowing that Owen was bringing Medi to meet us. It appears he decided to go up to the woods after Chapel, you know he likes his own company. I wish he wasn't so quiet. I can't believe he's seventeen already. If only he had a little of Owens' confidence. Soon they will both be planning to leave Cefn Glas as well.'

'One thing's certain,' said Peter, 'they must both decide their own destinies as I did mine. I came here with nothing and you were the best thing that ever happened to me Anna. My life has been well blessed.'

He put his arm around her shoulder and as they climbed the stairs to bed she whispered to him,

'I wish it could always be like this.'

'Always is a long time,' was his reply.

CHAPTER 8

David Malone, the third child to be born to Anna and Peter was now a few months old and as his tall, sun-tanned father carried him, his face was filled with smiles. This beautiful little boy had made Peter's dream come true. Now the family was complete. They were returning home from a picnic, Elizabeth and Kate held hands as they ran ahead of their mother and father.

Anna wore a daisy chain in her dark hair, which Elizabeth had made for her earlier in the day. A large picnic basket swung from her arm now devoid of the food they had eaten that afternoon. She stopped as they reached the large iron gate to release the catch for them to pass through. Before closing it again little Kate climbed up and hung on to it tightly, enjoying the ride as it closed with a clanging noise. Her mother lifted her down safely saying to her,

'The gate must always be closed behind you so that the animals do not stray from the fields causing the farmer to search for them.'

The evening air was still warm as the sun began to set over the hill. It had been a good summer and soon it would be time for the harvesting to begin. Peter looked at the fields around him, it was good to be alive.

Soon the Harvest Festival would be held at Elim Chapel, where all could give thanks for another fruitful harvest safely gathered in. The children would take their gifts and flowers and fruit while the women of the Chapel arranged the stone windowsills with ferns and flowers in abundance.

A large loaf of bread shaped into a golden sheaf of wheat would stand on the table near the pulpit, having been delivered by the boy from the bakery. It would be displayed for all to see.

It was a busy time at Cefn Glas like many other farms around. Peter had asked Carwyn Thomas to release him from his work so that he could help Wil in his fields while Morgan did likewise, planning to bring with him a few more men from the village.

Owen and Huw could hardly wait for the work to begin and they arose almost before the sun came up. It had been decided that Morgan and Owen were to go with Wil, while Peter would take Huw with him to the lower pasture, and as the dawn began to break they all set out for an early start to the day.

By mid-day the heat caused the sweat to pour though their shirts as they clung to their bodies. Peter decided it was time to have a break and seconds later Huw was already taking a bite from a huge piece of bread covered with dripping, that tasty melted fat which had come from the meat his mother had cooked the night before.

Peter's throat was so dry as he reached for the bottle of water Beti had packed in a basket for them. His hands began to search for it but it wasn't there.

'What's the matter?' called Huw, his mouth so full of food he could hardly speak.

'My throat's on fire and I can't find the water in here,' he answered.

'Never mind,' munched Huw 'Mam will realise we've left it behind. I expect she'll bring it to us.'

'I can't wait that long boy, I must have a drink. I'll go back for it, I shan't be long,' said Peter rising to his feet.

'I'll run faster than you,' the boy replied. You have a rest, then you can decide where we'll start next.'

Before Peter could protest at this, Huw jumped up and began to run toward the gate and out into the lane. Peter then decided to carry on with the work where he had left off not noticing the boy in his haste had left the gate wide open.

As Huw reached the farmhouse he called out as loud as he could.

'Mam Beti, where's the water? You've forgotten to put it in the bag and we're dying of thirst up there!'

Beti looked up suddenly as she heard her son's voice. She was busy washing shirts in a large tub of water.

'I'll give you Mam Beti, my boy!' she laughed out to him. 'You're not too big for a clip across the ear for your cheek!'

She left what she was doing and began to dry her hands on her apron. Then she began to fill the bottle with cool water from the pump and as she handed it to him he quickly said,

'I can't stop any longer Mam, Peter'll be waiting for me. Parched for a drink he is.' As he ran out of the yard she called to him,

'Take your time boy!' But all she saw was a glimpse of his hand as it waved goodbye to her. Beti returned to her washing, chuckling to herself. Her youngest boy could always make her laugh. There he was, helping in the fields. Her Huw was becoming a man, growing up too fast.

Huw ran as fast as he could up the lane toward the field when suddenly he felt a sharp pain in his right side of his body. He must not let this slow him down he thought to himself as he continued to run. Peter would be waiting anxiously for his return. As he reached the gate he was surprised to find it was wide open. The scene before him made him halt in his tracks, as he stared at Peter hanging on to the branches of the big oak tree where he had tried to climb to safety. Beneath him stood an enormous black bull, its hooves tearing at the ground beneath him. The snorting animal, whose nostrils held a large metal ring through them, paced backward and forward allowing no means of escape.

The boy immediately dropped the bottle he was carrying, as he heard the branch of the tree begin to snap with Peter's weight. Without a thought to himself, he began to shout and flap his arms in the air, trying to draw the animal's attention away from Peter towards the direction of the gate.

He knew he could get the bull out of the field and then jump to safety himself so he shouted louder once more.

'For God's sake Huw, get out now!' yelled Peter, but the boy could not hear his cry as the bull turned in his direction tearing at the ground once more. Huw began to run as fast as his feet could carry him, while the earth shuddered as the huge animal tore after him.

He was nearly there, he thought. Once passed the gate into the lane, then double back locking the gate after the bull had gone and he would be safe.

Suddenly the searing pain in his side returned without warning. It was much worse than before as he began to struggle for breath. Then his steps began to falter as darkness overtook him and finally he fell to the ground exhausted.

The huge animal tossed his young body into the air again and again until it lay lifeless near the wide, open gate. Then the bull was gone!

Peter fell from out of the tree and ran breathless toward Huw as he lay there on the ground.

He lifted the boy's crumpled body in his arms and cradled it.

'God in heaven. Why?' he screamed out loud as he looked toward the sky. Not a sound could be heard only that of the gentle breeze as it sighed through the tall leafy trees, which minutes before had sheltered him.

Peter lifted Huw up and carried him sadly through the gate and out into the lane in search of help at the old stables nearby but it was much too late for Huw who had already departed from this world.

In no time at all several men were despatched in search of the rampaging bull while others went to break the news to Wil.

Peter sat there still in a state of shock until at last Wil arrived followed by Owen and Morgan. Never had he witnessed grown men cry when they saw the injured body of the dead boy. After hearing how it had happened Wil tried to compose himself.

'How am I to tell Beti?' he asked looking at each of the men around him. 'I cannot take him home like this. It will be the finish of her.'

'We've sent for Sam Matthews the Undertaker, Wil,' said one of the men. 'We hope we've done right. He'll know what to do when he arrives.'

Wil nodded, grateful that someone had taken this duty out of his hands.

'I must get to your mother,' he said to Owen, 'and you'd better see to Anna,' he said to Peter.

Owen walked over to where Peter sat and placing a hand on his shoulder said,

'Are you alright?' Peter nodded as he got up.

'You are right Wil. The news must be broken by both of us before they hear from someone else,' said Peter.

'You go on ahead Da,' said Owen. 'I'll stay here and arrange everything with Sam on your behalf.'

Wil began to leave knowing that however hard it would become, Owen would do what was right and proper for Huw. As for himself, how he would find the words to tell Beti he could not rightly imagine.

Peter borrowed a horse and rode off in the direction of the cottage but as he reached there he found Anna waiting outside for him.

She called out anxiously, 'Is it true Peter? Has our Huw been badly hurt.'

How had she heard he wondered? He had not reckoned on the news travelling so fast throughout the village. Without waiting for his reply she turned on her heel to go back inside saying to him,

'Mog Richards called to me as he rode past to say there'd been an accident. For God's sake what happened? I'll get the children ready, we'll be needed at Cefn Glas.'

Peter followed her into the cottage, then caught her by the shoulders and swung her around to face him as he said in a hushed tone,

'Anna, I'm afraid it's too late my love.'

Immediately she could see the look in his face and Anna knew then that her brother was dead.

'He's gone?' she asked, dreading to hear his answer. Peter nodded to her with tears in his eyes.

'Oh my God!' she cried out as she almost collapsed to the floor as Peter's strong arms caught her and led her to sit down in the chair.

'How did it happen? Who was with him?' she asked fighting back the tears. Peter was lost for words not knowing how to begin to tell her the story, but before he could reply Anna stood up and began to move about quickly gathering things together.

'Has Mam been told?' she asked. 'You call the children, they are upstairs playing. We must hurry Peter!'

Peter could see she was in a state of shock. It would be time enough for her to learn the truth of what had happened when they got to Cefn Glas. So he replied,

'Your father has gone to tell her. I said we would get there as soon as we could. Morgan has gone for Marged. And Anna,' he hesitated for a moment then added, 'We shall both have to be brave for everyone's sake.'

She did not reply. The fear of having to face her parents in their grief had completely numbed her.

There was an air of sadness as they reached Cefn Glas and saw Owen standing in the doorway. Anna caught around him hugging him tightly for a second as she asked,

'Where are they both?' Owen shook his head saying, 'Mam is in there but she'll not say a word to us. As for Da, he's out in the barn as far as I know. I've only just returned.'

'Everything's taken care of then I gather?' asked Peter watching Anna go inside.

'For now, at any rate,' replied Owen. The two men followed Anna while the children went to play in the yard.

Beti sat in silence near the fireplace; she did not raise her head as they approached her. Anna knelt down beside her mother.

'It's me, Anna,' she said softly, but there was no response as her mother rocked to and fro in the chair.

'I'll go to find your father,' said Peter, and Anna replied,

'Tell him I'm here will you?'

Owen came to stand near her and nodding in Beti's direction he said, 'She's been like that since Da broke the news to her.'

Then they heard a knock at the door. Owen turned to answer it and found Medi Preece standing there.

'I came as soon as I heard. Is there anything I can do?' she asked gently.

Her arrival surprised both brother and sister. Owen did not know what to say but Anna stood up and said,

'I'll be grateful if you would look after the children Medi. It was difficult to leave them with anyone and I'm sure they'll be glad to see you.'

Medi, grateful to be of help in some way or another nodded to her but before turning to leave she said,

'Are you alright Owen? This has been a terrible shock for everyone especially grandfather. He's been everywhere, making enquiries as to how the bull escaped from the field. It's been caught at last and now it's on its way to the slaughterhouse. He told me to tell your father that he shall be calling to see you as soon as he can.'

'No, I'm not alright,' he said, 'and I don't care what's happened to his precious prize bull. As for my brother, it's too late for him!'

Medi held back her tears and said sadly.

'I'd better go to look for the children then.' Owen gruffly replied, 'Very well.'

'Don't blame Medi,' said Anna, 'It was good of her to think of us. Try to understand how she must feel, after all she didn't have to offer her help to us.'

Owen felt guilty that he had spoken to Medi in such a way. He would have to apologise to her later he decided.

Anna returned to her mother and sat down beside her once more and as she squeezed her hand gently, Beti looked up at her.

'He's gone Anna,' she said. 'My Huw will not be coming home again.'

'Hush now Mam,' said Anna stroking the hair back from her mother's forehead. 'Everything will be alright you'll see.'

Softly her mother's words came to her. 'He was so happy Anna. When he left, he was laughing and singing and teasing me in his way. Why did it have to happen? What am I going to do without him?' she asked.

Anna began to cry.

'I don't know how it happened, Mam, or why. Peter's not told me. It's empty I feel from the moment I knew our Huw was dead.'

Beti looked toward Owen and it was he who finally told Anna.

'Huw died because he thought he was trying to save Peter from the bull.'

Anna gasped, 'Oh no! Is it true?'

Beti nodded her head sadly, and then both women listened to Owen as he slowly began to relate the story of how it had all happened to Huw.

Soon it began to dawn on Anna, she had lost the brother she loved but Peter was alive because of his actions. Anna turned to her mother and hugging each other tightly they began to cry together.

She then heard Peter's voice.

'It's no good Anna, your father is out in the barn and I cannot persuade him to come in.'

Anna stood up, wiped the tears from her eyes and with renewed strength she ran into her husband's arms.

'Why didn't you tell me how it happened Peter?' she asked. 'The shock of it! How awful it must have been for you.'

'I shall never be able to forget it Anna, and I shall never forget Huw either,' was all he could reply.

Clinging tightly to him she replied softly.

'We both owe him a great debt. Now I must go and find my father, leave him to me. I'll talk to him.'

Then she left quietly through the door leading to the yard where she crossed in the direction of the barn.

Leaving the sunlight behind her she entered the coolness of the barn and it took a few seconds for her eyes to become accustomed to the light.

'Da, it's me,' she called out. There was no reply. 'Are you there?' she called again.

Suddenly a sob filled the air causing her to turn to the right and then she saw his shadow as he sat on a large bale of hay in the corner.

'Come now,' she said gently. 'You can't sit here all alone when you are needed so badly inside.'

His hand reached out to touch hers and as she clasped it tightly he began to sob and his body began to shake. He looked like a child who needed comforting when it knew it had done wrong.

'Why did it happen Anna?' he cried. 'Huw had everything to live for, he was so young. He went out to do a man's work but he was only a boy. Now there are no goodbyes, nothing left to be said now he's gone.'

'He was a man,' said Anna proudly. 'He gave his life for Peter because he loved him like a brother, and now my children still have their father and I, my husband. I shall miss him, God only knows, but I shall never forget the sacrifice he made for us. Now come inside Da, we must be strong for the others.'

Wil nodded at last, 'You are right merchi,' he said. 'My family need me now.'

As they walked back out into the sunlight, father and daughter gathered strength from each other as they returned to the house filled with sadness.

'Where's your mother?' Wil asked Owen as he entered the kitchen. 'Peter persuaded her to go upstairs to lie down. I'm worried about her Da, she's hardly spoken a word and it seems as if she can't believe what has happened,' said Owen.

Peter came down the stairs.

'Go to her Wil,' he said. 'She has need of you. I can do no more.'

Wil did as he was told and climbed the stairs slowly. He had only just left the room when Morgan arrived with Marged and John. The sisters embraced and once again grief overtook those present.

Owen then began to tell the other men what arrangements had been made to bring Huw's body home the next morning.

'Sam Matthews said that he will see to everything,' he whispered so as not to upset either of his sisters further.

Suddenly, they heard their mother cry out from the room above.

'I must go to her,' said Marged, rising from the chair.

'No, let her be,' said Anna. 'Da is with her and it's best they are left alone to comfort each other for now Marged.'

Eventually their mother's crying died down and soon their father came down the stairs.

'She's quiet now,' he said. 'Cried herself out she has.'

Marged went to him and placed her arms about him weeping quietly. On seeing his mother so sad, the little boy climbed on his father's knee and began to cry.

'Now then John,' said Morgan. 'Let's go and find your cousins is it? They can't have gone far.' The child nodded as they left the room.

'We can stay as long as you want us to Da,' said Marged.

'That's good,' replied Wil. 'We shall need someone here in the morning to be with us when they bring our Huw home.'

'Then I'll take John with me when we leave,' said Anna.

Wil sat down in the rocking chair and put his head in his hands, the tears began to flow fast.

'It was a terrible sight. I shall never forget it. My boy. My boy!' he cried.

Marged bent to comfort him. But Anna touched her arm gently leading her away.

'It's best that he cries Marged. Let him have it out of his system,' she said.

Some time later, Medi brought the children to them. They immediately ran to Wil sensing something was wrong with their grandfather who was always so happy to see them.

Wil began to talk with each of them. 'Well, what have we here then?' he said taking a small bunch of wild flowers out of Kate's hand.

'They are for Mamgu,' said Elizabeth. 'Shall we give them to her?'

'Not at present merchi, she's sleeping,' said Wil. These children were a blessing to them he thought to himself.

Suddenly there was a knock at the door. Owen went to answer it and as he opened the door he found Carwyn Thomas of Bryn Cethin standing there.

'Good evening,' he said politely. 'Is your father here? I'd like to speak with him.'

'You'd better come in then,' said Owen in not so polite a tone. Wil stood up and as both men shook hands Carwyn Thomas said, 'I hope I'm not intruding Wil. I've come to pay my respects and to let you know how sorry I am for the tragedy.'

Before he could continue, Marged stepped forward and in a loud voice said,

'Sorry is it? Who let the animal out of your field and why are you not out looking for the scoundrel who did it instead of standing here. We do not want your pity.'

Wil became astounded at this outburst. What was Marged playing at? They were all shocked and upset but there was no reason for her to speak like this.

'Be quiet Marged. Let Mr Thomas have his say,' he commanded.

Marged sat back down. Carwyn Thomas then continued.

'If there is anything either I or my family can do, you only have to say. As for the bull, it has been captured and destroyed.'

Then it was Owen's turn to speak.

'You have helped already by having your valuable animal put down, so that it will not kill again. As for your offer of help, we are already indebted to Medi.'

It was only then as Owen spoke that Carwyn caught sight of his granddaughter as she stood near the children at the other end of the room.

'What are you doing here Medi?' he asked, surprised at her presence, but it was Anna who replied.

'We are grateful to Miss Preece who came immediately to offer her services. She has taken care of the children. We are indebted to her.'

'Then you can return with me,' said Carwyn Thomas speaking to his granddaughter.

'Your grandmother will be worrying about you.'

Medi walked over to where he stood and as he again extended his hand to Wil he said,

'Please give my condolences to Mrs Lewis and tell her that my wife and I would like to attend the funeral service if you will allow us. Never fear Wil, however long it will take I'll get to the bottom of this tragedy.'

Wil thanked him then turning to Medi he thanked her also.

'I shall call to see Mrs Lewis again,' she said as she left with her grandfather.

Anna walked with her to the door.

'Thank you for your kindness Medi. I shall not forget it,' she whispered.

As she went back into the room Anna found an argument taking place.

'Now Marged. What are you saying? The man is as sorry as we are and I do believe he will try to do his duty to find out what happened,' said Wil.

'Well I think it was a cheek, coming here to offer help. It won't bring our Huw back, you are too trusting of that family Da,' said Marged angrily. Seeing the hate in his sister's eyes Owen was bewildered at her attitude.

'What's got into you?' he said. 'What has that family ever done to hurt you in any way?' he asked.

Marged annoyed at his question left the room without answering and quietly climbed the stairs fearing her actions had taken her too far.

The next person to call at the house was Goronwy Evans. Peter shook hands with the Minister then showed him into the front parlour where Wil joined him.

'Do you think your mother will wish to see him?' Peter asked Anna.

'I think she's best left alone for the time being,' answered Anna making her way to the stairs. 'I'll tell her we're about to leave Peter. The children look tired and so am I. We need to return home,' she said.

As Anna climbed the stairs sadly she began to cast her mind back over the years. It seemed like only yesterday that they had played here together as children laughing and tumbling down these same old stairs. They were happy times, but now, all of a sudden the happiness the house had held was gone.

Holding back the tears she entered the bedroom to find Marged sitting quietly on the edge of the bed, watching her mother sleeping peacefully at last.

'How is she now?' whispered Anna

'She's cried herself out. She's completely exhausted,' answered Marged. 'Who was that at the door?' she asked.

'It's the Minister. Da is with him in the front room. This is why I came to say we are leaving Marged. The children are getting tired.'

Marged arose from the bed and followed Anna out onto the landing saying,

'I'll come downstairs with you as I shall want to say goodnight to John if he is to go with you.'

As they reached the top of the stairs, Anna halted and placed an arm on that of her sister's, then said,

'Marged, take my advice, you must keep calm. You can't afford another outburst like the one you had downstairs. Surely you can see that. You will only put yourself at risk.'

Marged pulled her arm free. Her eyes flashing in temper she whispered so as not to wake her mother.

'Why do you side with them Anna? I want nothing to do with any of the Thomas family, certainly not Medi Thomas. She's no good for our Owen. You are blind to it all!'

Anna could see that she had failed to reason with Marged and so she replied.

'Come now, let's not argue among ourselves. We are all in a state of shock and we must keep our minds clear for we shall both be needed here these next few days.'

They descended the stairs, one behind the other and as they entered the kitchen the sisters heard Elizabeth say,

'I'm tired Dada. Where's Uncle Huw? Is he coming home with us?'

The innocent talk of the child silenced each of them.

Peter picked her up in his arms.

'Now little one, it's time to go home,' he said kindly.

Marged called her father from the front room and excusing himself to the Minister, Wil followed her to the kitchen.

'We'll be here in the morning Da,' said Anna as she kissed him on his cheek. Wil took her in his arms hugging her tightly to him. Anna looked into his eyes, which were now sad and drawn. His body seemed to stoop before her and he seemed to have aged ten years in just one day.

'At a time like this, I thank God for all of you,' he said.

Then one by one they left, leaving Marged and Morgan to cope with the situation until the morning came.

CHAPTER 9

As the funeral day dawned, people came from miles around to pay their respects to young Huw Lewis of Cefn Glas who had died due to such tragic circumstances.

The family, who loved him, mourned him as he was laid to rest in the grounds of the Chapel he loved. Beti and Wil were besides themselves as they each tried to comfort one another. As the time came for them to leave, Peter held back, and as he stood at the graveside he bowed his head in his own silent prayer to the boy who had given his life for him.

As soon as they reached Cefn Glas the women busied themselves making tea and serving food to the mourners who had returned to the house with them.

Owen immediately went to find Medi who was already making her self busy in the kitchen.

'Thank you for being here,' he whispered to her. 'I could not have seen this through without you.'

Medi touched his hand, but before she could reply her eyes caught sight of young John as he passed by in the other room.

'Your nephew John, he reminds me of someone,' she remarked to Owen.

'Perhaps you see him like his mother,' said Owen looking after the boy.

'No, it's not that,' she replied. 'It's just that there are times when I see a familiar look about him that puzzles me.'

The couple did not notice Marged as she stood nearby listening to their conversation.

Her heart began to race wildly. Had Medi seen the resemblance to her own uncle? Marged could see how the boy had changed as he grew older. He was a constant reminder of the past as his features had begun to resemble that of his father Rhys Thomas.

Anna was always there to reassure her that this was not so, however, she had become more and more terrified that one day her secret would be revealed. The one thing she was certain of was that she and Medi Preece could never become friends. Of that she was sure. Hopefully, Owen would eventually come to his senses and break his relationship with her. It was all Marged could hope for.

From the opposite side of the room Anna stood watching her sister closely and she knew that if Marged was not careful her hatred would eventually consume her.

Her attention was turned in the direction of Peter who had stood near Beti most of the day ready to comfort her, and she was grateful of the close relationship between her husband and her mother.

As she watched them, she promised herself that when this day was over she would endeavour to give more time to him and their family of little ones come what may.

o o o

The harvest Festival at the Chapel went ahead as planned with the children looking forward to taking their gifts of fruit and flowers there. Despite the sadness she still felt in her heart, Anna knew she had to make the effort to attend with them, and as she sat with Peter in the family pew she looked at her little ones with pride.

Elizabeth and Kate sat quietly; holding bunches of sweet smelling flowers in their hands. Peter sat beside them holding their baskets of fruit, which Anna had neatly arranged that very morning. David slept soundly in Anna's arms.

Elizabeth began to fidget, waiting for the service to begin. Peter spoke to the child, gently saying that it would not be long now.

Anna also longed for the service to commence. She had found it hard on entering the Chapel, and had to hold back the tears, which came so quickly to her eyes. Was it just one week ago this place had seemed so dark and dismal as the funeral hymns rang out for the departure of her beloved Huw?

Now this same Chapel had been transformed into a multi-coloured scene of fruit and flowers, which also adorned the stone clad windowsills, while golden sheaves of corn, decorated each wooden pillar.

A huge loaf of bread shaped and plaited into a sheaf of wheat stood on the table beneath the tall pulpit.

Blodwen Evans began to play the first cords of music on the organ and soon some of the old harvest hymns were sung by both adults and children alike. Then her husband, Goronwy Evans, began to pray giving thanks to God for yet another fruitful harvest gathered in.

The time arrived for the children to step forward to the pulpit with their gifts. Elizabeth held her sister's had tightly and with a look of pride on her face she handed her gift to the minister. Kate, on the other hand, had become reluctant to part with the flowers she carried. The minister knelt down beside her and after a few kind words in her ear he persuaded her to hand him her gift.

'Well done!' said Peter to his daughters as they returned to their seats. Anna nodded and smiled to them as she gently rocked the baby in her arms.

After the service had come to an end they stood outside waiting to shake the minister's hand.

'Where are Wil and Beti? I thought they might have come with you,' he said.

'I'm afraid it's a little too soon Mr Evans' Anna replied. 'The service was lovely but would have been so upsetting for Mam. She is still very much in a state of shock, as are we all. Huw always loved the Harvest Service you know.'

Goronwy Evans nodded silently then said, 'Tell them I shall call to see them soon.'

Anna turned away and began to walk toward her brother's newly covered grave.

It was still covered with wreaths of flowers, which had remained fresh from the week before.

Peter followed her holding the baby in his arms. Then they stood together in silence while Elizabeth and Kate played among the gravestones oblivious of their parents' sadness.

'I still can't believe it Peter,' she said as she linked his arm in hers.

He did not answer immediately, but then he felt the need to brighten the sad moment as he suggested they would call with the children to Cefn Glas on their way back home.

'Yes let's do that,' said Anna as she called to the two little girls to follow them.

Beti had cooked so much food the previous day and now there was no one there but Wil and herself to eat it. The only way she could cope with her grief was to keep herself busy. Owen had gone out walking with Medi, and as both she and Wil sat in the fireside chairs they had suddenly lost their appetites. She was therefore delighted to hear the happy chatter of the children as they approached the back door to the kitchen. The two girls ran to their grandfather eager to tell him about the Harvest Service but he sat in his chair quiet and withdrawn, taking little notice of either of them.

Beti called Anna into the next room.

'Your father is taking this hard,' she said. 'He was so strong for my sake in the beginning, but now I can't bear to watch him grieve in this way. He found a little boat he'd carved for our Huw. You remember the one? Since then he's not spoken to me. He doesn't want to mention Huw's name and gets quite nasty when I talk about him. It's nearly driving me crazy Anna.'

They returned to the kitchen where Anna immediately began to talk to her father.

'The Minister asked after you Da. He'll be calling to see you soon, so he said.'

Her father did not reply.

The sounds of the children's laughter as they played in the garden with their father filtered through the air.

Wil looked up. 'Can't they be quiet out there!' he grunted.

'Now then Da,' said Anna turning on him, 'Our Huw would not have wanted all this!'

'How do you know? Have you ever lost a child?' was his answer.

Anna turned angrily toward her father.

'God forbid that I ever will,'she said. 'Huw was your son but he was also my brother. Have you asked yourself how we feel? Mam, Marged or I? And Owen also? They were friends as well as brothers!

How do you know how we get through the day without him? You think only of yourself and of how much you miss him. We all need each other at this terrible time. We need you Da, and we can't carry on without you.'

Suddenly her father placed his head in both hands and began to cry but Anna never moved to comfort him. It was her mother who knelt beside him and placing her arms around him Beti said,

'She's right Wil. Things can never be the same without him but we must have faith in each other to carry on.' She touched his forehead brushing back a damp curl from his face.

'Are you alright now?' she whispered to him.

'In time Cariad, in time,' was his reply.

He got up from the chair. Quietly leaving the room he went up the stairs to the bedroom, leaving both Anna and her mother standing there.

A few seconds later Wil returned. In his hand he carried a small wooden boat.

'I've something here for the children. It belonged to our Huw. You'll stay for tea merchi?' he asked Anna. 'I'll show them how to sail it on the stream later on,' he said gently.

'Why don't you take it out to them now Da while I help Mam set the table,' said Anna.

Wil nodded and left the room.

'You have a way with him Anna and I'm, grateful to you,' said Beti.

Anna said nothing in return though she was pleased at her father's action. Deep down, she knew however that it would take a long time before they would begin to feel like a whole family again.

CHAPTER 10

Summer quickly came to an end, and as the leaves began to turn colour on the trees Anna dreaded the approach of autumn. As she walked in the direction of the village she noticed each leaf as it fell on to the pathway in front of her. The parcel she carried felt heavy in her hands, and so she placed it on the ground for a second or two.

'Hello there Anna. Are you going my way?' a voice called out to her as she rested herself. She was relieved to see Medi Preece sitting in a small carriage holding the reins of a small dapple grey pony. Medi immediately stepped down and taking the heavy parcel from Anna she lifted it into the back of the carriage.

'I'm taking some sewing to Mrs Seth Lloyd,' said Anna, gladly accepting the offer of a lift as she climbed up beside the young girl.

'Then we'll go to the village together,' replied Medi. 'Grandmother wanted some supplies and I needed to get away for a while. How are Mr and Mrs Lewis? I expect they find it very strange without Huw?' she said gently.

'It's kind of you to ask Medi. They are both trying hard to carry on but the old place is not the same without him. Sometimes we imagine it all seems like a nightmare and we wait for him to walk through the door once more,' said Anna sadly.

'Owen has taken it hard also,' said her young companion. 'He gets upset even at the mention of Huw's name.'

Anna looked at her, and the girl's words made her realise that she had not given any thought to how her brother must be feeling.

Suddenly feeling guilty at having neglected him she said,

'They were so close you know. Owen and Huw. He must have missed him beyond a doubt. I am grateful to you Medi that he's been able to confide in you.'

Medi nodded, but stared ahead as the pony trotted on.

Anna continued to speak.

'I don't wish to interfere, but I have to know what your true feelings are for my brother. It is obvious that he loves you in a very special way, and he has been hurt so much over Huw that I don't want to see him upset by anyone again.'

Medi pulled gently at the reins and the pony came to a halt. She turned to Anna, then answered.

'I love your brother dearly, and not since my mother died have I felt so needed by anyone. We've already talked things over, and I've offered to ask my father if Owen can come to work for him. But it would mean him leaving Cefn Glas and that he will not do, so near to your mother and father losing Huw. I don't expect him to choose between me and them, and I told him last evening that he has to decide for himself my heart is sad but I'll not influence him in any way.'

'Thank you for being honest with me Medi. Maybe I can talk to him, but you are right about one thing. He has to make up his own mind on the matter,' said Anna.

Medi pulled gently at the reins once more and the pony trotted on, the remainder of the journey was spent in polite conversation but Anna's thoughts were more than troubled ones.

Later that evening, as she and Peter talked together, they discussed what Medi had said about Owen.

'Do you remember what I told you a while ago Anna? The time will come when Owen would decide where his future lay? Maybe the time has now come and a decision has to be made,' he said.

'I know what you are trying to say Peter,' she answered. 'But how will they manage without him at Cefn Glas?'

'Your father can afford to employ someone and it will do Owen good to get away. Huw's death has affected him deeply. It will be hard on them of course but this is his chance to better himself. Besides if he loves the girl he must make the right decision.'

Looking at Peter as he ended his sentence Anna felt the need to ask.

'And what of Marged? If Owen goes, if he accepts the work, it will take him into close contact with Rhys Thomas. After all he is Ryland Preece's partner.'

'That is for Marged to work out,' said Peter. 'Then I need to go to Cefn Glas in the morning, perhaps he will listen to me,' she said earnestly.

o o o

Owen picked up the heavy spade and forced it into the hard ground and as he began to dig the earth turning the soil over and over again, his mind began to wander into the past. They had always worked in the garden together he and Huw planted the seeds and watched them grow. With each turn of the spade the dark rich soil fell beneath his foot. He paused for a moment, then looking toward the sky he said out loud.

'Where are you Huw? God! I miss you!'

He remembered the last time they were here. Huw's throaty laughter, the golden curls tumbling over his forehead, and that slight stubble which had begun to form on his chin. He had teased him about it. Those things, like him, were now gone forever.

Owen carried on digging, oblivious of the sounds around him. He paused then, and as he gazed around the land he began to ask himself the one important question on his mind. How could he leave? He was needed here, but his love for Medi was so great he was torn between staying and making a future with her.

Then he heard the garden gate creak open. He turned around to find Anna standing there.

'I didn't hear you coming Anna,' he said putting the tool down on the ground. Then wiping his sweaty hands on the leg of his trousers he said. 'My mind was far away, thinking of our Huw and the times we spent together up here.'

'I'm on my way up to the house, and as I heard you digging, I thought I'd come to speak with you first,' said Anna.

'Nothing wrong is there?' he asked his sister, his face full of concern.

'Medi told me of her offer. I think it would be good for you to get away Owen. We all miss Huw, but we have to carry on and lead our own lives. Surely you realise that? You have plans to share with Medi. She loves you and I know you love her. The farm is doing well and it is about time Da hired some help with the work.'

Owen listened to what she had to say then replied.

'I feel I am letting them down, and with Huw gone, it wouldn't be fair but I cannot give Medi up either. Anna, what am I to do?'

'Grasp the chance in both hands. If you really love her then that's all that matters. Would you like me to have a word with the folks? I could pave the way for you?' she said.

'No. Thank you Anna. This is something I have to do for myself. My mind is made up.'

Then bending to pick up the spade once more he continued digging the ground. As he looked down at the rich earth Owen did not hear the gate closing quietly behind his sister as she left him. His thoughts now were only of the future.

Owen had visited the Big House, Bryn Cethin, once before. Medi had invited him to tea on the same Sunday as the Harvest Festival had taken place at Elim Chapel. He was glad to accept the invitation although he felt a little uncomfortable at the time. Both Carwyn Thomas and his wife had welcomed him but he had the feeling that it was more through a sense of duty over Huw's accident that he had been invited at all.

Despite Medi's protests, he had made an excuse to leave that time; however, here he was being invited yet again. This time he had decided to make an impression on them. He loved and wanted their granddaughter and this was utmost in his mind.

He arrived, dressed in his best suit with starched collar to his shirt. As he was ushered into the sitting room he began to feel nervous once more, but as soon as he saw her standing there before him he began to relax.

Medi looked more than beautiful. She wore a cornflower blue dress with ribbons at her throat that matched the sea blue colour of her eyes. God! She was lovely he thought.

Carwyn Thomas rose to greet him shaking him by the hand.

'It's good to see you again my boy. How are things at Cefn Glas?'

Owen replied that both his parents were as well as could be expected under the circumstances. Neither man mentioned the recent accident, and suddenly there was silence in the room.

This was broken as Leah Thomas began to speak.

'Well then, I think it's time for us to take tea.'

With that statement she began to pull on a long velvet sash which hung attached to the wall. It immediately rang, summonsing the maid to the room.

'We are ready now Jeni,' said Leah Thomas. The maid scurried back to the kitchen and soon returned carrying a large silver tray on which was arranged a tiny milk jug and sugar basin and a large silver pot which held the tea. She set it down on a small table beside her mistress, then curtsied and left the room.

Taking a delicate bone china cup and saucer into her hands Leah Thomas then asked, 'Do you take sugar Mr Lewis?'

'Yes please,' Owen replied.

She poured the tea into the cup, then set it to one side as she began to lift the tiny lumps of sugar with a minute silver tongs, eventually dropping them one by one into the tea.

Medi stepped forward and taking the cup and saucer from her grandmother, she handed it to Owen who held it steadily in his large hands, afraid that he might drop it.

As the old lady began pouring the tea into the remaining cups, Owen's attention turned to his surroundings. He had not paid any attention to it during his last visit but this time he felt more relaxed and as his eyes wandered around the room he began to notice how lavishly it was furnished.

It was a fairly large room, painted green and blue in colour. Heavy velvet drapes hung from the wide windows. These were held back with huge tassels of silk. A large oak dresser stood at the far end of the room and on it were displayed many fine pieces of china and glassware such as he had never seen before.

Further along stood a tall ornate clock, which struck the hour then the half-hour. Carwyn and Leah Thomas sat either side of a beautiful oak fireplace, it's panels delicately carved with leaves and flowers. On its mantelpiece stood two huge china vases identical in shape and colour. Silver frames stood in line, holding photographs, one of which Owen guessed to be Medi's mother, it looked so much like Medi herself.

Above the mantelpiece hung an elaborate mirror, its edges carved in the same pattern as that of the fireplace.

'Do you like the room?' asked Leah Thomas as she noticed the young man's gaze.

Feeling very embarrassed at her question Owen began to stammer but then Medi came to his rescue.

'I expect Owen finds it quite different to his home grandmother, although I must say that I think the sitting room at Cefn Glas is charming.'

Thankful for Medi's intervention, Owen soon began to feel at ease. Every now and then he was conscious of Medi smiling toward him and he knew his visit was going well. As she offered a plate of sandwiches and cake to him she brushed his hand slightly in an effort to let him know this.

When they had ceased eating, Carwyn Thomas began to speak.

'There is something you should know my boy,' he said gravely. 'I've made many enquiries as to how that dreaded bull of mine got loose and I've finally found the answer. It appears that a passing traveller or tinker as they are called had been given work in one of my fields. He was caught pestering some girl from the village and my lads reckoned with him. It appears he released the bull for revenge but I'm afraid he was long gone before the accident occurred.

I have tried to trace his whereabouts but my efforts have been in vain. He has disappeared. I would be grateful if you could convey this to your father.'

'I appreciate you efforts sir,' said Owen, 'and I'm sure my father will thank you himself. Our home is so empty without Huw, but we are all learning to accept it somehow. They say time is a great healer, but all we can do for now is to carry on for each other.'

Carwyn Thomas nodded he head sadly. Leah Thomas sensed the sadness now beginning to overtake them and so she attempted to change the subject gracefully.

'Medi has told us of your love of the sea Mr Lewis. It seems strange for someone who has worked the land to be fond of the sea also.'

'I've always loved the sea, and the ships, which sail on it. As children my father often took us to visit relatives who lived near the coast, and I have never forgotten it. I've never been on a ship though,' he added.

'Medi's father and my son Rhys are in the shipping business you know,' continued the old lady.

'Yes I'm aware of that, Medi has spoken about her father quite often to me,' answered Owen.

'Enough of this talk,' said Carwyn Thomas. 'Come, I'll show you around the grounds. We'll leave the women to talk amongst themselves.'

Owen bowed to Medi and her grandmother then followed his host out of the room.

Leah Thomas noticed the look in the eyes of the young girl as they followed Owen Lewis.

'It seems you are set on this young man then?' she said.

Medi's eyes turned in the direction of her grandmother as she answered.

'Yes I am.' Then taking the old lady's hand in hers she asked quietly,

'Will you speak to father for me? Let him come to meet Owen for himself then he will find what a kind, loving man he is. I love him dearly, but I also love my father. One day, I hope that he will accept Owen and consent to our marriage. However, if he does not, then I shall go to Owen as his wife, if he will have me.'

'You'll settle on being the wife of a farmer?' said her grandmother. 'Think hard Medi. You have had a very different upbringing to him.'

'As long as I am with him, sharing his life, that is all that matters,' she answered.

The old lady watched her closely, detecting a note of determination in her voice. Medi was so like her mother Rowena. She had known what she wanted out of life and taken it in both hands, leaving the countryside to live in the city with Ryland Preece. Her marriage had been a happy one, marred only by her untimely death. It would not be too difficult to persuade Ryland, who worshipped his only child and would want nothing but her happiness.

Smiling at her granddaughter she hugged her tightly.

'Leave it to me, I shall do what I can,' she said.

With joy in her heart, Medi planted a kiss firmly on the old lady's forehead then ran off in search of Owen and her grandfather.

o o o

In the weeks that followed, Owen and Medi continued to see each other and as each day passed their love grew stronger.

Soon it was time for Owen to meet Ryland Preece at Bryn Cethin House, and he knew his background and family would come under scrutiny. However he was determined to make a good impression of himself to the man whose daughter he loved dearly.

Introductions having been made, Medi left the two men together in the sitting room. Owen sensed immediately that Medi could do no wrong in the eyes of her father but he also knew that Ryland Preece was nobody's fool. He began to answer the questions put to him, and as their conversation deepened, Owen realised that all this man required of him was a guarantee of his daughter's happiness.

Ryland on the other hand had begun to realise the feelings of this young man standing before him. Given the chance it was possible for Owen Lewis to prove himself in business. He would have to leave his family and the village of course, but this would be the sacrifice he would have to make. At the mention of Medi's name, one only had to see the look in the young man's eyes to know how much he loved her.

They spent the next hour talking and making plans until at last Medi was summoned to the room.

Breathless, she ran through the door and from the joy seen in Owen's face she knew that all was well.

Her father spoke directly to both of them giving his blessing for the courtship to begin. Owen was to be offered work with Ryland Preece's firm and he had barely completed his sentence when Medi threw her arms around his shoulders to hug him tightly.

'Thank you father. You'll not regret it,' she cried.

Owen shook hands with the older man. Medi's shouts of glee soon attracted her grandparents who were invited to share the good news. Leah and Carwyn Thomas had come to like the boy and they too were delighted at the match.

All that remained was for Owen to share his plans and good fortune with his own mother and father. How would they accept the news he wondered?

'Shall I come with you Owen?' asked Medi as she walked him to the great front door.

'Thank you, but no. This is something I have to do for myself Medi,' he replied.

'Then I'll pray that everything goes well for you my love,' she said, kissing him tenderly.

She stood watching him ride into the distance wishing she was already at his side.

During the visits made by Anna to Cefn Glas over the weeks that had passed, she had taken every opportunity to speak to her parents about Owen and Medi. She would try to prepare them for the day when he would have to make his decision to eventually leave the family home.

So it came not as a shock to them when Owen announced that evening of the plans already agreed with Ryland Preece.

His mother had cried of course, while Wil his father, talked long into the night of what this new future would mean to his son. They were both very fond of Medi, and eventually they agreed that it was the best thing that could happen to Owen. However, both Beti and Wil had certain misgivings about their son eventually becoming one of the gentry.

Finally, they gave him their blessing and Owen was relieved that all was well between them.

Marged was horrified to hear the news however and could not wait to discuss it with Anna

'I don't understand it. How could they be pleased for him? When they are married we shall lose sight of him altogether,' she cried. 'First Huw, now Owen! How are Mam and Da going to manage without him? As for the Thomas family, I shall never accept them, neither will I accept Medi Preece!' Marged cried.

'That's not fair!' replied Anna firmly. 'We all stood by you and you received help and understanding in your time of need. Now it is Owen's time. He has his own life to lead and it is not up to you to question it. Surely we've seen enough sadness in our lives. We should be happy for him.'

'I might have known you'd take sides with him Anna. I have nothing more to say except that I shall not go to the wedding when it happens. It is obvious that Rhys Thomas would be there and I cannot be under the same roof as the man. Not even for one day!' shouted Marged.

In a calm, controlled voice Anna replied, 'I understand how you feel Marged. However, are you willing to take the risk of having to tell Morgan the reason why you will not go? And Mam, Da and even Owen? Peter and I alone have held your secret all this time. It was your choice to keep the truth from your own husband. It was all a long time ago. Rhys Thomas knows nothing of John's existence and providing you can control your feelings, he need never know.'

Marged knew in her heart that Anna was speaking the truth, but she felt far from reassured as to what the implications might be. The sisters decided to take the children to Cefn Glas with them where they hoped to hear further news from both their parents.

Finally Marged returned home having made the decision that she would meet the future as it came. She had too much to lose otherwise.

CHAPTER 11

The same dream occurred to Anna again and again, until it finally turned into yet another nightmare. She could see Peter as he scrambled from the bull's fury into the branches of the tree. She could hear Huw's screams as his delicate body was hurled through the air and the final thud as it landed on the ground.

She sat up in bed, shaking and sweating until Peter again held her tightly in his arms to reassure her it was only a dream.

Lately, Anna had begun to feel tired and depressed. Questions that seem to have no answers to them began to nag at her. Was Owen right in the decision he had made? Would her parents cope without him? The uncertainty of how Marged would react at the forthcoming wedding of Medi and Owen. Even the children, who always demanded a great deal of her attention had finally begun to wear her body down.

She realised that she still grieved for the brother she had lost, but the others still depended on her strength to help them through each day without Huw. Peter, though trying to be patient with her, found it difficult on times to cope with her moods. Today was one of those times.

'Are you going to Cefn Glas?' he asked as she sat sewing dresses for her two little girls who were to be Medi's attendants at the wedding.

'I may go there tomorrow,' she replied. 'Why do you ask?'

'Owen has asked me to speak at the wedding. I'm not very good at speechmaking. Could you ask him to call and maybe we can work something out together?' answered Peter.

As she put the needle down for a second, it pricked her finger causing a drop of blood to flow.

'Goodness Peter, now see what you've made me do. Have I to arrange everything with Owen as well?' she said angrily.

Peter was surprised at her irritable manner. What had come over her? This was not his Anna speaking to him.

'Will you ask him to call, Anna,' he asked, his voice a little more sternly than before.

'Yes, if I see him there,' was her curt reply.

The following day did not see a change in her mood, so Peter decided to go to Cefn Glas himself. Taking the children with him he set out early, leaving Anna to put the finishing touches to the bridal dresses.

On arriving at Cefn Glas, Wil had immediately taken charge of the children who he introduced to the two new farm hands he had just taken on.

Peter sat in the kitchen with Beti who began to sense there was something on the lad's mind.

'You seem quieter than usual Peter. Not worried about being our Owen's best man are you?' she asked.

He did not reply and so she said again:

'Is there something wrong, Peter? Sometimes, sharing a problem makes it seem a lot simpler, but if you don't wish to share it with me, I can't help you.'

Peter hesitated, then spoke.

'I'm not sure mother,' he said.

He had never called her 'Mam' like the others, and it had taken Beti a long time to aquaint herself to the word. However, she could see by his face he was deeply troubled.

'It's Anna,' he went on,' I realise she grieves for Huw as much as anyone, but she's not been herself of late and I can't seem to help her any more. She has little enough patience for anyone and it's so unlike her. I'm that worried, I had to talk with someone.'

'I suppose we are to blame as much as anyone Peter. Her father and I have relied on her too much. Both Owen and Marged still turn to her for advice, that much I know. Maybe she needs time to herself. I've an idea. Bring the children here early on Saturday so that the two of you can get away by yourselves. Maybe a ride, or a picnic? She'd like that. I'll ask Wil to get the buggy ready for you.'

Grateful for Beti's suggestion, he asked,

'Do you think she'll come?'

'Leave it until the very last minute to tell her, then she'll not have time to refuse,' said Beti.

'You are good to us mother,' Peter said fondly, feeling at last that an answer to his worries was now in sight.

It was late on the Friday evening that Peter made his move and finally told Anna of the plans he had made with Beti.

'What nonsense Peter. How can we leave everything? I've had no time to prepare anything!' she protested.

Peter, however, ignored her pleas and continued,

'I thought perhaps a picnic near the sea. Your father has the buggy ready for us and your mother has planned the food we shall take. What more could we want? The sea air will do us good.'

Peter had taken her completely by surprise. How and when had he made all these arrangements?

'Please say you'll come Anna,' he pleaded, 'we have so little time by ourselves.'

It would be so good to get away, even for a short while she thought to herself.

'Very well, I'll go with you, but you must promise that we shall not return late. There are the children to think of.'

'I promise,' was his reply.

Anna kissed the children farewell one by one as they ran off to greet their grandparents. The peaceful existence at Cefn Glas was soon to be shattered by their very presence.

'Be good children now,' she called after them.

David turned to look back at her then began to cry but Wil was there trying to persuade him out into the garden. The girls' laughter could already be heard as they played on the swing nearby.

'Thank you for everything Mam,' she called out to her mother.

'Get away with you, before I change my mind,' laughed Beti as she listened to the noise continuing in the garden.

The horse and buggy transported Peter and Anna away, giving them at last the temporary freedom they had both longed for.

He put his arm around her shoulder while his other hand held the reins.

'Today is for us,' he said gently

Anna rested her head on Peter's shoulder while he looked down at her and smiled.

o o o

The small seaside cove was deserted as Peter lifted her down from the buggy. Then tethering the horse to a nearby tree, he placed a large bag of oats and a bucket of clear water for the animal's use.

Carrying the basket of food and a large woollen rug, they clambered down a rocky path which led to the beach. Anna slipped once or twice and as he caught he in his arms they laughed at each other. As they reached the sandy shore she began to smell the fresh sea breeze and taste the salt in the air. The clouds moved gently in the blue sky above causing rays of sunlight to escape through at varying intervals. The slight breeze shook her dark curly hair as it shone like a raven's wing.

Peter looked closely at Anna. The years had not changed her. She was still as lovely as ever. She dropped to her knees, spreading the blanket out over the warm sand before her.

'This place brings back lovely memories of my childhood,' she said lovingly.

'We always came here when we were children. We'd hide among the dunes playing hide and seek. I can almost hear the voices of the past whispering to me in the tall grasses. Is it the same for you Peter? You never speak of your childhood. Were there times of happiness in your life with your family?'

'There were happy times, but there were sad ones also,' he replied as he stooped to pick a pebble up from the sand. 'Let's not talk about families today Anna, let's just be ourselves.'

He threw the pebble as far as he could out toward the sea, there it landed with a quick 'plop' as it disappeared from view.

Anna unpacked the basket of food and soon all that was left was a few crumbs, which were soon devoured by several greedy seagulls.

'Let's take a walk,' said Peter holding his hand out to her.

They climbed a small winding path, which took them to the cliff top. There they sat down on the grass. The view was breathtaking, even the horse standing in the shade of the tree looked so minute in the distance.

'I feel as if I am sitting on top of the world,' Anna cried out.

Turning to Peter she said quietly, 'I'm so glad we came here.'

She lifted her hand to shade her eyes as she looked out toward the sea.

Suddenly, Peter took her in his arms and pulled her roughly toward him, his kisses immediately arousing the passion she felt within her.

'I love you Anna Malone, you are everything to me. There are times I hate to share you with anyone, not even the children,' he said.

'I'll always be yours Peter, no matter what happens,' she replied.

'Will you Anna? Even when I'm long gone from this earth?' he asked.

'Don't say such things! I'm frightened when you talk like that. Please don't spoil this moment Peter,' she pleaded as she began to feel a chill coming over her body.

She jumped to her feet saying,

'Let's hurry, it may be warmer down below on the beach.'

Anna then led the way as Peter followed without question.

The sand felt warm beneath their feet and as Peter lay down on the blanket with his coat for a pillow he soon began to drift off to sleep.

Seeing him lying peacefully there and not feeling tired herself, Anna decided to walk to the sea's edge. It was so quiet here except for the piercing squawks of a few seagulls overhead and the sound of the waves lapping as they reached the shore.

She took off her laced boots and stockings and waded delicately into the cool water, all the time lifting her long skirts so that they would not become wet.

The sea was calm and as she looked down she could see her toes quite clearly through the water. Tiny silver fish darted by, there and gone in one second. She began to walk along the shore splashing her feet in the water now and then. Suddenly she stood and looked back to where she had left her boots on the sandy shore, and she felt surprised when she realised how far she had come. She turned and walked back on the warm sand enjoying each moment of complete solitude. Picking up her boots she returned to where Peter still lay fast asleep. Then she lay by his side resting her head in the curve of his arm and soon she too had fallen asleep.

Peter stirred, then slowly opened his eyes. The sun was now quite hot in the sky. No longer were there clouds to be seen. Beads of perspiration trickled down onto his face and then to his neck. He turned around to find

Anna lying by his side. She was fast asleep. He kissed her forehead gently brushing the damp curls aside with his lips.

She began to stir slightly, but did not wake. He could hold back his emotions no longer as he took her gently in his arms. He moved his hand to caress her full breast and as her lips parted he bent forward to kiss her.

'I love you Anna,' he whispered again and again.

Her eyelids fluttered and as they began to quietly open she realised what was happening and clung to him saying,

'Hold me Peter. Don't ever let me go.'

'Hush now,' he whispered as he began to kiss her mouth again. Then murmuring soft words of love to her he began to caress the more sensuous parts of her body.

'Stop Peter!' she cried out, 'not here, we can't surely?'

'There's no-one here Anna, just You and I,' he said reassuring her.

Immediately she felt herself giving in to him until in absolute passion he entered her again and again. In one final moment she lifted her face to the sun and as their bodies moved in unison she felt her very soul reaching out to the heavens above. Their bodies lay together, exhausted. All their energy had been completely spent.

It was a while before either of them spoke, then Peter stood up and began to take off the remainder of his clothes.

'I'm going for a swim. Are you coming Anna?'

She shook her head and lay back on the blanket as she watched him run toward the shining water.

His voice called out,

'Anna, come on! The water's great!'

She looked around again at the deserted beach, then stepping out of her long dress and petticoats she ran naked down the warm sandy shore to join him in the water.

They swam and splashed each other and laughed like little children. Finally they ran back to lie in the sun drying their wet bodies together.

Then they make love again but this time it was gentle, and as they lay in each other's arms they did not want the day to end.

Soon, however, it was time to leave and as Peter shook the dry sand from the blanket Anna hurried about collecting colourful shells to take home for the children.

They climbed the path, weary this time. As he hitched the horse to the buggy Anna stood looking toward him. It had been a wonderful day, one she would never forget.

Peter climbed up on to the seat and as he held his hand out to help her he asked,

'Are your ready, my love?'

With tears in her eyes Anna nodded as she quietly sat down beside him.

o o o

The two men got up from the table, then Owen followed his father out into the yard where the daily chores of the farm waited for them.

The next few hours flew by and soon Beti was calling out to them that it was time to get ready.

As Owen reached the foot of the stairs he found his mother waiting there for him. Beti held her arms out to him and he hugged her tightly,

'Be happy my son. That is all I want for you,' she whispered to him.

'Thank you Mam. I know I'm doing the right thing,' said Owen with tears in his eyes.

'Then hurry now,' she said, 'or your bride will arrive there before you!'

Owen nodded to her, laughing as he raced up the stairs to get dressed for his wedding to Miss Medi Preece.

o o o

Marged entered the chapel looking nervously around her to see who was already there. She saw Owen and Peter sitting together in the front pew near the pulpit, and immediately walked toward them joining her mother and father who sat directly behind them.

Morgan and John followed her and sat nearby. Marged noticed the sadness in her mother's eyes. Beti had not found it easy to come to her chapel since Huw had gone and today she had come with very mixed feelings. Anna sat with David thinking only of the arrival of her two little girls who were to accompany the bride.

Suddenly Marged became aware of someone looking toward her from the seat opposite to where she sat. As she turned around, their eyes met.

Rhys Thomas caught her glance, and in that short moment he had remembered the shy little parlour maid. What a time he'd had with her!

His thoughts however were interrupted by the arrival of his niece, the bride, as she entered the chapel on the arm of her father. They were followed by two little girls, carrying baskets of flowers.

On being told of this wedding between his niece and the farm boy, he had registered his disapproval. However, he knew better than to incur the wrath of his parents by staying away from the wedding ceremony. So there he stood, listening to the young couple take their vows but all the time his thoughts were with the young woman sitting opposite him.

The wedding ceremony now complete, the couple left the chapel to shouts of laughter and congratulations from the people who stood around them. Medi noticed there was one face missing from the well-wishers, and as she looked around she saw Beti standing at the nearby grave of her son. Silently she walked toward her and taking Beti's hand she placed the bouquet of flowers in it. Beti looked at Medi with tears in her eyes and slowly she knelt down to place it on the grave beneath her. Then the two women walked back arm in arm to join the others waiting at the chapel door. The poignant scene had not gone unnoticed as both Owen and his father had seen Medi as she had joined Beti. Owen then led his bride to an awaiting carriage which would take them on their journey to Bryn Cethin where the festivities would be held.

Anna and Marged ran after them throwing handfuls of rice over them, calling out good wishes along with the others. As the carriage pulled away Marged halted where she stood,

'I don't know if I can enter that house Anna. Not while Rhys Thomas is there!' she said.

'Now Marged, remember what I told you. I will be nearby at all times. You have to take courage, it will be over all too soon. You'll see,' said Anna gently touching her sister's arm.

As they entered through the great oak door at the front of the house, Marged felt herself looking around the spacious hallway. Over the years it had hardly changed at all. However, this time it was strange for her to find herself the guest and not the servant.

Anna suddenly disappeared and for a moment Marged found herself alone. As her eyes began to take in the rich surroundings she heard a voice whisper to her,

'Brings back old memories doesn't it?'

She quickly turned around to find Rhys Thomas standing there, but before she could make her escape, thankfully John appeared on the scene calling to her.

'There you are Mam. Uncle Peter is about to speak and they are waiting for you.'

Rhys Thomas looked closely at the boy who tried to hurry his mother away. Was there something familiar about the lad?

He then glanced toward Marged who hastily followed her son into the drawing room. He decided he would seek her out later. Then they would have time to talk.

'Are you alright Marged?' asked Anna. 'You look so flushed. I'm sorry I left you but you know Peter. He just wanted to be reassured once more about his speech.'

'I want to leave this place Anna. The sooner the better,' whispered Marged wiping her brow with her lace handkerchief. 'Rhys Thomas has spoken to me and now that he's seen John I'm sure he's guessed something!'

'You are imagining things Marged,' whispered Anna back to her, but before they could continue their conversation Peter began to make his speech to the happy bridal couple.

For the remainder of the afternoon Marged remained at her husband's side, thankful that Morgan suspected nothing of the deep thoughts which continued to upset her.

Looking around the room full of people Marged's eyes began to search for her son.

'Where is that boy?' she asked her husband.

'He was here a moment ago,' answered Morgan, 'Don't worry, he'll be back soon.'

Marged, not satisfied at this, went in search of her son.

Rhys Thomas however had found the boy as he wandered about in the garden, and had taken the opportunity to talk with him.

'Hello lad! Are you having a good time?' he asked.

John nodded politely at this tall dark stranger who sat down beside him.

'How old are you then?' Rhys Thomas continued.

'I'm eight,' answered the boy.

Rhys looked closely at the boy. Eight years old!

How many years ago had it all happened here in this house. Dare he hope this boy was his? He certainly resembled both himself and Carwyn Thomas, his father. There was definitely a familiar look about the boy's eyes. Rhys was convinced of it.

Marged stood at the door in silence as she watched Rhys Thomas talking and laughing with her son. Her temper arose within her. She stepped forward and said out loud,

'John, what are you doing here? Your father and I are ready to leave!'

'Can't I stay a little longer Mam?' the boy eagerly asked his mother. 'Mr Thomas has told me about the ponies here. I can come to ride one if I wish!'

The boy's voice was full of excitement.

'I said we are leaving now!' said Marged.

'Go this minute!' she demanded.

Unaccustomed to the sharpness in his mother's voice, the boy ran off to find his father, but the tears were already smarting his eyes.

Rhys Thomas turned sharply toward Marged.

'There was no cause to speak to the boy in that manner. All he did was talk with me,' he said angrily.

She turned on her heel and prepared to walk away but Rhys Thomas ran after her and taking her roughly by the arm said,

'He's mine, isn't he?'

Her eyes flashing like lightening, she turned to face him,

'What makes you think that?' she replied, trying to remain calm while her whole being trembled with fear.

Rhys Thomas knew from the look on Marged's face that what he had suspected about the boy now had to be true.

'I've never been more sure of anything. The boy is mine!' he replied confidently.

'Try and prove it. You'll never succeed. Now let me go. My husband and son are waiting for me!'

She tore her arm from his as she turned again to walk away, but he followed her saying,

'I won't have to prove it. Already he begins to resemble my family. Does he also bear the same dark mole on his right shoulder that both my father and I carry?'

Marged did not reply. She dare not reply, for she had noticed the small dark blemish on the skin of her child's tiny shoulder immediately she had given birth to him.

She turned once more and faced the man she would hate for the rest of the life.

'He is not yours,' she lied, ' Stay away from my son or you'll be sorry if we ever meet again.'

Rhys Thomas would not be deterred, and with a warning to her he said,

'You will see me again. One day, who knows, I may even prove he's mine!'

Marged hurried away, her heart beating wildly. The sooner she left this place the better it would be for all of them.

As they journeyed home, Morgan began to notice how quiet Marged had become. It had been an emotional day for all of them and now the excitement had seemed to die down. John on the other hand, had talked constantly of the man who had told him about the ponies and of the grand house he'd seen.

'Mr Thomas said that I could go there any time I wished,' he said.

'You can put it out of your mind John, because you'll not be going back there ever,' said his mother sharply.

John began to cry but Marged scolded him even further.

'Leave the boy be,' said Morgan. ' I don't know what on earth's got into you today, Marged!'

Then soothingly he spoke to his son,

'Your mother is tired John. It has been a long day for all of us. We'll soon be home now.'

The boy lay down in the back of the cart, but in his mind he was still back at the house with its rich surroundings and promises of adventure.

When at last John was ready for his bed, he kissed his mother goodnight.

'Sorry, John,' she said, ' I didn't mean to upset you but you must realise that it would be impossible to dream about things which are out of reach to us.'

He nodded to his mother, but Marged realised how tense he had become in her arms.

As soon as John had left the room, Morgan decided to question her.

'I have to know what's wrong Marged. What has made you so angry? Unless you tell me, then I cannot help you. Today should have been a happy one, though I realise that you had your thoughts about Huw and the accident. But it seems as if you are at war with the whole of the Thomas family. Remember that Owen is one of them now.'

Immediately Marged burst into tears. Morgan was right. Her guilty feelings had begun to eat away at her, and she knew the time had come to tell him all that had happened. The years had passed and never once had he mentioned or questioned who John's father was. Now it was up to her to tell the truth, but how would it affect their lives from here on in?

Slowly she began to relate the story from beginning to end, and gradually she watched his face change with the anger that took hold of him.

Finally, when she finished there was a silence, which remained for several seconds. Then quietly he said,

'So Anna and Peter are the only ones who knew the true story? All these years they've helped you keep the secret. But why?'

'I always had the fear that Rhys Thomas would one day find out about John and try to take him from me,' she said sadly. 'Today he's guessed the truth and though I've denied his accusations I'm sure he's not believed me. And what of John? He seemed so at ease talking to Rhys. It hurt me so. Do I tell him the truth Morgan? You are the only father he knows. Will I always have to live the lie for the older he gets the more of the Thomas family I see in him.'

Marged began to sob, then taking her into his arms and holding her gently Morgan replied,

'I'm a simple man Marged. I've loved John as if he were my own and it's sad I've been that we were not blessed to have a family of our own. We've been happy together and I promise you Rhys Thomas will not come here to make trouble. If he does, I'll show him what trouble is. What happened was a long time ago, he will not come back into our lives. He has his lifestyle, we have ours and it's just as well that I know nothing of this else I'd have killed the man in that very house today.'

Marged looked at this man whom she loved dearly and silently thanked God for him.

'I fear so much for what he is capable of Morgan. Rhys Thomas is a man who usually gets what he wants,' she said sternly.

'It will not do his image any good Marged. Especially if folk find out what harm he did to you. As for John, when the time comes we shall tell him together.'

Morgan looked at her. He loved this gentle woman and her son. They were his life, and no man would ever take them away from him.

'I shall always love you Marged. We shall see this through. Now dry your eyes and be content that all will be well,' he said.

Marged knew in her heart that this strong man would stand by her and for now her son would be safe. However, deep down, she still had feelings that sooner or later Rhys Thomas would again try to enter their lives in one way or another.

CHAPTER 13

The excitement of Owen's wedding had now ended and life at Cefn Glas began to return to normal.

Beti and Wil, though kept busy by their daily routine, soon began to realise that life would never be the same without their children.

There were times they felt so alone, and often as nightfall came and they sat by the fireside together, there were few words they had to say to each other.

Anna and Peter's lives on the other hand were full with the love of their little ones, who had now begun to grow up very quickly. Anna felt sure she was once more carrying Peter's child. The child she knew had been conceived that day as they made love on the warm, soft sand of the beach where they had lain.

She had held back her news for now, as Peter had not been well. He had failed some days to work in the fields, suffering from a heavy cold, which had begun to affect his lungs.

They did not have riches. Their lives were blessed only by their children, but how would he take to the news of another child when it was becoming a struggle to rear the others?

Anna's chance came at supper time after she had taken the children to bed.

'You're very serious Peter, surely you are pleased at the news?' she asked quietly.

'Of course I'm pleased,' he answered ' it's just that we already have to go without so much, and with another baby on the way I'll have to find work that will earn us more money.'

Anna's heart felt heavy. She knew he spoke the truth but surely they would find a way to manage?

'The other children are growing so fast Peter, it will be good to have a little one around the house again. It will be alright, you'll see,' she tried to convince him.

Peter took her in his arms and held her tightly to him so that she could not see the worried look on his face.

'Yes, Anna, you are right of course. Together we will manage,' he said.

However, Peter had made up his mind. At the first opportunity he would approach Carwyn Thomas with a view to apply for his old job. Driving the cattle to market would indeed bring more money into the house. Anna would not be pleased, but with winter approaching he would make sure his children would not go without food in their bellies.

The very next day Peter walked up to Bryn Cethin but Carwyn Thomas did not hold the answer to his problem.

'I'll keep you in mind of course Peter, but I'm not needing another drover yet. There's plenty of work on the land,' he said.

Peter returned to the cottage downhearted and as he reached the kitchen door he heard Marged's voice.

She had not been a visitor since Owen's wedding.

'There's a stranger you are Marged,' he said greeting her.

'I stayed away from the village until I knew Rhys Thomas had left,' she replied quietly.

Peter sensed there was something wrong and immediately Marged began to pour out the story of what had happened on the day of the wedding.

'So Morgan knows the truth at last!' said Peter. ' Many's the time I've wanted to confide in him, but for the promise both Anna and I made you I would have done it too.'

'How did he take it Marged?' asked Anna.

'I shall always love him and be indebted to him for understanding, but if he had laid his hands on Rhys Thomas I think he would have killed him,' was her reply.

Then quietly she added,

'I shall never be free of Rhys Thomas for I fear he will still try to claim my child. Now enough of my troubles. Anna has told me about the baby, Peter. I'm so pleased for both of you.'

Peter immediately chose to change the subject by suggesting Marged stay for tea with them, but she declined his offer saying she had to return to Cefn Glas where Beti and Wil would be waiting for her.

As they walked her to the gate and waved her goodbye, Anna took his arm in hers,

'It's such a pity they had no children of their own. Morgan would have made a good father. We are so very lucky,' she said.

Peter stood at her side but he did not reply.

o o o

The weeks passed and Anna's time came at last. She gave birth to a little boy. They named Peter John. The children loved their baby brother from the very beginning, and Peter despite all his previous fears, adored his little son.

His luck had changed at last when Carwyn Thomas sent word that he urgently needed a drover to go to market. Peter was a trustworthy man, liked and respected by the others. He would fit in well with the men. Anna's protests fell on deaf ears as she saw Peter's determination to accept Carwyn Thomas' offer.

'The money is good, Anna. I won't be away that long, and if I am ill again, we shall have something put by. You already do more than your share of baking and mending for other people to help out. Now that we have Peter John, you must let me go,' he insisted.

Anna knew it was hopeless to argue with him, and so the night before he was due to leave, she packed some food for him to take with him on his journey. He was right of course, but her love for him was so great, all she wanted was for him to be near her always.

As dawn broke, Peter crept quietly downstairs so as not to wake Anna and the children.. It was a damp and misty day outside as he peeped through the kitchen curtains.

Anna lay awake, listening to his hushed movements below. She knew he couldn't let him go without saying goodbye and so she quietly crept downstairs behind him.

On hearing he footsteps approach him he turned around,

'What are you doing here, Anna? Go back to bed, it is still quite cold,' he said.

She shivered slightly, and reached out for a shawl, which hung from the back of a chair. Peter picked it up and placing it around her shoulders he said,

'It's time for me to go. Give me a kiss now, then I'll be on my way.'

She lifted her face to his as he kissed her gently.

'You'll be alright?' he asked.

She nodded, ' Take care of yourself and hurry back to us,' was all she said. Then she watched him leave through the door of their little cottage.

Her whole body felt frozen as she jumped back into bed trying hard not to wake the baby as he slept soundly in the wooden crib nearby. Try as she might, she could not warm herself. Her feelings were ominous, all she could do was to pray for his safe return. Soon the children would be awake and asking for their father, she would have to set her feelings to one side for their sakes if nothing else.

As they sat at the table to eat their breakfast it was David who chose to ask,

'When Dada returns, will he buy me a pony? John says he shall ride ponies at the Big House when the man comes back.'

'I doubt that Dada will have enough money to buy a pony David!'

On seeing the look of disappointment in the child's face she added,

'Never mind, perhaps we shall get you a white rabbit. You've always wanted one haven't you?'

'Yes, yes,' cried the little boy with delight, the idea of John and the ponies finally disappearing from his mind.

'Then we shall see when Dada returns,' promised Anna relieved at last that the children's minds would be occupied with the idea until their father's return.

o o o

Peter walked briskly down the lane pulling his muffler tightly around his neck to keep out the cold which had begun to tug at his face and nostrils. Suddenly, he began to cough and as the cough worsened he slowed his pace and stopped walking for a second or so. His chest began to wheeze slightly. Dear God! he thought. Don't let this happen to me. Not now!

He took a few gulps of fresh air and in a moment his panic was over. He began to pick up his stride as he headed for Bryn Cethin. He hoped that the day would turn out fine and dry. The next few days would be tough ones but they would be well paid for the work they had to do. Carwyn Thomas was a hard taskmaster but a fair man to work for.

'Hello there, Peter,' called Twm Shenkin. 'You on this ride then?' he asked.

Peter nodded, then looking around for Carwyn Thomas he asked,

'Where's the boss? I thought we were having an early start.'

Rubbing his hands together to keep them warm Twm replied,

'It seems he's not well up at the house. Evan Evans has gone to see what's happening. He's been gone a while, but knowing Evan as I do he's probably drinking tea with one of the parlour maids, that he is!'

Peter smiled at the man who was prone to exaggerating now and then, but his attention was then drawn to the others who stood around mumbling their discontent.

'You go up there Peter,' said Twm. 'There's a bit of shape about you boy. Try to find out what's happening, none of the lads here will go.'

Peter looked around at the men who nodded in agreement with Twm. Then he set off in the direction of the house.

He knocked loudly on the kitchen door but when no-one came in answer he called out,

'Hello there!'

'Come in, come in,' a woman's voice rang out.

Taking his cap from his head Peter folded it and placed it in his pocket, then stepping through the doorway he entered the house.

He walked through a narrow hallway to find himself in the kitchen where he came face to face with Leah Thomas as she stood arguing with Carwyn, her husband. Evan Evans stood alongside them watching as Leah Thomas tried to persuade her husband not to travel.

'You cannot go this time,' she pleaded, 'You'll be carried home in a box. You're much too ill.'

Carwyn Thomas began to cough until his body started to shake.

Then looking towards Peter for support, the mistress of the house continued,

'Perhaps you can persuade him. Although he has been ill in bed he is determined to take the cattle to market this time. It seems he has the notion that only he can deal with Wil Hafod at the Auction. He's in no fit state to go!'

Peter had never seen Leah Thomas so angry. Evan Evans stood to attention, wringing his cap in his hands but not uttering a word. So Peter stepped forward and directing his words to Carwyn Thomas he said,

'She's right you know sir. You are very ill. Surely one of the men can see to the business for you. Give the order and we shall be on our way.'

Leah Thomas looked grateful for his words while the old man finally nodded his head in defeat.

'Very well Peter, but you must be the one to do the business in my place. Go to Wil Hafod, he will get a fair price for the herd and in turn he will sort it out with you.'

Evan Evans gasped as he heard the old man give Peter his instructions. Peter agreed to take the herd and as the two men departed, Carwyn called after him,

'And Peter, take no nonsense from the men. Evan will tell them that I have put you in charge.'

Peter followed Evan out into the yard where the men stood waiting. Evan Evans stood talking with them.

Peter looked at the faces of the other drovers then spoke,

'I daresay that you have been told that Mr Thomas has taken to his bed. He has put me in charge and if anyone has anything to say, then say it now. If not, we'll be ready to move.'

The men shifted uneasily, a few of them muttered together as they stood in the corner. Twm Shenkin could foresee a bad mood developing among them and so he spoke up.

'We all need the work boys and I know what you're thinking 'bout Peter Malone. Who the hell is he to be taking over? But, is there any one among you who is willing enough to do the business at the other end? We know Peter Malone to be a fair man. He'll get a fair price for Mr Thomas, then we'll get our share also.'

Peter was grateful for Twm's support, and as each man went to his duties, Peter climbed up on to Carwyn Thomas' horse and gave the order to be off. However, he could not fail to notice the evil look in the eyes of Evan Evans.

Men and cattle moved slowly through the heavy iron gates out into the lane leading to the road. It was still quite early and the sky was dark with threatening clouds. It would be many miles and long hours until they would finally reached their destination.

o o o

The journey seemed endless but it had gone smoothly, much better than Peter had hoped for. Once the men had accepted his leadership he knew he would not let Carwyn Thomas down.

As darkness fell, he could feel a spot or two of rain as it touched his face and head.

Damn, they weren't far off now he thought. If only the rain would stay away for another hour or so he prayed.

As the rain fell faster and faster he knew they were in for a soaking before they would reach the market town.

The men tried hard to coax the cattle to move faster, but as if they knew their fate, the animals bunched together trying to shelter from the driving rain.

'Get along there!' shouted one of the herdsman, but the stubborn cows refused to budge. Each man used all his strength and effort to get them to move and finally they were on their way once more.

Peter, along with the other men was now soaked to the skin, and with great relief they at last saw the lights of the town in the distance. They drove the cattle into the stockyards and Peter gave the order to pen the animals.

'I'll leave the rest to you Twm,' he ordered as he set off to find the man called Wil Hafod. Twm nodded to him, the rain running from his cap down over his face.

'I'll look for lodgings for us when I've finished here,' he called after Peter, but the driving force of the rain carried his words away before Peter could hear them.

The cold tore into Peter's wet clothes as they clung to his body. He searched around for the man, wanting desperately to get the business over and done with so that he could get out of these clothes.

He found Wil Hafod in a nearby public house.

'So the old man's not well then? Never fear lad, you can rely on me,' said Wil. 'Are the usual terms of sale to stand is it?' he asked. 'I need to know if I'm to have an early start tomorrow.'

'Yes,' said Peter as he began to shiver all over. 'I'm to leave it in your hands and you're to settle your share. He must trust in you greatly.'

'Carwyn Thomas and I have done business together for many years my boy. Now get yourself off and change those clothes. You're not looking too well yourself. I'll see you first thing in the morning,' said Wil Hafod.

'I'll be away then,' said Peter his teeth now beginning to chatter as his body felt the cold once more.

He turned down a lane, which led to some houses nearby. Then he caught sight of Evan Evans standing in a darkened doorway.

'Where are the men?' he called out to him. ' Have they all found lodgings?'

Evan shouted back,

'As far as I know they are all settled in. As for myself I've only just managed to get a place but there's no more room here.'

'I'll carry on then. I'm bound to find somewhere!' Peter shouted.

'Well, good luck to you, it's a bad night that it is,' called Evan as he watched Peter hurrying away.

A door opened behind Evan and a voice called out to him,

'Can you see him then?' Twm Shenkin peered out into the dark, wet night. 'I want him to know that there's place here with us,' he said anxiously.

Evan looked Twm straight in the eye and said,

'No I didn't come across him after all. He must still be with Wil Hafod.' Then he pushed himself passed the older man, shouting,

'Shut the bloody door will you? I'm wet enough as it is!'

Twm closed the door reluctantly, praying that Peter had found a safe haven in this hell of a night.

Evan Evans stripped off his wet clothes, secretly satisfied that the so called ' boss' Peter Malone was still searching for somewhere to shelter, while he turned into his warm bed and finally fell asleep.

Peter tried several lodging houses, but in vain. Tired and soaked to the skin he turned into a stable yard where he found a shelter among several bales of hay. Pulling an old piece of sacking over his body, exhausted, he fell asleep, oblivious to the sound of the rain as it poured down on the tin roof above him.

It was some hours later that the dense cold suddenly awoke him. Why was he shivering and at the same time his head ached and his body felt on fire? He knew he had to get help from somewhere but as he tried to lift his body from the ground he collapsed again to the floor as darkness overtook him.

Later, much later, he awoke to the sound of children's voices.

He called out, 'Anna, are you there? Where are the children?'

In his mind he knew he was back at home, safe at last! But it was all a dream as he drifted yet again into the darkness.

'Careful now, lift him gently,' said the voice, which belonged to the man known as Griffiths the Milk.

Dewi Griffiths and his brother Ifor carried Peter's limp body carefully across the road and into the dairy where Dewi's wife was busy heating a bucket of water over the fire.

'It's lucky you went to the stable early Ifor,' she said. 'The poor boy could have died. Carry him over here and let him lie near the fire.'

Rachel Griffiths hurried away to fetch warm blankets while the two men began to strip Peter of his wet clothes. Soon he was enveloped in the warm covers and as the heat began to penetrate his body he tried to open his eyes, but it was such an effort that he failed each time.

Eventually he succeeded, and as he opened each eye, he looked at his surroundings but had no idea where he was. He was just grateful to feel warm and dry. He felt a soft hand lift his head and a mug of hot tea touch his lips but he had to struggle to swallow the warm, sweet liquid.

'Where am I?' his voice croaked. 'I must go, I have to get home.'

Peter tried to get up but his strength failed him.

'Hush now,' said the voice, 'you can't go anywhere in this state. Rest now, you'll soon be able to go home.'

'You don't understand. Anna's waiting there for me,' Peter insisted as he tried to sit up once more.

But the woman's voice was soothing and as the warm liquid began to trickle down his throat his body finally relaxed in the makeshift bed in front of the fire.

Griffiths the Milk searched Peter's clothes and found a piece of paper with Wil Hafod's name, written on it. So he'd sent Ifor to market and Wil in turn had notified Twm Shenkin who found his way to the dairy as soon as he could.

Peter began to open his eyes as Twm called out his name. He tried to answer him, but he failed to speak as his chest now started to wheeze and he felt he could hardly breathe.

'Don't worry boy. You'll be as right as rain, you'll see. Wil Hafod has everything to hand. He'll be here as soon as he can. How did you get in this state? Last night I sent Evan to find you, there was room at our lodgings but he came back alone,' said Twm.

As ill as he was, anger flashed in Peter's eyes as he heard the man's words.

Twm saw the look and immediately realised what Evan Evans had done.

'He did find you then!' he said angrily. Peter did not reply.

'Wait until I get my hands on him,' said Twm clenching his fists tightly.

'No!' said Peter in a voice no more than a whisper, ' just get me home to Anna. I'll settle with him again.'

'You're not fit to travel lad. Stay here and in a few days time we'll talk about going home,' said Twm.

Peter grabbed at Twm's coat, trying to lift himself. He urged,

'Promise me you'll take me with you.'

Twm sensed the strain in his voice, it was as if the lad could foresee something bad happening to him.

'Don't worry Peter, I'll get you home somehow. Now you have to remain warm while I make some arrangements. I'll try to find a wagon and I'll be back as soon as I can.'

Peter relaxed his grip and lay back down satisfied that his friend would not fail him.

Rachel Griffiths stood in the doorway shaking her head.

'If pneumonia sets in, he'll never see his home again.'

'I've promised him merchi and something's telling me I have to try. I'll be back later,' said Twm.

Then he left in search of Evan Evans. Twm didn't have to search far as he found him in the stockyard giving orders to some of the men. As Twm approached him he yelled out,

'Where the hell have you been Twm Shenkin? The business is almost done, no thanks to Peter Malone. He's not shown his face near here!'

'Never mind about the business,' answered Twm. ' It's not the only thing that's almost done,' Peter Malone has nearly died thanks to you!'

'I don't know what you're talking about,' said Evan gruffly.

'Don't lie to me man. I sent you to find him last night. We were to share our lodgings. You found him and told him otherwise, then you let him search in that rain until he collapsed,' shouted Twm.

Evan Evans shook his head furiously denying the allegations.

'If anything happens to him, you'll have me to reckon with,' said Twm. But the younger man began to push him away as he yelled,

'What's it to do with you? Carwyn Thomas should have put me in charge, not Peter Malone!'

'So that's it, is it?' said Twm. ' Damn you for being the fool that you are!'

Then raising his right fist he punched Evan in the body knocking him to the ground.

'Get up you coward, put up your fists like a man,' he demanded.

Evan Evans made no attempt to get up from where he lay.

Twm turned his back on him and walked away while the other men stood around in amazement.

Griffiths the Milk helped Twm to lift Peter into a cart filled with dry hay and they covered him in blankets.

'Go careful with him now,' ordered Rachel Griffiths as she placed a pillow beneath Peter's head, and began to tuck the blankets around his body.

'I've done all I can for you, but if I had my way you'd remain here a while longer,' she said to him.

Peter smiled, and tried to thank her for her kindness but another bout of coughing overtook him as his body began once more to shake uncontrollably. Twm climbed up into the seat and as he pulled on the reins the horse and cart began to move away.

Rachel Griffiths wiped the tears from her eyes and as her husband stood beside her he said,

'Come now, you did all you could for the lad.'

'Yes, but I fear he will not last the journey,' was her reply.

upsetting this lovely young woman who was already sick with worry as she looked at Peter's ashened face.

'You did right to bring him home Twm,' said Anna gratefully to him as he ended his tale.

Peter's eyes slowly began to open.

'Anna,' he said weakly.

'Yes cariad, I'm here,' she replied. ' Hush now, you must try to sleep. You are home safe at last.'

He smiled and closed his eyes again knowing this time it was not a dream.

The sound of the latch turning on the kitchen door drew her attention and as she saw her mother and father enter the kitchen she ran toward them.

'We came as soon as we could,' said Wil. ' How is he?' he asked Twm, but Twm just shook his head sadly.

Beti went straight to the chair and placing her hand on Peter's forehead said,

'What this lad needs is a good poultice on his chest. Put the kettle on to boil, give me the bellows, I'll have the fire going in no time. We'll soon have him well again, you mark my words.'

Anna was grateful to her mother, for fussy though she was, Beti would take things in hand. Wil on the other hand remained silent until he could take Twm to one side where he hoped to get an explanation as to how this had happened to Peter.

'Make a pot of tea Anna, I'm sure Twm is half frozen after such a journey,' said Beti.

Anna hurried to the pantry and as she left, this gave Wil the opportunity to speak with Twm. Once more the tale was told but this time Twm included all that Evan Evans had been capable of. Wil clenched his fists in anger as the story began to unfold. He swore to settle the score for Peter one way or another. Pray God the lad would recover for he looked desperately ill.

'I've left a message for Doctor Pugh. We called there on our way over,' Wil told his daughter.

Beti meanwhile had opened Peter's shirt and was now placing the warm poultice on his chest covering him quickly again. Then giving instructions to get him to bed she watched Wil and Twm carry Peter up the stairs. Anna began to fill a stone jar with warm water from the kettle and fastening the top tightly to it she followed them and placed it under the bedclothes next to Peter's body.

As Wil and Twm went quietly back down the stairs Doctor Pugh arrived at the door. He lost no time as he made his way to the bedroom where he began to examine Peter in the room lit by candlelight.

'Keep him warm and carry on with the poultices. He has a fever and it is too soon yet to say whether he has a touch of pneumonia. Give him a little soup if he feels like it but that is all. I'll come back in the morning Anna. Now try to rest, we can do no more for the time being,' he said gently to her.

Anna sat at the bedside, a large blanket covered her shoulders and body, which had begun to shiver in the cold.

'Drink this,' said Wil offering her a cup of hot tea. 'Let me take a turn to sit with him.'

'I'll stay a while longer if you don't mind Da. He may call out for me,' she said not wishing to leave her husband's side.

Wil went down the stairs.

'I'm so worried Beti. She won't leave him, and what if the worse happens?' he asked.

Beti did not answer him. Soon the dawn would break and she would be kept busy seeing to the children's needs. This was the only way she had learned to cope with the unexpected.

Anna had fallen to sleep in the chair when she was suddenly awakened by David's small voice as he cried out,

'Dada's home, he's in the bedroom!'

'Hush now,' she whispered to the little boy as she took him by the hand and led him from the room.

'Have you asked him about the rabbit Mam? What did he say?' said the child full of excitement.

Elizabeth stood in the doorway of the adjoining room and before Anna could answer her little son the girl said,

'He's ill isn't he Mam? I heard the doctor as he left.'

Anna led the two children into the bedroom where Kate now lay awake. She sat on the bed and spoke to each of them,

'Dada has a bad cold, so you are all going to Mamgu's until he is well again.'

David began to cry,

'But I don't want to go away from you.'

'It will be such fun' she tried to convince him, 'and if you are good, then I shall ask Grandpa Wil to get you the rabbit.'

Satisfied at this, David began to jump up and down with joy.

'Now get dressed, try not to make a noise or you'll wake Peter John. Mamgu and Grandpa Wil are waiting for you,' said Anna.

'I'll see to them Mam,' said Elizabeth, and Anna knew she could depend on her as she returned once more to her husband's side. Soon she could hear the children's laughter as they went downstairs to where their loving grandparents waited for them.

The house had become silent, after the children left. Anna missed their presence but it gave her the time she needed to be at Peter's side.

Later that morning Doctor Pugh called again, only to tell her that there was little if no improvement in Peter's condition. Anna continued to sit with him, wiping his fevered brow now and again, as he tossed and turned in the bed. She heard her father's footsteps on the stairs and quietly went to meet him.

'How is he? Is there any change?' Wil asked anxiously.

Anna shook her head as she turned back into the room. Wil pulled up a chair and sat down beside her.

'The children are fine Anna, and I have sent word to Marged. She'll come as soon as she can, then you'll be able to rest.'

Then seeing the tiredness in her face he asked,

'Shall I stay the night to keep company with you.'

'It's kind of you to offer, but I'll be alright Da. Mam will need your help with the children, especially with the baby there.'

'Things will be better tomorrow, you'll see,' said her father trying to reassure her.

'I hope you are right,' Anna replied.

'I'd best be off now. Twm Shenkin will call later on and if you need my help, he'll come for me,' said Wil as he walked toward the door. He stopped, then turned back.

'You know how much Peter means to your mother and I. Don't you?' he asked.

Anna nodded as she was too full of emotion to speak.

'I'll see you in the morning,' said Wil as he made his way down the stairs and let himself quietly out through the back door of the cottage.

Anna nursed Peter through the endless day coaxing him to take sips of water to quench his thirst. Twm Shenkin arrived later and she was grateful for his company. He gathered logs for the fire and sat with Peter while she managed to eat a little food herself. After he left, Anna wrapped herself in a woollen shawl and settled down in the rocking chair by the side of Peter's bed. A candle flickered in its holder as it stood on the dressing table, its flame barely lit up the room. It gave enough light however for her to see how frail and weak Peter looked and she prayed he would be better by the morning.

A few hours later she suddenly awoke from her sleep. Feeling cold and stiff from sitting in the rocking chair she got up to peer through the curtains. It was still quite dark outside. Not knowing what time it was she returned to the rocking chair.

Then she heard him whisper to her,

'Don't leave me Anna, I need you beside me.'

'I'm right here Peter,' she said. 'Hush now, you must try to sleep.'

'I'm so cold,' he cried, breaking into a coughing fit once more.

She pulled back the bedclothes and climbed in beside him. His body felt ice cold to her touch and as she settled down beneath the sheets she placed her arms around him and began to cradle him gently. Soon she felt his body warming to her own and slowly they both drifted off to sleep locked in each other's arms.

Anna slept peacefully with Peter beside her until suddenly a clanging sound awoke her. She eased herself gently from the bed and looked out of the window only to see Mattie Rees on her milk round.

Pulling a shawl over her shoulders she hurried downstairs stopping to pick up a jug from the kitchen table. As she stepped outside, the wind caught her breath for a moment and she was unable to speak to the young girl.

'What will it be today Anna?' asked Mattie Rees. Before Anna could reply, the girl went on, 'I hear Peter's poorly then? Such a nice man he is, I hope he'll be better soon.'

Taking the jug from Anna's hand she waited for a reply.

'I'll have a whole pint today Mattie,' said Anna watching as the girl measured a pint of milk from a large churn which stood at the back of he cart. Mattie handed the jug back to Anna.

'What's wrong with him then? Cold on the chest is it? Poor thing! There's a lot of it about you know.' The girl chatted away but all Anna wanted to do was to return to the warmth of her home.

Not to hurt Mattie's feelings she said,

'Doctor Pugh is about to call later and I hope he'll say that Peter has improved. Thank you for asking after him.'

'Well, I'll best be off then. Got a big round to do today,' said Mattie returning to the cart.

Anna waved to her then hurried back inside feeling that the cold air had chilled her very bones. She hurried to light the fire and set the kettle to boil. She could do with a warm cup of tea, then she would see to Peter's needs.

Doctor Pugh called at the cottage quite early, bringing with him several potions to ease Peter's condition. But the news was not good as he informed Anna that Peter was suffering from pneumonia. Complete rest was the answer. Poultices were to be applied both day and night, and he advised that the children stay away from the cottage so that his orders would be carried out.

Beti and Wil persuaded Anna that it would be for the best, and so the children stayed at Cefn Glas a while longer. Marged stayed to help her sister, taking turns to nurse Peter through the days that followed. In his delirium he often talked about his native land. His boyhood days in Ireland, and of the family he had left behind, and of his mother whose name was often on his lips. Anna tempted him with small amounts of food but he ate little. Gradually, as the days passed, Peter began slowly to improve. Doctor Pugh was convinced it was Anna's love and devotion for her husband that had made him pull through.

However, Peter would never again be the man that he was.

The children had now stayed at Cefn Glas for almost a month, coming only to see their father when they were allowed to. But today they were to return home.

As he sat on the edge of the bed looking at his face in the mirror, Peter could hardly recognise the stranger who looked back at him. The face was thin and gaunt, the eyes sunken and his chin was covered with a thick reddish beard. Was this person really him? Had the illness altered him that much?

The children would never recognise him, so he called out for Anna to bring him hot water. He would have to shave before they arrived.

Anna appeared carrying a bowl of water and his shaving brush and razor. Peter's hand began to shake as he picked up the towel to place around his neck.

'Here, I'll shave you,' said Anna lathering the brush with some soap. 'Sit still, I don't want to cut you,' she laughed as she lifted his face and gently began to scrape away with the razor.

'What's going to become of us Anna?' he asked. ' How am I to work?'

Question after question came but Anna chose not to reply, as she carefully completed the job she was doing. He took her hand in his, and his eyes sought hers.

'Answer me Anna!' he said.

'Be thankful you are better. We'll get through this somehow Peter, but for now the children are the most important thing to us. They'll be here soon. Now let me help you dress,' she assured him.

He knew the subject was closed for the time being, but sooner or later he would have to bring it up again.

His flannel shirt hung loosely on his body and his trousers required a belt to hold it up around his waist. He had lost a tremendous amount of weight. Anna watched him as he looked at himself in the mirror.

'We'll soon fatten you up again,' she said trying to encourage him. ' Twm is bringing a turkey for Christmas and Owen's killing us a pig. We'll have plenty to eat that's for sure.'

'I don't like charity,' he answered angrily. ' I've always been able to provide for us and now I'm like this. What good am I to anyone!'

'It's not charity, Peter,' she said calmly.

Before they could continue this discussion, they heard the children's' laughter and knew they had arrived.

David was the first to arrive in the bedroom. He carried a large white furry rabbit in his arms.

'This is Snowy,' he said, introducing the timid animal to his father. 'Grandpa gave him to us. When you are better, will you build a hutch for him to live in Dada?'

Before Peter could reply David disappeared through the door.

Next to arrive was Kate. As she peered around the doorway, Peter beckoned to her.

'Aren't you going to give me a kiss then?' he asked.

The child was timid on entering the room, as she had heard so many tales of her father's illness she did not know how to approach him. Peter held his arms open toward her and she ran into them hugging and kissing her father, almost taking his breath away.

Elizabeth followed, carrying Peter John who she handed to her mother before sitting on the bed next to her father. In a grown up voice she said,

'It's good to be home at last! Are you feeling better Da?'

Peter looked at his eldest child and nodded to her. How tall she had grown. Suddenly tears began to fill his eyes. He composed himself however as David came running back into the room.

'Now, downstairs with you!' ordered Anna. ' Dada mustn't get too tired. There's a saucepan of stew waiting for you with lots of your favourite vegetables in it. Ask Mamgu to warm it well and perhaps Dada will feel like some later.'

David, who was always ready for food, turned on his heel to leave the room but the rabbit he carried immediately jumped out of his arms and disappeared underneath the bed. The children all fell about laughing as they tried to coax it from its hiding place.

'What's going on up here?' called Wil as he climbed the stairs to the bedroom where he found the children on all fours still trying to retrieve the rabbit.

'It's good to hear laughter in the house again,' said Wil. ' Come with me. We'll fetch a dock leaf from the garden. Perhaps he'll come out if he sees his dinner waiting for him,' said Wil to the children who began telling him what had happened.

He winked his eye at Anna as the children followed him out of the room one by one.

'I think the noise is a little too much for Peter,' she said gratefully to her father.

It was Elizabeth who re-appeared carrying the large green dockleaf. She knelt down and held it out to the rabbit, which immediately came from underneath the bed to munch greedily on it.

Elizabeth quietly bent to kiss her father on his cheek before she left the room carrying the white rabbit in her arms. Anna and Peter watched her leave and smiled at each other in silence. They were a family once more.

CHAPTER 15

Christmas arrived at last and with it came a light fall of snow, which began to cover the earth.

Branches of holly filled the windowsills of the little cottage, their bright red berries clinging to the prickly green leaves gave a festive look to each room.

Kate reached out to touch one, careful that it would not prick her little fingers she said,

'Look how the berries shine, Dada.'

Peter picked her up and placing her on his knee replied,

'My mother, back in Ireland used to say that if the holly berries shone bright red then we were in for a hard winter.'

David came to sit at his father's feet while Elizabeth pulled up a stool beside him.

'Tell us stories Dada,' he pleaded. 'The ones when you were a boy and all the things you used to do at Christmas time.'

They never tired of their father's stories and although they'd heard them time and time again, each one seemed like the first time.

Peter began to tell them about his brothers and sisters and although they were poor, the love and affection they had for each other had made them feel rich in the end.

'You miss them Dada, don't you?' asked Elizabeth trying to imagine how life would be without David and Kate beside her.

'Yes, I miss all of them and it was a hard decision to leave but I knew if I did there would be one less mouth to feed in the family,' replied Peter.

He noticed how serious each of their faces had become and so on a lighter note he continued,

'I do not regret my decision. If I'd not come to Wales and met your mother, then we wouldn't have had all of you. And that would never do would it?' he laughed.

The children hugged and kissed him in turn, laughing as they did so.

A knock came at the door. Elizabeth went to answer it and returned followed by Twm Shenkin who carried in a large turkey which had been cooked, earlier on, in the village bakehouse.

'We've been expecting you Twm,' said Anna taking the outsized baking tin from his arms. You're looking frozen with cold, sit yourself down and I'll fetch a warm drink for you.'

Elizabeth pulled the stool up in front of the fire.

'Sit here Twm, you'll soon be warm,' she said. Then she went to help her mother spread the tablecloth over the table ready for supper. Anna returned carrying a large mug of parsnip wine which she handed to Twm.

'There, that'll warm you,' she said.

Twm envied Peter and Anna their little family as he had none of his own, and as he drank the sweet liquid and felt the heat from the fire warm his bones. He was glad they had made him welcome.

'You'll stay to supper then, Twm?' asked Anna as she already prepared to lay an extra place at the table.

'It's very kind of you missus but I'll not impose on you,' he answered politely.

'Nonsense,' said Peter. 'Where would we be without you? You are always welcome at our table Twm.'

'Yes, do stay!' pleaded David while his sisters cried out in unison.

'Very well then,' said Twm giving in, grateful to share their company on Christmas Eve.

When the meal had ended, Twm helped the children hang their father's long stockings by the fireplace. Anna had already taken the baby upstairs to bed, and when she returned, it was to find the other children singing carols softly to their father and his friend. She stood in the doorway with tears in her eyes, thankful that Peter's health had improved enough for him to enjoy this little scene.

'Nadolig Llawen,' they called out as they climbed the stairs hoping that in the morning they would find the stockings filled with all good things.

'Merry Christmas,' said Twm and their parents back to them.

'I'd best be on my way,' said Twm. 'Thank you for supper Anna. I enjoyed it very much gel!'

'You'll come for dinner tomorrow?' asked Anna hoping that Twm would accept.

'It's kind of you to ask but I'll be off to my sister's. She'll be expecting me you know,' he replied.

Anna nodded, she'd forgotten he had a sister in the next village.

Twm halted at the door and picked up a small bag he'd carried. To Anna and Peter's surprise he began to take out several small gifts he'd made for the children.

A small wooden rabbit he'd carved for David and some peg dolls for the girls and lastly he took out a monkey on a stick, which he'd bought for Peter John.

Anna was so delighted that she leaned forward to kiss him on the cheek, thanking him for his kindness to them. Embarrassed at it all, Twm stepped into the cold night air calling out 'Nadolig Llawen' as he left.

Anna and Peter then began to fill the stockings with fruit and some nuts and raisins. Peter placed a few coins in each of them and these immediately fell right down into the toe of the stocking. Finally, Anna put a bag of sticky taffy, which her mother had made and now they were full.

Peter hung them up at the fireplace.

'It's a poor time for us,' he said. 'We've not been able to afford much since I failed to work Anna.'

Putting her arm around her husband's shoulder Anna said,

'We are richer than many Peter. We have the children, our family and friends like Twm and we have each other. What more would we want?'

Anna helped him climb the stairs and soon they were settled in bed. She lay awake for what seemed an age, until she became satisfied that Peter, and the children were fast asleep. Then she got up, quietly lit a candle and crept back downstairs praying that she would not wake anyone.

She lifted the latch on the door leading under the stairs where she had hidden the warm scarf and gloves that Mam and Medi had made for Peter some weeks before. Then she took out two dolls. No-one would recognise them as Elizabeth and Kate's old dolls. Their hair had been washed and combed and they each wore new dresses she'd made for them. Then she reached for a bag which held new ribbons and combs that she'd bought with money from the sale of eggs at the market. It also held some toy wooden soldiers she'd bought only yesterday.

Yes! These will do nicely, she thought as she carried them into the kitchen.

Finally, she reached in her pocket of her night-gown a took something out of it. This was to be for Elizabeth. A she wrapped the tiny piece of lace she thought back to the old lady who had given it to her.

'For luck!' That was what she'd said, but where was their luck now? Had it run out at last?

Anna dismissed the thought from her mind as she put each present on the kitchen table. Then she hurried through the cold night air thankful to return to her nice, warm bed.

It seemed no time at all before David stood by the bed waking her.

'Can we go downstairs, Mam?' the small boy asked eagerly.

The room was still dark and Anna could not tell what time it was. Eyes still heavy, she reached out toward him.

'Come in here, it's so cold David,' she whispered. ' Don't wake the others, it's far too early to get up yet.'

Peter stirred on the other side of the bed but he did not wake.

'I'm not cold,' the boy insisted to his mother but did as he was told and climbed into the bed. Soon he drifted off to sleep and it was some hours later that Anna awoke to find the two girls peering through the doorway wondering where their brother had disappeared to. Anna got up and pulling a shawl around her shoulders she persuaded them to return to their room while she went downstairs to light the fire.

Soon the sticks began to crackle as the fire began to light in the grate. She would have to hurry especially if the baby were to wake. The fire roared up the chimney and its flames began to lighten up the room where Anna could see the presents waiting on the table. Peter began to cough and so she hurried back up the stairs where she found that the children had now climbed into bed with their father as he was once more attempting to keep them occupied with another of his stories.

'Are you getting up,' she called from the doorway. 'I think I see something in the stockings at the fireplace.'

Three excited children jumped from the bed and ran to their mother's side.

'I'll follow you down shortly,' said Anna as she heard the baby crying from the adjoining bedroom. She went in and picked up Peter John from his cot, then she carried him to Peter's room.

'I don't think I'm able to get up yet Anna,' said Peter as he lay back on his pillows.

Anna could see how pale and drawn he looked as he lay there.

'Go down to the children, they need you now,' he said.

'Very well,' she replied, ' But I'll be back as soon as I can.'

She cuddled the baby to her as she went down the stairs.

Peter began to cough again, the spasms taking hold of him so that he could hardly breathe. When it was over, he lay there exhausted, but his mind began to think back to Christmases long passed. He was the one whose task had been to rise up early, light the fire and then take the excited children downstairs where their eager faces would be lit by the flames from the fire. Now all he had was memories, would it ever be the same again he wondered.

o o o

'Where's Dada?' asked Elizabeth looking over their mother's shoulder.

'He'll come down later when the room becomes a little warmer,' said Anna as she joined the children around the fire. One by one they gathered around their mother, and each in turn hugged the baby and wished him a Merry Christmas. Then they returned to open their stockings. Kate let out a squeal of delight as she poured the contents of the stocking into her lap while David on the other hand began to delve further and further into the depths of his until at last he found the coppers hidden in the toe.

'Are these for us also Mam?' asked Elizabeth noticing the presents on the table.

'Yes,' said Anna with a twinkle in her eyes.

'Then we'll carry them upstairs so that Dada will be with us as we open them,' said Elizabeth in her grown up voice.

David and Kate followed her upstairs and into the bedroom. As he heard them approach, Peter sat up in bed. The children laid their parcels down on the patchwork quilt in front of him.

'Our stockings were full of presents,' said David to his father, ' and now we've brought these up here to open Dada.'

'What a good idea,' answered Peter wondering how Anna had managed to hide all these things.

As the children began to open the presents, Anna arrived carrying Peter John who she placed on the bed beside her.

'Open this one,' shouted Elizabeth, 'It's for you,' she said, handing Peter a parcel packed in brown paper.

Peter undid the string and opened the parcel to find a bright green woollen muffler.

'It's just what I need,' he said. ' I shall wear it when we go for long walks together.'

Each gift was carefully unwrapped and each child in turn shouted with glee at the presents before them.

Finally, all that remained was one small package, which Anna held out to Elizabeth.

'Go ahead, open it,' she said to her daughter.

Elizabeth very gently opened the package and to her delight out fell a small piece of delicately crocheted lace. She knew this was the piece of lace that her mother treasured and now it was hers.

'It has brought me much love and good luck cariad. I pray it will do the same for you,' said Anna.

'I shall keep it always Mam,' said Elizabeth as she hugged her mother tightly.

'Where is your gift Mam?' asked Kate as she tugged at Anna's arm.

'I've no need of gifts,' laughed Anna, ' not while I have all of you around me.'

Elizabeth had quietly slipped away unnoticed and she returned carrying a large, heavy object in her arms. It too had been wrapped in thick brown paper.

'What's this?' cried Anna as the girl place it in her lap.

'Open it,' shouted David with excitement.

'Yes, open it Mam,' echoed Kate.

Anna undid the string, her fingers trembled as she struggled with several small knots. As she opened the paper it revealed a large black iron bakestone.

'It's just what I wanted,' she laughed out loud.

'Now I'll be able to make the best Welsh cakes in the county.'

'Grandpa Wil had the blacksmith make it for us to give you Mam,' said Elizabeth.

All the while, Peter sat silently in the bed, then he reached under his pillow and brought out a small parcel which he handed to Anna.

She looked puzzled, then she quietly began to open it. Inside was a small box and as she opened its lid she gasped,

'It's beautiful Peter, but how?'

Inside lay a small tortoiseshell comb, which Anna immediately placed in her long dark hair.

'Mr Thomas paid me the money he owed me and Elizabeth went to choose it,' he replied. 'It's beautiful, just like you.'

David, not to be outdone by all of this, ran out of the bedroom and returned carrying Snowy the rabbit in his arms.

'Here you are. This is from me,' said the little boy handing the rabbit to his mother.

They all laughed at him but Anna took her son in her arms and hugged him,

'Thank you David. I always wanted a rabbit of my own,' she said, ' but I'm afraid I'll need someone to look after it for me.'

'Don't worry Mam, I'll look after it,' the boy said eagerly.

Peter smiled and the little girls giggled together. Anna began to scold them. This had been a precious moment between mother and son. One that she would always cherish. Laughter filled the air once more, it was to be a good Christmas after all.

CHAPTER 16

The month of January had come and gone and now the damp, misty month of February was almost passed. Peter felt no better, his strength had failed him. Anna was at her wits end as she prayed for his health to improve.

Twm Shenkin, loyal as ever, sat with him for many an evening, saddened that he could no nothing more for his close friend.

Carwyn Thomas sent parcels of food for the children but Peter knew nothing of this. Anna hid the truth from him knowing it would sadden him further that he could no longer provide for his family.

Twm had made it his business to inform Carwyn Thomas of the truth of Peter's illness, and it was to his credit that Evan Evans had been sacked on the spot. However, the dastardly coward had sworn that one day he would get even with Peter Malone and his family. Of that he was certain.

That very morning Wil called at the cottage and decided to take the children for a walk. Anna had made them wear their warm woolly caps and scarves as the day was cold and frosty. Soon she heard their voices as they returned.

'The pond is frozen over,' said David pulling off his gloves to warm his hands by the fire.

'My old bones are frozen as well merchi,' said Wil pulling up a chair at the table. 'I feel snow in the air. We could be in trouble come lambing time,' he muttered.

Anna poured a mug of warm tea and handed it to her father.

'Look at these Mama,' cried Kate holding out a small bunch of snowdrops. 'I picked them for Dada,' the child said.

'Take this tea up to your father, Elizabeth,' said Anna holding out a steaming mug.

Elizabeth took the mug and went upstairs. Suddenly her voice called out,

'Mam, come quickly. Dada's not well!'

Anna ran from the room while her father was left with the children.

Elizabeth stood at the top of the stairs,

'I was talking to him when suddenly he slumped forward in the bed. Is he alright Mam?' she asked.

Anna ran past her to where Peter lay. His hands were cold and his breathing was shallow.

'Go quickly, fetch Doctor Pugh. Tell him Dada's taken a turn for the worse,' she cried.

Elizabeth ran downstairs and out of the house as fast as she could.

'Is everything alright Anna?' called Wil from below while little Peter John clung to him in his arms.

She ran to the stairs and looked down.

'Peter's collapsed,' she said, ' I've sent Elizabeth for the doctor. Can you manage there?' she asked.

Her father nodded and returned to the kitchen with the children.

'Can you hear me, Peter?' she asked as she pulled the blankets around his shoulders to keep him warm. He did not respond to her voice. Anna stayed with him for a little while anxiously waiting for the doctor to arrive. Soon it became apparent that the children would be better off at Cefn Glas with her mother, and so she quickly got them ready and Wil left with them.

Then she returned to Peter, wiping his brow and gently speaking to him all the while, but there was still no response.

The palms of her hands perspired and the beat of her heart raced wildly as she prayed,

'Dear God, don't let me lose him now!'

It seemed ages before she heard the sound of a pony and trap as it pulled up at the door.

Doctor Pugh rushed upstairs followed by Elizabeth who had now begun to cry.

'Will he be alright Mam?' she asked looking at her father who seemed to be sleeping peacefully in his bed.

'I don't know merchi,' said Anna truthfully. 'Now go downstairs and warm yourself by the fire, you look frozen.' The girl did as she was told.

Anna went back inside the room but Doctor Pugh led her outside to the landing and shaking his head sadly he said,

'I'm afraid he's had a relapse Anna. I'm so sorry. I can do nothing more. It was doubtful he would ever recover after such an illness, and now I'm afraid his heart is very weak.' His voice trailed almost into a whisper he added,

'Will you be alright?'

Anna nodded, tears running softly down her face. He picked up his bag and left saying he would call later in the day.

Elizabeth stood in the doorway as she watched the pony and trap disappear, then she turned and faced her mother,

'I heard what he said Mam and I want to be here with you.'

'I need you to be with the others Elizabeth,' said Anna sadly. 'They will not understand what is happening, and my mind will be at rest if I know you are there to help them. Do this for me, will you?'

Elizabeth nodded, then asked,

'Can I see him before I leave?'

Anna took her by the hand as they climbed the stairs together, each one trying to be brave for the other.

Elizabeth stood at the bedside and as she took her father's hand in hers she kissed it tenderly. Then tears streaming from her eyes she ran from the room leaving her mother alone with him.

As soon as Elizabeth arrived at Cefn Glas with the news of her father, Wil returned to the cottage. This time, Anna must not be left on her own.

Wil sat in the silence of the kitchen with only the ticking of the clock to keep him company. Now and then he ventured up the stairs to see if there was any change in Peter's condition. Anna sat beside him talking softly all the while until she finally gave in to her father and lay down on the bed in the next room to rest herself.

Wil took his turn to sit at the bedside. A deep sadness overcame him as he looked toward the man who had become like a son to him. It was so unfair that he should be soon taken away from them.

Suddenly, he thought he saw Peter's eyes as they moved slightly. Yes! He hadn't imagined it! His eyelids definitely had moved. Will hurried to the next room and called out,

'Anna, come quickly, he's opened his eyes at last!'

Anna jumped from the bed, her heart pounding within her. She ran to her husband's side almost pushing her father out of her way.

'Peter,' she cried. 'Peter, can you hear me?'

Peter's eyes opened again and he smiled as he whispered.

'Mother, is that you?'

'No cariad, it's Anna. I'm here beside you,' she replied, taking his hand gently in hers.

'Anna?' he asked again.

'Yes, my love. I'll always be near you.'

Peter nodded his head and smiled again. Then quietly slipped away from life leaving her to face the future alone.

PART TWO

A NEW BEGINNING

CHAPTER 17

Anna shivered slightly as a small bird flew from its nest in the trees above. The sound it made brought her mind back to the present day. The day when she finally had to part with her beloved Peter.

The mist, which had previously enshrouded the little chapel and the gathering of mourners, now began to lift as the sun's rays poured through the dark grey clouds above.

She glanced at the faces of the people around her and although she tried to concentrate on what they were saying, her mind would not accept the fact that it was Peter they had come to lay to rest.

Her mother and Marged had tried to persuade her to remain with them at Cefn Glas during the funeral, but her mind was made up. She would be with her husband to the end of his journey.

Goronwy Evans, the minister took her arm as they walked away from the graveside. Anna's head nodded as he quietly offered words of comfort to her. Then she joined the other members of her family for the journey to Cefn Glas where her children waited for her. She was grateful to Marged and Medi who had combined their efforts to provide refreshments for all who would return from the funeral. So many people had come to pay their respects to her.

Though she was filled with grief, her tears would not come. She would not allow herself to break down in front of the children who needed her now more than ever.

'Take the children into the garden, will you John?' said Anna to her nephew who had now grown quite tall in stature. The others loved him and would listen to all he said. They were becoming so excited at the attention everyone made of them that Anna felt she needed a few moments on her own without them.

'You look tired Anna. Drink this,' said Medi handing her a cup of tea. Then Medi who was several months pregnant, eased herself into a chair nearby and they sat and talked for a few moments together.

Wil stood in the corner of the room watching the two women. He wished the words would come so that he too could comfort the daughter he loved but so far he had failed.

Owen went to join them and as he sat beside Anna he said,

'I have something to say to you Anna, and I know this may not be the time or the place, but I need to put your mind at rest.'

Anna listened intently to what her brother had to say.

'It's regarding the cottage,' he went on. 'Medi's grandfather, Mr Thomas, is unwell and cannot be here today, and so he wanted me to tell you that he'll not be looking for a new tenant for the cottage. Neither will he expect you to pay rent to him, such was his respect for Peter and the way he came by his illness.'

These words coming from Owen almost brought tears to Anna's eyes. Tears of relief when she had dreaded being turned out of her little home.

'Will you thank him for me, Owen?' she asked. 'Please tell him how very grateful I am to him,' she said.

She took Medi's hand and squeezed it.

'Does anyone else know?' she asked. 'I've told Mam and Da. They are disappointed that you may want to stay at the cottage, as they hoped now that you and the children would decide to live here at Cefn Glas. The decision must be yours of course,' he added.

'There is no decision to be made Owen. I shall stay on at the cottage. Peter's memory will be there with us,' she said.

Later, as some of the mourners began to depart, Anna noticed a tall young man looking at her from across the room. His face was full of sadness and although she felt they had met before, she could not place where or when. He had probably come with someone. Peter knew so many people, she thought to herself.

As she reached the door and began to shake hands with those about to leave it became time for his turn to stand in front of her.

As he took her hand in his, he held it slightly longer than was necessary. Then in a quiet voice he spoke,

'Words will mean nothing to you now, but be sure that I know what you are going through. Time will heal your pain and it will get better, I promise you.'

With that, he released her hand, then shook hands with Wil before he left.

Anna stared after him. His words felt shallow to her ears. They had done nothing to reassure her that she would feel any better than the sadness she now felt. She mentioned this to her mother and it was Beti who told her who the stranger was.

'He has cause to say that, merchi. His wife, Morwenna who was a relative of your father, died not so long ago. She left him with three little ones to rear. Your father's cousin Martha helps him with them. They live over in St Clears. His name is Iestyn Roberts.'

Anna then remembered having met Morwenna at a wedding some years before. She was a pretty girl with fair, curly hair. Now she too was gone. No wonder the stranger had been able to speak those words of comfort to her. He had probably been through exactly the same nightmare as she was now having to experience.

'It's hard when a man if left on his own, isn't it?' asked Beti.

Anna nodded, thinking how fortunate she was to have all her family's support to help her through the difficult times ahead.

The following day, Wil tried to persuade Anna once more to move in with them at Cefn Glas. He argued it would be for the sake of the children but knowing how strong willed his daughter was, he finally gave in. He was satisfied Carwyn Thomas' offer was a genuine one and that Anna would feel secure in the cottage. Her mind was made up, there was nothing more to be said.

And so it was, Anna returned to her little cottage to carry on with life, empty though it seemed and made bearable only by the love of her children. She spoke to them often of Peter and there were times they laughed and cried together, but as each day passed they began to give her the courage she needed to carry on. They each had lovely memories held within their hearts.

Elizabeth, staunch like her mother, Kate who had her father's features, David who had become very quiet but possessive and the baby Peter John, too young to realise his loss. People in the village were kindness itself. Anna took in sewing and sometimes baking to make ends meet.

Twm often called at the cottage bringing with him a fresh chicken or a rabbit he'd caught. She would make a stew while he played with the children, thankful for his company now and then. He too had grieved for the friend he'd lost.

Marged and Morgan called as often as they could and Wil or Beti were daily visitors.

Anna had not seen Owen or Medi since the funeral but they'd received news that Medi had given birth to a little girl. They had named her Rowena after Medi's mother.

Slowly, Anna began to feel that some small measure of happiness was finally returning to her family.

Her newly felt security did not last however, as Carwyn Thomas of Bryn Cethin died shortly after, passing away quietly in his sleep.

Almost at once it was rumoured that his son Rhys would soon return to manage his father's estate. If this were true, what would happen to the cottage she wondered.

'I can understand how you feel Marged,' said Anna trying to allay her sister's fears. 'Maybe the years have changed him. If he returns, there is nothing we can do but accept the position.'

'It's easy for you to say Anna,' she said. 'But if Morgan finds out, he may return, I don't know what he'll do to him. My fears are for John also. You know what happened the last time,' she added.

'Let's try to be positive Marged. We'll just have to see,' replied Anna.

'Well, I thought you'd better find out from me Anna, but Da heard that Rhys Thomas has already contacted Evan Evans and put him in charge until he can get here. I hope that old man Thomas put it in writing the promise he made you about this cottage, else you'll find yourself in trouble also.'

CHAPTER 18

Marged walked down the lane, which led to her sister's cottage. The basket she carried felt heavy on her arm as it was filled with things she's brought for Anna and the children. John had decided to stay at Cefn Glas with his grandparents and Beti had packed the basket with eggs and bacon, cakes and pies, for Marged to take with her.

As she reached the cottage gate, she called out to Elizabeth and the others as they played in the garden. The children ran to her and each one hugged their aunt in turn. David had already taken a peak in the basket she'd set down on the ground and squealed with delight at the things he'd found inside it.

'Mam is in the kitchen,' said Elizabeth. 'I don't think she's very well today Aunt Marged so I've brought the children out here to play.'

Marged picked little Peter John up into her arms and held him tightly, but her thoughts were with the young girl who had matured since her father's death thinking only of her mother and the help she could give her.

'I'm so thankful you are here Elizabeth,' she said. 'It makes it much easier for me to leave here knowing how capable you are with the children. Now then, I'll go inside and find out what's ailing your mother.'

As Marged placed the basket on the kitchen table she found Anna almost close to tears.

'I forgot you were coming today,' said Anna.

'Well now, that's nice isn't it?' said Marged.

'I didn't mean it to sound that way,' answered Anna. 'It's just that I have a lot on my mind at the moment.'

'Well then, out with it,' said Marged as she put the kettle on to boil. 'We'll have a cup of tea, then perhaps you'll tell me what is wrong.'

The sisters sat at the table and for the next few minutes they began to chat about things in general when suddenly Anna burst into tears.

'Come now,' said Marged. 'Whatever's wrong. It cannot be a bad as all that.'

Anna wiped away her tears as she began to tell her sister of Evan Evans' recent visit to her.

'Damn the man! He's got a nerve coming here,' said Marged. 'Wait until I tell Morgan, he'll sort him out! Or better still, we'll go and see Da. He's waiting for the chance to get even with the scoundrel.'

'No!' cried Anna. 'You mustn't do anything yet. I have to speak with Owen first. He'll know what to do. He may even persuade Rhys Thomas to reconsider his decision.'

Marged shook her head in anger,

'I doubt it very much Anna. Rhys Thomas is capable of anything and once his mind is made up he'll not change it. Mark my words! Who better than I should know?' she asked.

But Anna was determined to do as she had decided.

'Promise me Marged. You'll not tell a soul?' pleaded Anna.

Marged could see how upset her sister had become again, and so she relented and gave her word that she would remain silent.

Soon it was time for her to leave and as she fastened her bonnet to her head, Anna caught her arm and held it tightly.

'Remember Marged, you have promised!' she said.

Marged nodded, and Anna became convinced that her sister was telling the truth. As she reached the end of the lane Marged turned to wave again to Anna and the children as they stood at the garden gate. Marged however, had plans of her own and as she reached the crossroads she decided to turn in the direction of Bryn Cethin. She would see Rhys Thomas herself and plead her sister's cause. What would she say to him and how would she find the right words to convince him? She would have to gather courage to enter the house, which held so many terrible memories for her.

Marged paused at the great front door, swallowed hard then taking the cast iron knocker in her hand she knocked twice. Bethan Jones the maid answered her knock and looked curiously at her.

'Wait here please,' she said as she went to find her master.

She returned, then instructed Marged to follow her to the drawing room where Rhys Thomas waited. Marged stared at the drawing room door, and her insides began to shake.

'What am I doing here,' she thought. 'I must be crazy!' But it was Anna's happiness that was at stake. She must try to reason with him.

Rhys Thomas stood up as she entered the room. Marged noticed immediately that he had not lost his good looks. The passing years had been more than kind to him. She did not fail to notice however, that her son certainly resembled his real father. Her heart beating wildly she began to speak.

'Good day, Mister Thomas. I'm sorry to disturb you but I would like to speak to you on a matter concerning my sister Anna Malone who lives in one of your cottages.'

Rhys Thomas could not take his eyes off the woman who stood before him. She still held an attraction for him.

'I am aware who you are and I am also aware of her case,' he answered slowly.

'Then you know that your man Evan Evans has called at the cottage to evict her and her children?'

He nodded to her.

'Surely you knew of your father's promise to my brother Owen?' she asked.

'And that is?' he said coldly.

'He promised Owen that Anna could live at the cottage rent free for as long as she'd want. It was to repay her husband Peter, but you'd best be asking Evan Evans about it. He played a large part in your father's decision,' she said.

'She sent you?' he asked.

'No, I came of my own free will,' Marged replied. My sister doesn't know I am here. Mister Thomas, the children are young and with their father now gone, my sister works hard to keep the family together. I am asking you, please reconsider. Let her remain at the cottage and if it's rent you want we'll have it for you somehow!'

Marged stood facing him, hating herself all the while for having to plead her sister's case.

Rhys Thomas knew the chance he had been waiting for had finally come. This woman had played right into his hands.

'My wife and I have no children of our own and so I cannot be expected to feel anything toward your sister and her family. However, I would be willing to reconsider her case if you would allow your boy to come and spend some time here with me.'

'My son!' she gasped.

'Don't you mean our son,' he replied looking at her for some reaction in her face. Then he added,

'Your sister keeps the cottage if he is allowed to stay here now and then! Those are my terms!'

'You must be insane,' she cried out. 'I've told you before, you are mistaken! He's not your son!'

Rhys Thomas grabbed her by the arm,

'He's mine. I know it. He even looks like me. You can't deny that. Think it over, would you deny him his heritage? This house, these lands and me?' he asked jubilantly.

'Never!' she said. 'He'll never be yours!'

Rhys Thomas knew then, he had achieved what he'd always believed. The boy really was his!

'Then your sister had better be ready to leave, unless you come around to my way of thinking,' he replied.

Marged turned her back on him and stormed out through the door, tears flooding her eyes. She could not wait to get out of this house and away from the man who had tormented her.

Rhys Thomas remained seated in the drawing room. Then hearing a noise coming from outside he went out into the hallway. He looked up toward the huge staircase above and saw his wife Eleri, standing there. She looked down at him with contempt in her face. She'd heard it all as she stood outside the drawing room door.

Rhys Thomas however, was jubilant! His secret was out at last. His wife could do nothing. As for himself, he had great plans in store for the boy who was now his son!

CHAPTER 19

Owen stood with his back to the fireplace and as he gazed around the room he noticed that little had changed in it. All the old familiar things he'd loved were still there. His mother and father weren't ones for change at Cefn Glas.

He turned his head in the direction of the window and as he heard the children's laughter he was pleased that they sounded so happy after suffering such grief. Anna was to be admired in the way she'd reared her children. Then his thoughts turned to Peter. He missed him as much as he had Huw.

Beti came into the room carrying her baby granddaughter. She was followed by Anna and Medi who also began to coo to the beautiful child.

'Is Marged coming today Mam?' asked Owen.

'I'm hoping she'll be able to come,' answered Beti. 'We left a message that you were calling here today.'

Anna held out her arms to the child and Beti handed Rowena to her. As Anna began to rock her to a fro the baby soon fell fast asleep, and while Anna and Owen chatted together the other women went into the kitchen to prepare tea. It was not long before Marged arrived on her own. It appeared Morgan and John had gone fishing.

'Don't tell Da mind,' she said. ' They went to Chapel this morning but as it was such a nice day they decided to go down to the lake this afternoon. They spend a lot of time together you know. It wouldn't do for Da to find out. You know how he feels about the Sabbath!' she added with a twinkle in her eye.

Owen laughed and giving her a brotherly kiss he said,

'Da will never change Marged. Surely you know that? Well now, what do you think of Rowena?' he asked his sister.

'She's beautiful Owen, and so like you,' she complimented him.

'God forbid!' Owen laughed but he was secretly pleased at the compliment paid him.

He left the room for a second to see how the women were coping with the arrangement for tea. Marged grasped the chance to speak with Anna,

' Have you spoken with Owen yet?' she asked. ' What has he said about the cottage?'

Anna shook her head sheepishly,

'I shall speak to him later. Now is not the time, Marged.'

'You cannot put it off any longer Anna. I'll help in the kitchen and when I send him back here to you then you will have the opportunity to talk with him.'

Anna knew her sister was right but how was she to approach Owen?

She rehearsed the words in her mind and as they sat facing each other the words soon became a reality, as Anna unfolded the story of Evan Evans to him.

Owen's face became a scowl, and when Marged returned to join them it was to find her brother in a dreadful temper to say the least.

'Who does Rhys Thomas think he is?' he said angrily.

'Keep you voice down Owen. I don't want you upsetting Medi. It is family after all,' said Anna pleading with her brother to stay calm.

Owen took little notice of her and said,

'Mister Thomas gave me his word, now it seems it was all for nothing. I shall call at Bryn Cethin later to take the matter up with him but there'll be no pleading with him Anna. Don't you worry he shall have to see it my way. Everything will turn out alright in the end.'

Anna gave him a look of relief. She knew that Owen would stand by her. All was not lost yet. However, neither of them reckoned on Marged.

'It will be of little use Owen,' she said sadly. 'You will be wasting your time. Rhys Thomas will not listen to reason.'

'How can you tell Marged?' he asked. 'When I remind him of his father's promise to Anna and the debt owed to Peter, I'm sure he will reconsider.'

'For God's sake Owen, why don't you listen to me?' asked Marged raising her voice. 'The man doesn't care!'

Owen also looked hard at his sister who had now begun to pace the floor clenching her hands together until the whites of the knuckles began to show. It was obvious that Marged knew a lot more than she was prepared to say and so he asked,

'Why are you so certain?'

Marged stood quite still, her face had become pale and distraught as she said,

'Because I know him better than you. I have already been to see him, and I have pleaded for Anna but he will not bend!'

Anna gasped! What had Marged done? Her sister had betrayed her!

'When did you see him, Marged?' she asked, not being able to look her in the face.

'I called on him after I left you at the cottage. I'm sorry Anna but I felt I had to do something and I failed you miserably,' said Marged sadly.

'Well, I'll not fail you Anna,' said Owen. ' He'll have to listen. I'll make him listen!'

Marged could see what was about to happen, and she knew the time had come to tell her brother the truth.

'I have one more thing to say to both of you. Rhys Thomas did agree to reconsider, on one condition. That is, if I am prepared to send John to Bryn Cethin to stay there now and then with him. But I shall never allow it to happen. Now do you see what an evil man he is Owen?' she asked.

Anna remained silent, the room began to spin before her as she clutched the arms of the chair she sat in for support.

'Talk sense Marged. Why John for God's sake?' Owen asked.

Marged lowered her voice and whispered in shame,

'Because Rhys Thomas is John's father.'

Owen began to look at his sister in sheer disbelief but as he turned to look at Anna he knew in his heart she was telling the truth.

'You too Anna?' he asked. 'You knew all this time and never told me?'

Feeling as if he had been betrayed he went on,

I always believed it was one of the boys from the village. All these years you both kept it from me. How could you?' he cried.

'Don't judge us too harshly Owen,' said Anna as she leaned forward to touch his arm, but he quickly pulled it away.

'Marged has her reasons why she wanted to keep it a secret and she has had to live with them,' said Anna in her sister's defence.

'What if you had known? What then Owen?' she asked. ' You would not be married to Medi now and you certainly wouldn't have this child to cherish,' she said looking down at the baby fast asleep on the couch nearby.

Owen looked at Rowena, the child he adored as she slept peacefully and he knew then that all Anna had said was true but it did not alter the fact and so turning to Marged he said defiantly,

'Answer me one thing. Did you give yourself freely to him?'

Marged hung her head in shame and began to quietly cry.

It was Anna who was left to tell Owen the true story and when she had finished, her brother remained silent.

Then he spoke,

'Rhys Thomas shall pay for this. He has disgraced you and made your son a bastard!' he said to Marged. ' Now he intends to blackmail this family. He'll pay before the day is out!'

With that statement Owen strode from the room and ran through the front door out into the yard where he mounted his horse. The sound he made as he rode away brought Medi and his mother to the doorway to find out what had happened.

Marged did the first thing to come to her mind. She ran out into the garden shouting to her father that they had to stop Owen and that she would explain what had happened on their way to Bryn Cethin.

A bewildered Wil jumped into the buggy alongside Marged as she flicked the horse's reins and they too sped away, leaving Anna to face her mother and Medi with the truth that had been hidden for far too long.

A mile or so up the road Wil pulled hard on the horse's reins causing the animal to stop with a jolt. There was murder in his heart as he learned of Rhys Thomas' deceit, but at that moment he was more afraid of what Owen, would do to the coward of a man. There were so many questions he wanted to ask Marged. So many answers to be found, but now was not the time or the place for them. They had to get to Bryn Cethin and try to stop Owen, if it were at all possible.

Owen burst through the front door of the Big House just as Bethan Jones the maid came running to answer his incessant knocking. He ran past her shouting,

'Where is he? Where's Rhys Thomas?'

Before the startled young girl could reply, Owen darted from room to room to find them empty.

Bethan Jones cowered in the hallway as she cried out in fear of the madman,

'The Master's down at the stables, Sir, I'll fetch him now!'

'Never mind, I'll go myself,' shouted Owen. He turned to leave and as he ran through the hallway he found himself face to face with none other than Rhys Thomas whose huge form now blocked the doorway.

'What's this, Owen?' Rhys asked, wondering why the lad was in such a state. 'Nothing wrong with Medi or the child is there?'

Owen looked at the man. How on earth could he act in such a polite, sympathetic way?

'I've come on family business which has nothing to do with my wife or child,' he said as calmly as he possibly could. So calm he was, he could hardly recognise his own voice.

Then he continued,

'I've come about a matter which should have been dealt with a long time ago had I been made aware of it.'

Rhys knew that Owen was attempting to be polite to him while all the time he could see anger in the lad's eyes. He would have to play it carefully here he thought.

'Come, let us go into the drawing room and we'll share a glass of port' said Rhys politely. Then his eyes strayed to Bethan Jones who had remained standing at the foot of the stairs listening to all that was being said.

'Get back to the kitchen where you belong girl!' Rhys shouted to her.

Bethan curtsied and ran thankfully below stairs where she was about to tell Cook all she had witnessed.

Rhys tried to take Owen's arm and lead him forward to the drawing room but Owen shook his arm free.

'What I have to say can be said here and now. You know why I've come don't you?' he asked.

'Indeed I do not,' answered Rhys. ' Oh! I see now, it must be about your sister. What is her name? Ah yes! Anna Malone isn't it?'

Owen ignored him and continued,

'You're not half the man your father was and never will be. When he gave his word he stood by it and was respected for it. Peter Malone gave his life in service to your father and in return your father promised that my sister, Anna, could live at that cottage rent free. Now you are planning to evict her!'

'Well, if that is all this is about, then of course she must stay there. I can see that there has been a terrible misunderstanding. Now there's no need to get upset my boy,' said Rhys thankful that Owen had finally calmed down.

The he turned once more to enter the drawing room in the hope that Owen would follow him.

Owen, however, reached out and placed his hand on Rhys' shoulder,

'That's not all!' he said. 'My sister Anna is only one problem I have dealt with. My sister Marged is the other!'

A vast change came over Rhys' face as he realised what Owen was about to say to him.

In a calm voice, which registered his every word, Owen began,

'You bastard! You disgraced my sister all those years ago and now you want the boy so badly that you are prepared to use blackmail. But you'll never have your way. I'll see to that! John shall never be yours!'

Rhys could not deny the allegations so he said,

'She never told me about the child. How could I know? Ask her, she'll tell you!' he said.

'And if you had known? What then?' asked Owen feeling no remorse for the man.

'I could not have married her. She would never have been accepted here,' Rhys argued.

'So you had your fun and damn the consequences is it?' said Owen. 'It would have been beneath you. Are you saying that Medi has married beneath herself also? I am her husband after all,' asked Owen.

Rhys Thomas did not reply but glanced at Owen scornfully.

'You will never take advantage of myself or my family again. I shall promise you that much,' said Owen defiantly.

The argument ensued and as tempers began to flare Rhys caught Owen by his arm swinging him around to face him. Owen was caught off guard and as Rhys hit out, he ducked in time but came back with both fists flying. He clenched his right hand and his fist landed clean on Rhys' jawbone sending him sprawling to the floor.

Rhys jumped up and lashed back at Owen and the fight that followed was second to none. Chairs were overturned in the hallway, which brought the cook and Bethan Jones from the kitchen to witness blow by blow.

Leah Thomas and Eleri, Rhys' wife, peered over the landing above, frightened to find out what all the commotion was. Eleri shouted to Bethan Jones to get help from the stables but before anyone arrived, Rhys Thomas lay sprawled on the floor, his hands and face covered in blood.

'Get up you bastard!' shouted Owen again, 'I'm not finished with you yet!'

Owen could hardly stand up himself. His left eye had begun to turn purple in colour from the large swelling around it.

At that very moment, Wil came running through the door, and as he witnessed the scene before him he knew there was no more to be done here.

His son had done it all for him. He put his arm around Owen's shoulder and tried to support him as they walked slowly to the door.

'I'm not done with him yet Da,' said Owen looking back to where the servants tried to lift Rhys Thomas from the floor.

'I think you've done enough my boy,' said Wil proudly.

Father and son walked past Margėd who now stood in the doorway. She looked toward the crumpled body of Rhys Thomas and as their eyes met she felt no pity for him. Then she turned on her heel and left the house in jubilation.

The women waiting anxiously at Cefn Glas were relieved to see the others return.

'My goodness Owen, what have you done to your face?' said Beti rushing to soak a piece of flannel under the cold water tap. She held it out to him and he placed it gingerly over his eye.

'Don't worry Beti Fach!' said Wil. ' You should see Rhys Thomas.'

Owen went straight to his wife's side. ' I'm sorry Medi,' he said. ' I know how you feel toward your family but I couldn't let him get away with this. Will you forgive me?' he asked.

Medi took her husband's bruised face in her hands and kissed it gently.

'Anna has told us everything,' she said. ' You did what you had to do. I wouldn't believe it at first but now it answers many questions I've long since asked myself. I suppose I've always seen a resemblance between Uncle Rhys and John but I knew it was impossible. I shall have to go to Bryn Cethin now. I hope you understand Owen.'

He looked at her, surely she did not intend to go to her uncle's side?

'Grandmother Thomas will need me now,' she said giving her explanation. 'This will surely come as a shock to her as well as us,' she said gently.

Owen nodded, then kissed her.

'I shall be alright here Medi,' he assured her.

Then it was Wil's turn to speak.

'I'll take you there,' he said to her. 'If I know Bethan Jones she'll have told half the village by nightfall and Leah Thomas will need you by her side merchi.'

Medi was grateful to him as she gathered her things quickly together.

Marged remained sitting quietly in the corner. Her father was right. Her secret was out and by morning tongues would wag once more. The years had passed but soon her name and that of Rhys Thomas would be on the lips of the village gossipmongers.

As if to read her thoughts Wil turned to her,

'We saw this through once before Marged, and we can do it again, and this time when you go to Elim Chapel, there will be no shame that is yours,' he said.

'I shall never go to Chapel again,' she said quietly.

Now, it was Anna's turn to speak.

'In view of all that has happened today I have come to a decision,' she said.

They all became silent and listened for her to continue,

'I have decided to return to Cefn Glas if you'll still have us. Maybe if I'd paid attention to Evan Evans then this might not have happened today. I am to blame,' she said.

Wil and Beti joyful at her decision came to embrace her.

'As soon as your belongings are packed you'll be welcome to move here. As for Evan Evans, don't blame yourself merchi. He always threatened he'd get even with this family and now he's lost,' Wil reassured her.

Anna nodded in agreement, but she began to shiver with the realisation that her little home and all that it stood for with Peter would soon become yet another memory.

o o o

The great front door stood wide open as Medi walked up the steps toward it. She turned and waved to Wil who sat waiting in the buggy, then she entered the house. No-one came to meet her and it was obvious that the servants had been sent home. As she walked down the hallway, Medi heard the sound of someone crying. It came from the downstairs sitting room and as she opened the door she found her Aunt Eleri sitting there in tears.

Then her attention turned to someone else sitting quietly near the fireplace. It was her grandmother. In her hands she held a fine lace handkerchief which she twisted and turned continuously around her fingers. She did not look up but continued to stare into the fireplace before her. Medi knelt down beside her.

'Grandmother, it's me,' she said softly.

The old lady looked up at last.

'Medi?' she asked. Then shaking her head again and again she added,

'You know what has happened then?'

Medi nodded, conscious that all the while her aunt had continued to weep. She took little notice of her however. He prime concern was her grandmother, Leah Thomas, whom she loved dearly. What this would do to the old lady was beyond compare.

Finally she asked,

'Where is Uncle Rhys? What has become of him?'

'He's badly hurt after his fight with Owen and Doctor Pugh has ordered him to rest. He's upstairs in his room. This shame he's brought on us, thank God your grandfather's not alive to see it,' sighed the old lady.

Eleri sat there listening to these words and began to cry again.

It was all too much for Leah Thomas, as she said,

'Losing your mother was bad enough Medi, but this! I shall never get over it!'

Medi wanted to cry at that very moment but was prevented from doing so by the voice, which rang out from the doorway.

Rhys Thomas entered the room and pointing his finger at his mother he said,

'You are partly to blame for all this!'

Medi could see from the injuries to his face that Owen had indeed given her uncle a beating he would never forget.

Rhys stood in the middle of the room as he continued with his allegations.

'You always favoured Rowena before me and when I couldn't provide you with grandchildren you lavished everything on her,' he said lifting his hand to point in Medi's direction. Then turning toward his wife he said angrily,

'And as for you! You could never give me children. How was I to react when I knew I had fathered a child at last. That boy is mine and I needed him.'

Leah Thomas looked at her son,

'You always got what you wanted. Even as a little boy and you never seemed to care how you came about it. If you had not taken advantage of that poor girl things may have been different. I never guessed that you were the cause for her to leave. Marged reared that child on her own despite everything that stood against her,' said his mother harshly.

'Be quiet, Mother!' he shouted. 'If I had not taken her then it would have been someone else. She was that sort of girl!'

Medi could listen no longer.

'How dare you!' she said. 'Marged has been like a sister to me. She doesn't deserve your slanderous tongue. Her father waits outside and I warn you to keep your voice down else you may find yourself taking another beating.'

'It's obvious that you've become one of them,' he said. 'Think of your breeding Medi, you should never have married into that family. I suggest you return to that no good husband of yours. You are no longer welcome here. Do you hear what I say? Get out woman!'

Before Medi could find the right words to say to him, her grandmother jumped up from the chair in a terrible rage.

Leah Thomas faced her son,

'No Rhys! It is you who are no longer welcome in my house. Through you, our good name will be dragged in the mud for miles around. You have turned against each one of us in this room. We who have loved you no matter what. But it has ended now, you will leave this house immediately and I never wish to see you again.'

Then turning to Eleri she continued,

'As for you Eleri, you must choose either to stay or to go with him. If you choose to go, then only God knows why, for he does not deserve you.'

The realisation of what his mother had said, finally began to dawn on Rhys.

'You can't be serious Mother,' he pleaded. 'Who will run the estate for you. Be sensible, we can sit down and talk it over. A lot of harsh things have been said but we can get over this.'

'There is nothing left to say,' said Leah Thomas to her son. 'Now pack your things and leave!' she demanded.

Rhys turned on his heel and left the room but a second later he reappeared and looking toward his wife said gruffly,

'Well, are you coming or not?'

Eleri Thomas glanced at the other two women, shrugged her shoulders in defeat and meekly followed her husband out of the room.

The scene had finally reduced the old lady to tears as she clung to Medi for support.

'What have I done my child?' she asked. 'I've turned away my own son but I cannot live here with him knowing what he has done.'

Medi held her grandmother tightly in her arms realising how frail the old lady had become.

Soon they heard the front door slam. Medi ran to the window in time to see her uncle's carriage as it pulled away from Bryn Cethin, the place which had always been his home.

Wil who had remained patiently in the courtyard witnessed Rhys Thomas's swift departure. Now he entered the house in search of Medi, as he feared for her safety. All around him was silence until he heard a sound coming from the end of the hallway. He peered around the door of a large room to find Medi trying to comfort the old lady who was sobbing uncontrollably.

'Thank God it's you. I'd almost forgotten you were outside,' said the girl. 'Grandmother has had a terrible shock. I think she needs a strong cup of tea. Will you sit with her while I make one?' she asked him.

'We could all do with one gel!' said Wil, as he pulled up a chair and sat beside Leah Thomas.

Medi left her grandmother's side. Then Leah looked at Wil sadly,

'What have we done to your family, Wil Lewis?' she asked. 'First your Huw, then Peter Malone and now this! Can you ever forgive us?'

Then softly she began to cry again.

Will took her hand in his,

'You are not to blame,' he said. 'God only knows how or why it happened. It has come as a shock to us all. I doubted my Marged for so long and now the truth has been revealed. I wish I could apologise to you for Owen's behaviour but if he had not settled the score with Rhys then if would have been my duty to do so. Your husband was a good man but I fail to understand your son at all.'

'My son!' she uttered. ' I never want to call him my son again. He has left, and I hope he will never return.' Then looking toward the doorway she asked,

'Is Owen not with you?'

'I'm afraid he's too ashamed to come here after all the trouble he's caused in your home,' replied Wil.

'He should feel no shame. I'm afraid he gave Rhys all he deserved. Tell him to come and to bring the baby with him. They are all I have now.' Then she looked directly at him adding,

'I would ask another favour of you Wil Lewis.'

'Anything,' he replied.

'Will you speak with Marged for me? Ask her if she will come to see me.'

'I shall give her your message, then it will be up to her to decide,' said Wil making no promises to the old woman.

Medi entered the room carrying a silver tray laden with cups and saucers. As she saw him about to leave she asked,

'You're not staying then Da?'

'No merchi, I'll be off now. Owen shall be with you shortly. His place is here with you,' he said.

Medi glanced at her grandmother and the smile on her face said that soon all would be well again.

Wil rode into Cefn Glas as Owen prepared to leave with the baby.

'Thank God you've come Da!' he said. 'Is Medi alright?'

'Yes son, she is waiting for you to join her,' answered Wil

He quickly began to relate all that had happened as and he ended his tale it was Anna who spoke,

'So Rhys Thomas has finally gone. How will the old lady manage now? Who will run the estate for her?'

'One thing is certain,' answered Owen. ' I shall not return to the firm to work alongside Rhys Thomas. We shall stay at Bryn Cethin for as long as Medi and I are needed. Surely now Anna, your stay at the cottage will be safe.'

'No Owen, my mind is made up,' said Anna, 'Whatever happens I shall return here to Cefn Glas where Mam and Da will help me to raise my children. It is time we got on with our lives.'

Wil and Beti were overjoyed at Anna's decision to say the least.

Marged, however, stood in the background, and although she was pleased for Anna, the events of the day had led her to believe that they had not seen the last of Rhys Thomas the man she would forever hate.

CHAPTER 20

Wil Lewis' words had come true. Bethan Jones, the little maid at Bryn Cethin had lost no time in spreading the news of the fight, which had taken place at the Big House.

Owen Lewis had beaten his wife's uncle half to death, according to her, and what was more - Rhys Thomas the master had been named as the father of Marged Lewis' son John.

By market day the gossip had spread from stall to stall, down on the street corners where women clutched their shawls around their shoulders, fearful of missing one word of the affair.

Davy Griffiths stood by the bar of the Market Tavern adding his version while others listened intently to him. Davy was known for his vile tongue and so he added a few words for good measure. Dic Watkins the landlord had heard quite enough and so he warned Davy to leave the gossip to the women and let the men carry on with their drinking. Davy did not heed the warning and continued to voice his opinion loudly.

Finally, Twm Shenkin who had been sitting quietly in a corner could stand it no longer. He jumped up from his chair shouting,

'Right then! One more word about Wil Lewis and his family and I'll take the lot of you on. Just step outside anyone of you and we'll settle it outside. As for Rhys Thomas, if ever I catch hold of him I'll tar and feather him, I promise you!'

Not one person in the room dared reply to Twm's threat as he had been known as quite a boxer in his younger days. So the conversation quickly turned to other matters and the afternoon's drinking continued.

Market day or not, Marged had decided to remain at home. She was aware of the gossip and she intended to shelter her husband and son from it. Morgan had become almost insane when he was told what had befallen Owen at Bryn Cethin. It took both Wil and Owen to calm him down and it was decided that the time had come to tell young John the truth of his birth.

'What will he think of me?' Marged asked her husband. 'He's still only a boy.'

'John is old enough to understand and he must hear it from us and no-one else,' said Morgan.

That evening John sat in silence as he listened to his mother and father and as the story unfolded he began to shake his head again and again. He knew they spoke the truth but he did not want to believe what he was being told. As his mother ended the tale she said,

'So you see John, that is why Mister Thomas made such a generous offer for you to visit him to see the ponies and the farm. He wanted you there at Bryn Cethin with him. I never had the courage to tell you he was your father. I was too ashamed.'

Suddenly the boy cried out,

'He's not my father! He never could be and I am not like him.'

Then he ran toward Morgan crying,

'You are my father, the only father I know. There can be no-one else. Ever!'

Morgan placed his arms around his son and held him tightly. John then lifted his head, looked toward his mother and asked,

'Mam, you are not ashamed of me, are you?'

Marged held her arms open to him

'You are the only good thing to come from all this, John. It is I who am ashamed,' she answered tearfully.

'Don't cry,' he said, turning to her. 'I love you so much Mam.'

Marged knew then that they had done the correct thing. John knew the truth now, and they would weather the storm together.

The following morning her father called to see them and they told him that John now knew everything about himself.

'He's handling it quite well,' said Morgan, ' but how his friends at school will react will be another matter.'

'That is why I've called,' said Wil. 'I have decided we shall all go as a united family to Chapel on Sunday. We've always held our heads high in the community and if we face the gossips together we shall beat them in the end.'

Marged was horrified at her father's suggestion. What good would it do?

'I couldn't face them Da,' she said. 'I can't put John through it either. We shall stay away.'

'No, your father is right,' said Morgan. 'You are the innocent party Marged. It's time to put this to rest once and for all.'

They were in deep conversation and had not noticed John as he arrived at the door.

'I'm not afraid to come with you Grandpa,' he said boldly to Wil.

'Spoken like a man' said Morgan, proud that his son had made a stand.

'Will you come then Marged?' asked her father.

'No, Da. I cannot,' was her reply as she avoided the look in John's eyes.

'Then I shall come for you on Sunday,' said Wil to the boy, then speaking to his daughter he said,

'That is if I have your permission Marged.'

'John must do as he wishes,' she said as she turned away from them.

Sunday came, and as they prepared to go to Chapel Beti felt quite sick. Were they doing the right thing? She had no concern for herself, only for John. Wil appeared quite confident.

'The Lord is on our side,' he had told her. If only she could believe it!

Goronwy Evans stood waiting for his congregation, most of which had already arrived. He was not alone, Twm Shenkin stood alongside the minister. As soon as he saw Wil he took him to one side saying,

'The Chapel is full Wil. I think you should know before you go inside.'

'That is exactly how I wished it to be Twm,' said Wil gratefully.

Twm nodded and took his place inside. Goronwy Evans shook Wil's hand.

'It's a pleasure to see a full turnout of the Lewis family today. Owen and Medi are inside, and you've brought young John with you. Welcome boy!' he said. However he noticed that the boy's mother and father were missing.

Wil ushered his family through the door and as they made their way to the family pew they became conscious of the whispers around them. One by one they filed into the dark oak polished seats with the exception of Wil who took his place with the other deacons at the front of the pulpit.

Goronwy Evans then took his place at the pulpit himself, while his wife Blodwen sat at the organ in readiness to hammer out the first hymn on the keyboard.

The minister stood to announce the first hymn to the sung but before he could do so a sound came from the rear of the chapel and he halted for a moment. Some latecomer, no doubt, he thought. As he looked up from his hymnal, he saw Marged and Morgan Harries entering the chapel. Then they walked together down the aisle to join their son John.

Beti and Anna quickly moved along the row to make room for them. Wil looked from where he sat and nodded to them with pride in his face.

Opposite them sat Martha 'the voice' Llewellyn, aptly named for other things than having a deep contralto voice. She could not take her eyes off Marged and soon found great difficulty in finding the correct page in her hymn book.

Her best friend, and her only friend, was Eva Hughes the seamstress. She sat next to Martha and she cursed the day that she had decided to wear her new hat. She had made it specially for today with its fashionable dark veil covering her eyes. Now all she could do was to sit there as blind as a bat as it prevented her from seeing what was going on.

Eva's daughter Mari took a lace handkerchief and held it to her nose as she began to sniff into it.

'What's the matter girl?' asked Eva in a whisper.

'It's so sad Mam. That John looks a lovely boy doesn't he?' she answered.

Eva gave her daughter a nudge, ordering her to remain silent. The girl almost fell from off her seat.

Meanwhile Goronwy Evans nodded to his wife to begin and Blodwen began to play the organ. As she began the first hymn the congregation sang out loud but it was not with the usual gusto. However, Wil Lewis' voice was as loud as ever as he sang the hymn with great pride. When it had ended, the minister took the huge Bible before him and opened it to present his sermon. He had taken hours to prepare this text the previous evening. He looked around his congregation then folded his carefully prepared paper and placed it inside his pocket.

He had decided to change his sermon there and then.

In a deep voice, Goronwy Evans spoke out loud.

'I have taken my text today from the Gospel of St John. Chapter 8, Verse 7.'

'So when they continued asking Him, He lifted up himself and said unto them, 'He who is without sin among you, let him first cast a stone at her'!'

A number of people began to fidget in their seats as they heard the minister's words. He repeated the same words again then paused for a second. The sermon that followed was one of fire and brimstone. It was enough to frighten the devil himself!

While he spoke, Marged cast her mind back to the day she had accompanied her father to face the same deacons who sat there today. Now everyone knew of her shame and the true identity of the man whose name she had tried so hard to hide. Surely she had now paid the price? Not so, it seemed, as she watched the faces of people around her. Faces that still held shock and disgust written all over them.

Many were relieved when Goronwy Evans completed his sermon and the final hymn was sung. Then they all filed outside. Anna with her children, Beti with Owen, Medi and the baby and finally Marged followed by Morgan and John.

They waited outside for Wil to join them, and soon he was shaking hands with the minister thanking him for a well chosen sermon. Without further ado they walked back together to Cefn Glas.

'I'm proud of you Marged,' said Wil releasing the stiff white collar from his shirt. He gave a sigh of relief.

'You certainly gave us all a surprise,' he added.

'It was Morgan who persuaded me and I'm thankful to him now,' she said. ' I've been thinking over the message you gave me from Mrs Thomas and I've decided to call to see her at Bryn Cethin before we return home,' she told her father.

'I'm glad to hear it merchi,' said Wil

As they all sat down to eat, Wil looked around the table and prayed silently to God that they could at last live in peace. They had felt enough sadness to last them for quite a while.

Later in the day Anna suggested that John stay with them at the farm while Morgan took Marged to meet with Leah Thomas. As the couple reached Bryn Cethin, Morgan jumped down off the buggy then taking his wife in his arms to help her down he said,

'I won't be far away Marged. Just call out and I'll be there.'

Marged nodded nervously to him as she walked to the front door of the Big House.

She was immediately shown to the sitting room where Mrs Thomas sat in her favourite chair. The old lady attempted to rise to greet her but Marged motioned for her to remain seated. Words did not come easy to either of the women so Marged took the initiative and began to speak.

'My father tells me that you wish to speak with me' she said politely.

'Please sit down,' said the old lady motioning to the chair beside her.

Marged did as she was asked. Then Leah Thomas continued.

'I wanted the chance to apologise to you Marged, and I also wished to know why you did not come to me for help all those years ago. I would have stood by you and tried to have helped you in some way. You would not have reared the child on your own. I am deeply ashamed of my son and the heartache he has caused you.'

'It was my decision then, and it remains the same now. My son and I need nothing from you,' said Marged curtly.

'You cannot change the fact that the child is still my grandson, my own flesh and blood and I am prepared to do right by him. I understand how you must feel but I promise you that he will be provided for in the future,' said Leah.

'That is kind of you to offer your support now, but as I've already said, we want nothing from you,' said Marged firmly as she stood up and prepared to leave.

'Please don't go yet,' pleaded Leah Thomas.

'I must,' answered Marged. 'My husband waits for me outside.'

'Then let us part as friends,' said the old lady, rising from her chair at last. She held her hand out to Marged, who at last noticed the sadness and despair in her eyes. She realised this lady had played no part in all that had happened her, so she took her hand and shook it in friendship.

Leah Thomas nodded, then sat back down in the chair, satisfied that at last all was well between her and the woman her son had wronged.

As Morgan and Marged drove away from Bryn Cethin, Marged looked back over her shoulder and she knew in the heart that if the boy chose to visit the old lady she would not prevent him.

As the days passed by, Owen and Medi moved back to Bryn Cethin. They would manage the farm for Grandmother Thomas who was only too happy to welcome them there. As for the baby, she was the one little person who could bring happiness back into Leah Thomas' life.

Owen had finally parted from the firm, as he could no longer stomach being near Rhys Thomas who felt likewise towards him.

The old lady prayed that one day the young boy, John, would come to visit her, but she knew it would seem out of the question.

A few weeks later however, her prayers were answered. Owen met with John at Cefn Glas and invited him to visit them at the farm. John became excited at the prospect of seeing Bryn Cethin once again.

'You'd better ask permission to visit,' advised Owen. 'It might not go down very well with our Marged!'

'I'm old enough to make up my own mind Uncle Owen,' said the boy earnestly.

Owen looked at him as he said this. John reminded him of his brother Huw. Quiet in one way, but possessing a strong character underneath it all.

When Marged welcomed the visit, it surprised Owen greatly.

'He'll have to get it out of his system sooner or later,' she said to her brother.

'I promise you Marged, John will come to no harm,' said Owen.

'Then have him home by dark,' she said, showing her brother that despite what John had told him she was the one who was still in charge.

The sun shone brightly as Owen accompanied by John made their way across the well kept lawns at the front of the house.

A face seemed to appear at one of the downstairs windows, then it was gone again. Only the boy had seen the movement but it had not bothered him.

'Shall we start at the stables lad?' asked Owen eager to show his nephew the fine stock of horses there. John quickly followed his uncle, eager not to miss anything.

'You like it here, don't you?' he asked Owen who nodded.

'Yes, there's always so much work to do. It's hard work, but I'm happy to be back on the land, and your Aunt Medi wants Rowena to grow up in the place she's loved for so long,' replied Owen.

The face looked through the window once more, but from inside the house Leah Thomas could not see clearly in the distance. She thought she saw the shape of a man with a boy standing near him. Whoever it was, seemed to walk in the direction of the stables.

How strange! Almost everyone was out in the fields at work and as she could not recognise the figures she dismissed them from her thoughts. How tired she had become lately. She sat in her chair and soon nodded off to sleep. Some time later she awoke to the sound of voices approaching the room. Owen entered first, followed by a young boy she immediately recognised as her grandson. His features told her everything, he resembled her son Rhys when he was about the boy's age.

Pushing the boy slightly forward, Owen said, 'I've a visitor for you Grandmother.'

John, overcome with shyness, stood there nervously waiting for the old lady's reaction toward him. His feelings were mixed ones filled with his own curiosity toward the lady he knew to be his grandmother.

'Come in,' she said kindly.

The boy took a step forward, then hesitated, looked back over his shoulder for his uncle's support, only to find that Owen had already left the room. He was now on his own with the old lady. Before he could turn on his heel to run from the room, she spoke again,

'You must be John. I'm so pleased to meet you at last. It's very kind of your mother to allow you to visit us,' she said.

Leah Thomas held out her hand and to his surprise John took hold of it and shook it politely.

'You look very hot. Are you thirsty?' she asked. 'Sit down and I'll send for something cool for you to drink.'

He sat down beside her while she in turn pulled on a large green silk tassel which hung on the wall by the side of her chair.

A maid appeared and John marvelled at the way in which the girl had been summoned. She hurried away again returning with a large pitcher of lemonade and two glasses on a tray which she placed by the side of her mistress.

'Tell me John. What do you think of Bryn Cethin? Do you like it here?' she asked as she tried to coax him into conversation with her.

'Your Uncle Owen has worked very hard and I'm grateful to him for his help,' she said again.

Slowly the boy gathered courage to speak,

'It's a fine place, but I remember it from the last time I came here,' he said. 'T'was when Uncle Owen and Aunt Medi were married.'

'I'd forgotten that,' she replied as she handed him a glass of cool lemonade. The boy drank it thirstily and then placed the fine glass down on the try beside him for fear it would break. He had never drank from anything so grand before.

Within a short time the old lady and the young boy sat and talked with each other. Soon John began to feel more comfortable with her and he was surprised when his uncle returned to tell him that it was time for them to leave.

John nodded to Owen, then Mrs Thomas left her chair to say farewell to him.

'Thank you for coming to see me John,' she said holding her hand out to him once more. 'I hope to see you again you know you are welcome here.'

'I should like that,' said the boy politely.

Owen watched the tender scene, then said he would wait for John outside. John took the old lady's hand in his a shook it gently. She watched him leave the room but as he reached the doorway, he paused and looked back at her standing there. Then he said out loud,

'Goodbye Grandmother!'

With tears in her eyes, Leah Thomas knew then that she would see her grandson again.

CHAPTER 21

The weeks turned into months. Anna and the children had begun to settle at Cefn Glas. They had finally started to rebuild their lives. The children laughed again, and Beti and Wil made it possible for them to feel secure in their new surroundings. It was a time of healing for Anna, filled with loving memories. Her family surrounded her with love and affection, but now and then she would steel herself away to the Chapel where she laid flowers on Peter's grave. She would sit down on the grass beside it and talk to him. She would tell him how he was missed and how her love for him was as strong as ever. Each time, as she walked back home to Cefn Glas she felt an inner peace.

Owen and Medi were happy together and Anna had felt pleased that Marged had so readily accepted John's eager visits to Bryn Cethin. As for her mother and father, she would always feel eternally grateful to them for giving her and the children a home. Despite this however, she had tried to hide her true feelings for she knew that with all the love and support she received, she was still a lonely woman whose life had become an empty shell.

It was time for the annual Chapel Picnic and the children had been busily gathering blackberries from the bushes. Jams had been preserved and large plates of tart stood ready for them to take with them.

'Are you sure you won't change you mind Mam?' asked Anna. 'Do come with us!'

'I've plenty to do here cariad,' answered Beti. 'Besides you'll have Catrin Lloyd's company to look forward to. It will be a change to have someone your own age to go with you. All the children will be able to play together as well,' added Beti.

'I suppose so,' said Anna feeling disappointed at her mother's refusal. She, herself, was not keen to go on the picnic now that the day had arrived. Beti prepared the picnic baskets and as she filled them with fresh bread, cakes and home-made jam and bottles of lemonade, David stood nearby eyeing all that would be devoured.

Wil took Anna and the children to the Chapel to meet with the others. Quite a crowd had assembled there.

What food did you bring to eat?' asked Bleddyn Jones the fattest boy in David's class. Before David could reply, Anna called out to him.

Have you seen Catrin Lloyd? I can't find her.'

Bleddyn Jones stepped forward.

She's not going,' he said. 'She's sent a message to say that Gwilym has the chicken pox, so she's keeping the others away from here as well.'

David looked at his mother,

'Who shall I play with now, if Gwilym's not here?' he asked.

Bleddyn looked at the heavy basket David carried.

'I'll play with you,' he said eagerly. 'What did you say you had to eat then?' he asked.

David ignored the greedy boy's question. Anna disappointed at her friend's absence said,

'Don't worry, there'll be others to play with.'

Then lifting the smaller children on the haycart she put her disappointment behind her and climbed up with them. Soon they were off to the chosen site for the picnic which was a mile or so away.

They reached the popular wooded glade where there seemed plenty of space for the children to run and play. The leafy trees shaded them from the hot afternoon sun. Anna placed the baskets beneath one of the trees while Elizabeth knelt by a stream running by, as she placed the bottles of lemonade to stand on the, cool, river bed. They would be very welcome when the children got thirsty later in the day.

Kate helped her mother spread a woollen rug on the grass beneath the tree. Peter John began to crawl on it and sat to play with the multi-coloured fringe around its edge.

Blodwen Evans, the minister's wife, called out,

'Everything alright there Anna?'

'Thank you Mrs Evans, we are fine. It's going to be a lovely day isn't it?' answered Anna.

'Don't forget the races for the children later on. There are prizes for the winners you know. And I've just heard there'll be another Chapel from over at St Clears arriving for their picnic as well. So it should be a lot of fun,' she called out again.

'Did you hear that Mam?' asked David jumping up and down with excitement.

'Yes,' laughed Anna. 'Now let's have lunch then you can do what you wish.'

The food was soon unpacked and most of it eaten quickly, then Elizabeth retrieved the cool drinks from the river bed.

Kate wandered off to pick daisies but soon came running back to her mother with the news that the people from the other Chapel had arrived.

'Can we go to play now?' she asked.

Elizabeth got up from the rug saying,

'I'll go with her mam, you rest yourself here.'

'Me too!' shouted David running to catch up with his sisters as they walked across the field.

'David, stay out of trouble, will you?' shouted Anna.

'Yes Mam,' called the boy as he disappeared out of sight.

Anna began to nurse the baby, rocking him gently until he fell asleep on the blanket beside her.

The sun shone hot in the sky. Butterflies flitted here and there while a large bee buzzed around her head. Anna lifted her hand to brush it away. How she wished that she could undo the high lace collar on her black dress. She was still in mourning for her husband, but she quickly looked around and as no-one appeared to be in sight she undid several buttons at the throat which allowed her to breathe more easily. The sweat began to trickle from her neck until it reached down inside covering her breasts. She leaned her head back against the large trunk of the tree and closed her eyes. The sound of the nearby stream as it babbled over the stones and the haze of the afternoon sun caused her eyelids to close even further. As she drifted off to sleep she imagined she could see Peter walking toward her, his red curls blowing in the breeze.

She awoke suddenly as she felt someone tugging at her arm.

It was Kate. The child stood there with another little girl alongside her.

'Mam, I've found a friend,' she said excitedly. 'Her name is Rebecca but she's called Becky. Can she have a cake? I said she could!'

Anna sat up and smiled. It was good to see her daughter so happy. She reached inside the picnic basket and brought out some welshcakes which she gave to the two little girls.

'Now go and tell your mother where you are. Then you can return to play with Kate' said Anna, to her daughter's newly found friend.

'I haven't got a Mam,' answered the little girl solemnly. 'She's gone to Heaven a long time ago. My Dada is here though, and my two brothers,' she added.

A second later a man's voice called out,

'There you are Becky! I've been looking for you!'

Anna arose to her feet and came face to face with the stranger.

The both laughed as they began to recognise each other.

'Well if it isn't Anna Malone,' he said looking at her.

Anna immediately began to button the neck of her dress, blushing while she did so. It was not proper for him to find her like this.

'Forgive me,' she said hastily. 'I know we've met before but I fail to remember where.'

'We met in much unhappier circumstances,' he answered. 'I came to Cefn Glas the day your husband was buried. We met and talked before I left.'

'I remember now,' said Anna. ' You must be Iestyn Roberts.'

Iestyn nodded to her, then he asked if he could join her.

'The baby is due to wake at any moment,' said Anna looking down on Peter John as he lay sleeping on the rug.

This did not deter Iestyn however, as he made himself comfortable on the grass beneath the tree.

Kate and Becky decided it was time to join the other children and so they ran off leaving the grown-ups to chat together.

'You've come with the chapel from St Clears, have you?' asked Anna as she tried to make polite conversation.

'Yes,' he replied. 'It's just that I work long hours on the land, and I don't find much time to enjoy my children, so I thought it would be good to spend time with them today.'

'How do you manage on your own?' asked Anna, then quickly, she began to apologise.

'I'm sorry, I didn't mean to pry. It's just that my mother told me you had lost your wife. Please forgive me.'

'There's nothing to forgive,' he said. 'I'm not really on my own. Morwenna's mother takes charge of the children. She lives with us and a friend helps her as well, so you see I am very lucky Anna. May I call you Anna?' he asked.

Anna blushed and looked away. Then she took up the conversation again.

'I too am lucky. We moved back to Cefn Glas where my mother and father help me all they can. I looked forward to today also, as I feel the need to be on my own with the children sometimes.'

At that very moment the two little girls came running back. Kate immediately placed a daisy chain around her mother's neck, while Becky placed another on Anna's head crowning her dark curls in glory. Then they ran off once more laughing at each other, while Anna filled with embarrassment attempted to remove the flowers from her hair.

Leave them,' he pleaded with her. 'They look pretty on you.'

It had been a long time since anyone had paid a compliment to her and she began to blush again. Iestyn looked toward the two girls playing a few yards away, suddenly he said,

'I never know quite what to say to her you know. The boys I can manage, but with Becky I seem to fail miserably.'

'You must miss your wife very much,' said Anna.

'Yes, I do,' he replied with sadness in his voice.

The baby began to stir. Anna lifted him and held him gently to her until he awoke thoroughly. Then she began to feed him and he readily guzzled the bottle of fresh milk she held in her hand.

Iestyn watched her, thinking all the time what a wonderful mother she seemed to be. Fate had dealt both of them a terrible blow but like himself, Anna Malone would be strong enough to weather the storm.

Suddenly a voice called out It was David as he ran toward them,

'Mam, they are holding games at the far corner of the field. Can we move a little closer so that you can see me run?' he asked impatiently.

He waited for his mother's reply, all the time ignoring the stranger who sat on the grass beside her.

'Very well,' agreed Anna. Then gathering their things together she told David to run to tell the girls what was happening.

'Oh! By the way David,' said Anna, 'I want you to say hello to Mr Roberts. He's here with his children also. Perhaps you can meet them later.'

The boy stared at the man but did not speak. Then quickly gathering all he could carry, he walked away in search of his sisters.

'Forgive my son,' said Anna apologetically. 'He's a good boy but he's become very possessive of me since his father's gone.'

'I can see that,' said Iestyn folding the rug as soon as Anna had picked up the baby from it. He gathered the remainder of her belongings and carried them to a spot where they could watch their children enter the races.

Anna turned to him saying

'Thank you for your company Iestyn, I'm pleased we met once again.'

'The day is not over yet Anna,' he replied.

Anna had expected Iestyn Roberts to rejoin his children and it surprised her that he wished to stay within her company.

Before anything further could be said between them, they heard a great shout of laughter and excitement. As they looked up they saw several red-faced boys, their legs encased in old brown sacks jumping passed them.

In the lead jumped David. He was way ahead of the others and Anna could not help herself as she shouted out,

'Go on David, you can do it!'

Her son reached the finishing line, he had won the sack race!

Minutes later, two small boys, hot and very much out of breath ran up to their father panting,

'Did you see that boy from the Elim Chapel Da? He was so fast we just couldn't catch him! I said he was the best, but Jethro doesn't agree with me' said Daniel, Iestyn Roberts' youngest son.

Jethro, his eldest, had flopped down on the grass in an effort to gain his breath.

'He wasn't that good,' he panted. 'I nearly beat him!'

Daniel began to argue with his brother until Iestyn decided it was time for them to stop.

'Now boys, he did win after all. His name is David Malone and this is his mother,' said Iestyn as he introduced Anna to his sons.

'I'm sure there are other games you will excel in so why don't you go to see what they plan next?' their father suggested.

The boys not feeling very much refreshed, jumped up and ran to where yet another event was about to take place.

'You have two fine boys,' said Anna looking after them.

'Yes I'm proud of them,' he said.

It was Elizabeth's turn to be introduced to the man who seemed quite friendly toward her mother. She held out her hand politely as Iestyn Roberts took it and began to shake it.

'Would you like me to take Peter John with me?' she asked her mother.

Elizabeth was so pleased to see that her mother looked so happy and relaxed. It had been a long time since she'd looked like this.

No, merchi,' said Anna, 'run along and enjoy yourself with your friends. I'm just fine here and the baby's no trouble to me.'

Another hour or so had passed, and soon the warm afternoon sun changed its direction in the clear, blue sky. It was time now for them to leave.

As he shook her hand, Iestyn held it a little longer than it was necessary.

'I want to thank you for your company Anna. It's been such a long time since I've relaxed and enjoyed myself. Perhaps one day soon we shall meet each other again,' he said hopefully.

'I have enjoyed myself also, but I doubt that our paths will cross each other. We have both made time to value our children and to spend it happily with them. That is what is important to us surely?' asked Anna hastily.

'You are right,' he said. 'Well, give you mother and father my regards and tell them that if ever I'm in the village I'll be certain to call and see them.'

Anna was surprised at his statement. She knew her mother had said cousin Martha rarely left Iestyn or the children out of her sight since her daughter Morwenna had died. So there was little chance of them meeting again, but as they shook hands once more Anna felt a little disappointed at their parting.

As she walked away from him she was tempted to look back, and as she did so she found him still standing there watching her.

Iestyn lifted his hand to wave but she did not wave back. Her heart told her she dare not!

The moment they arrived back at Cefn Glas, Anna carried the baby up to bed while David ran inside eager to tell his grandmother of his success at the Chapel races. Beti listened to him intently, while all the time Kate also tried to gain her grandmother's attention.

'I met a new friend, Mamgu,' she pleaded for Beti to listen to her. 'Her name is Becky' the child said.

'Yes, and her father sat with our Mam all afternoon, that he did!' said David spitefully.

Kate stuck her tongue out at him and he replied by repeating the gesture.

'And what have you to say Elizabeth?' asked Beti, eager to know who the strange gentleman was.

'Don't ask her, Mamgu,' said David again. She was too busy with Morfydd and Delyth. They were playing kiss and tell with those boys from the other chapel from St Clears.'

'You little tell tale,' hissed Elizabeth as she took hold of a wooden spoon and began to chase her brother around the kitchen table.

'Stop this noise,' said Anna entering the kitchen to see all the commotion, taking place. 'I don't want the baby to wake,' she demanded.

The children knew better than to disobey their mother, as each became silent in turn.

'Now then, it's been a long day so get washed and it's off to bed with you,' said Anna.

Elizabeth, David and Kate kissed their grandmother and then their mother, but it was David who left with a mischievous grin on his face knowing that he had sown enough seeds for his grandmother to be curious as to who the stranger might be.

Eventually the two sat down together, and as Beti poured the tea into the cups, she could wait not longer.

'What's all this about a stranger? David seemed quite put out that you had spent some time talking with a man at the outing today,' she asked Anna, innocently.

'David is only a child,' was Anna's reply. 'But if you really want to know Mam, the man was no stranger. He was Iestyn Roberts, you told me about him, the day of Peter's funeral.'

Beti waited for her to continue but when she could see there was nothing further to be said, she took it on herself to ask,

And that is all?'

Anna glanced at her mother and with innocence said,

'Why the questions Mam? He was there with his children. It was their Chapel picnic, we met, sat and talked. He spoke about Morwenna and I about Peter. We enjoyed each other's company. There is nothing more to say!'

Beti looked at her. Why had Anna's words and the tone of the voice failed to convince her?

'I remember Iestyn Roberts. He's a fine man,' she said. 'They say he nearly went to pieces after his Morwenna died. If it were not for cousin Martha, and a friend of hers, he would have been in serious trouble. Martha looks after him and the children. Last I heard he was walking out with Sarah Madoc, Martha's friend. A widow she is, older than him though. Those children of his need a mother they do. God help them!'

Beti had finally parted with what little knowledge she had of the man.

'Well, he'll not find one here,' said Anna, 'so you needn't worry yourself Mam. It was a pleasant afternoon, but that's all it was!'

'I'm pleased to hear it merchi,' said Beti feeling slightly more satisfied at her daughter's explanation.

The conversation turned to other events of the day but later as Anna climbed the stairs to bed it was with mixed feelings in her heart. Who did she think she was fooling? Her mother or herself?

She had not wanted to admit to herself that her meeting with Iestyn Roberts had left her more than breathless.

He had stirred feelings within her that she thought were gone forever.

CHAPTER 22

In the weeks that followed, Anna gave little thought to her meeting with Iestyn Roberts. She resigned herself that their paths would not cross again.

She worked alongside her mother and father and what spare time she had was taken up with rehearsals for the Gymanfa Ganu at the Chapel, it was the annual Festival of Song.

Wil had persuaded his daughter to join the Chapel choir with him. He began to rehearse his solo part as he went about his daily duties. Soon even the children knew its tune off by heart. Practice was held at the Chapel Vestry twice a week, and as Watkin Williams raised his baton in his hand, there was much coughing and clearing of throats to be heard. This made way for a tuneful start to the anthem they were about to learn.

As Wil and Anna walked home that night he felt he had to ask her once again,

'How did I sound tonight merchi?'

'You were very good Da. There'll be no-one to touch you when the time comes for you to sing solo,' said Anna smiling, as she knew this was just what her father wanted to hear..

'Can you help your mother to take the refreshments to the vestry?' Wil asked.

Anna answered that she could do this. After all, it was the custom for the host chapel to invite members from visiting chapels to stay for tea after the service had ended. The ladies of the chapel would organise the event long before the time was due.

Visitors came from miles around to join in the festival, which was to be held on the following Saturday and Sunday alike.

The children were up from bed early in the morning. They each counted the hours until they would go with their mother and mamgu to the chapel.

Soon it became time to dress in their best clothes for the afternoon service to be held especially for the children. Then they set off.

As they entered the chapel they found it full to capacity. The service then began, and the organ played by Mrs Evans sounded more in tune than ever it did before. Even the smallest of children attempted to sing the hymns though sometimes words had to be mimed where they had been forgotten. Sweet music filled the air, and soon an hour had passed and it was time for the service to end.

Beti and Anna stopped to talk with some of the women while the children ran outside. Elizabeth however had decided to disappear for a few moments. She had discovered a secret place where she knew wild dog daisies grew, and soon she returned with them and placed them gently on her father's grave.

Her mother and grandmother stood watching her, then the other children ran to join her.

'She loved him very much didn't she?' said Beti as she watched the little girl tell her brother and sister all about their father who lay there in the grave.

'So did I, Mam,' whispered Anna. 'So did I.'

Anna joined her children at the graveside while Beti wandered through the gravestone around her until she stopped in front of one.

As she read the inscription yet again, tears filled her eyes.

'Oh! My son. I long to see you.' How old would he be now? She had missed Huw every day since he had died.

Beti looked back to where Anna stood and her heart ached for her. She had loved Peter so much but now her dear Anna was resolved to a life of loneliness. Dear Lord, why had it had to happen to both Peter and Huw?

Elizabeth called out to her and Beti went to join them on the walk back to Cefn Glas.

It was evening, and as Beti helped her husband to fasten the stiff white collar to the neck of his shirt he began to complain,

Don't fasten it too tight woman. I'll never be able to sing if I can't get my breath!'

'Now then Wil, this is nothing but nerves,' she said holding his jacket out to him as he slipped the coat over his shoulders.

'He's nervous, he'll be able to sing as well as anyone in the county,' said Anna trying to instil some confidence into her father.

Beti wanted to believe her daughter but aggravated the situation by saying,

'I hope you're right merchi. I don't want him making a fool of himself. There's glad I am that I won't be there tonight. I'd much rather stay home with the children!'

'You'll be at the Chapel to hear me sing tomorrow evening, won't you Beti?' asked Wil earnestly.

Beti smiled at him and putting his mind at ease replied,

'Of course I shall, you silly man!'

Then, as a final gesture she handed Wil his best bowler hat which he in turn placed on his head.

Wil then offered his arm to his daughter saying,

'Are you ready Mrs Malone?'

Linking her arm in his Anna replied,

'As ready as you are Mr Lewis!'

Wil turned to his wife, doffed his hat and said,

'Don't wait up Beti fach! We may be late!'

Laughter filled the air as Beti watched father and daughter walk arm in arm down the lane toward Elim Chapel.

o o o

Anna followed her father inside the chapel and went to take her place in one of the side pews where the choir had gathered. Wil sat with the deacons directly in front of her.

The chapel was almost full of people; some had come from miles around. There were lots of faces she recognised but there were a number of strangers she did not know. Representatives of other chapels had joined the congregation. They too had rehearsed the chosen hymns about to be sung at the Gymanfa.

Her father turned toward her and smiled. He was proud that at least one member of his family would be here to listen to him sing his solo piece this evening.

Anna nodded to him, but her attention turned to the upstairs gallery where the pews were filled with people.

Suddenly she saw a man sitting in the front row upstairs, and realised that it was Iestyn Roberts who was looking down at her. Their eyes met and he smiled and nodded in recognition of her. Anna had heard that his chapel would be represented here this evening but she had not dared to hope that he would be here himself.

Her heart began to skip a beat and she looked quickly around, anxious in case her face might betray what her heart now felt. What was she doing she thought? She realised she would have to avoid him at all cost. What was happening to her? Had her mind taken leave of its senses.

She thought of Peter who lay in his grave outside. He had been the love of her life, a life never again to be shared, despite the loneliness she had begun to feel.

Why then did she feel a stirring in her heart at the very sight of Iestyn Roberts? Anna desperately wanted to run outside but then the organ began to play and so she remained seated. The service had finally begun and so she decided she would avoid looking upward toward him again.

Soon the time came for her father to sing the solo part in the anthem, and proud though Anna was of him she could not relax and enjoy herself.

The feelings of guilt she held within her had stemmed the joy of the occasion and she felt relieved when the service came to an end.

Blodwen Evans, the minister's wife, came to seek her help. Anna was asked to make tea in the vestry before some of the visitors departed. She waved to Wil who was deep in conversation with Twm Shenkin and motioned to him that she would see him later. Then she followed Mrs Evans to the vestry where she found several of the ladies handing out plates of sandwiches and cakes to a number of people already seated.

Anna found a nearby table set out with rows of cups and saucers and she began to pour the milk from a jug into the cups in readiness to hand out the teas.

A hand reached out, touching her gently on her shoulder and a voice said,

'Here you are, I thought I'd missed you.'

Anna's heart began to skip a beat as she recognised who had spoken. Her hand began to shake and she quickly placed the jug of milk down on the table.

'Careful, you might spill it on yourself,' laughed Iestyn Roberts.

Then he began to notice how flustered she became and added,

'I thought I'd pay my respects to your father and yourself before I leave. Wil certainly sang well tonight, didn't he?'

Yes, I'm very proud of him,' replied Anna, trying hard to compose herself. 'Are the children with you?'

Iestyn could see how uneasy she had become and without answering her question he asked,

Is there something wrong, Anna? Would you rather I leave?'

Their conversation had been nothing other than polite and so she replied,

'No, there's nothing wrong. I was surprised to see you here, that's all.'

She prayed her voice would not reveal her true feelings as she was more than pleased that he had come in search of her. All the promises she made earlier on to avoid contact with him had now been forgotten. She picked up the jug of milk and began to pour it into the cups again as one of the ladies began to pour the tea and carry the cups away.

'I was hoping I would see you again,' he said. 'Will you walk with me to the gate when you are finished here?' he asked.

Anna looked around in fear someone had over heard what he had said. She did not want anyone to get the wrong impression. This man had only come to pay his respects. Then she replied,

'I'm afraid that's not possible. As you can see, I am quite busy here. But if you wish to speak with my father, I'm sure you'll find him waiting outside.'

'Very well. I'm sorry if I've chosen the wrong moment to speak with you. Now if you'll excuse me I shall go and pay my respects to your father. I apologise if I've upset you in any way Anna,' said Iestyn. Then he turned on his heel and left the room feeling very disappointed at her attitude. She could not have known how long he had waited to be near her again!

Anna watched him leave and immediately regretted how cold she had been towards him. What's the matter with me she thought? He was obviously just trying to be polite. How could he know how I feel toward him? She realised how foolish she had been and so she found Mrs Evans and made her excuses to leave the vestry. Then she went in search of him.

Anna found Iestyn talking with her father near the chapel gate.

'Here's Anna now,' said Wil. 'I understand you've already met?'

'Yes,' said Anna, all the while she tried hard not to look directly toward Iestyn Roberts.

Then Iestyn spoke,

'I've just been complimenting your father on his fine solo and I look forward to hearing him again tomorrow.'

'A glutton for punishment is it?' said Wil, slapping the younger man on his back.

Iestyn laughed,

'And I'll see you as well Anna?' he asked politely. 'I shall be bringing Becky and her grandmother along to the afternoon service and we may stay for the evening one as well. Becky hopes to meet with Kate again if she's here.'

'And the boys?' asked Anna.

'No they are far too boisterous. They will stay with my sister, I'll drop them off at her cottage on my way,' replied Iestyn.

'Then I suggest you come to Cefn Glas for tea,' suggested Wil. 'It's some time since I've seen my cousin Martha. We shall all return to evening service together my boy.'

Before Iestyn had time to accept Wil's invitation, Anna spoke up.

'I daresay Mr Roberts has to make other plans Da, and it doesn't give mam much time to prepare for visitors.'

'Nonsense Anna. Your mother will be delighted,' said Wil. 'It's settled then. We'll look forward to seeing you tomorrow,' he said taking Iestyn's hand and shaking it vigorously.

'Iestyn. Are you ready?'

Anna turned and found herself face to face with an older woman whom immediately took hold of Iestyn's arm and linked it with her own.

'Aren't you going to introduce us?' she asked Iestyn as her eyes began to wander up and down Anna's body.

Iestyn's face reddened, and Anna was not sure whether this was in embarrassment or temper. Then he said,

'Yes, of course. Mrs Anna Malone, may I introduce Miss Sarah Madoc, an old friend.'

'An old and dear friend,' said the woman as she held on tightly to his arm. 'Are we ready to leave now,' she demanded in a high pitched voice.

Iestyn pulled his arm free from hers. 'I'll be there in a moment Sarah. Why don't you join the others and wait for me over there,' he said.

His voice had now become a command and Sarah knew better than to argue with him and so she said politely to Anna,

'It's been a pleasure meeting you Mrs Malone.' Then she strutted away.

'A good looking woman if ever I saw one,' said Wil. ' You should set your cap there my boy,' he said to Iestyn.

'Now then merchi, we'd best be on our way. Your mother will be waiting for us. I'll say farewell to Twm Shenkin and meet you outside Anna.'

Anna nodded as her father walked away. Then she heard Iestyn speak, Please let me explain about Sarah' he said.

'There's nothing to explain,' she replied in a cool voice.

Iestyn knew then he would fail to convince her that Sarah Madoc meant nothing to him.

'I shall see you tomorrow then, Anna?' he asked.

'My father has invited you to his home and you will be welcome,' was all she replied.

Then Sarah Madoc's voice called out to him once more.

'You had better go, it seems the lady is becoming impatient,' said Anna beginning to dislike the woman even more.

'Tomorrow then?' he asked again.

Anna did not reply this time but turned on her heel and walked away from him in search of her father.

When they arrived home they both had to tell Beti all that had happened that evening. She was full of curiosity. Had her husband sang well? Were there many people at the chapel to hear him sing?

After all the news had been relayed to her Wil broke the other news, that he had invited cousin Martha, her son-in-law Iestyn Roberts, and the little girl Becky to tea the following day.

'How could you?' asked Beti, annoyed that she had not been told before hand. Now she would have to be up early in the morning. There would be extra baking and cleaning to do. And all on the Lord's day at that. It would never do for cousin Martha to find anything out of place in Beti's home. Beti knew all too well what a fussy person Martha could be.

Wil could not understand Beti's concern for her visitors and the next hour was spent in arguing with each other.

Anna decided she could take no more and so she made her excuses and went upstairs to bed.

Later, as she lay there in the darkness which surrounded her, she found she could not relax as her thoughts returned to the events of the day.

What sort of man was he? How could she think he would be interested in her? It had become obvious to her that there appeared to be something more than just friendship between Iestyn Roberts and the woman Sarah Madoc. Beti had been right all along, and Anna began to realise what a fool she'd been to think otherwise.

She knew also that she could not undo her father's invitation for Iestyn to visit them, so decided she would have to remain cool toward him, then he would realise that he held no interest for her.

With that decision firmly fixed in her mind she turned over and immediately fell asleep.

o o o

'Goodness gracious, Beti! There was no need to go to all this trouble,' said Cousin Martha admiring the parlour table set out in all its finery.

'We could easily have taken tea at the Chapel vestry with the others you know.'

Beti smiled sweetly at the older woman as she brushed a few crumbs from the table, which had been set in her best tea service. A lace cloth, its folds draped delicately down over the side had been taken from its box earlier that morning and ironed to perfection before its use.

On it stood plates of sandwiches, and lightly buttered scones and fruit cake just waiting to be eaten.

Beti glanced at her husband as if she were about to make a remark but Wil, fearing what she might say, quickly stepped in,

'It's no trouble, Martha. Why, Beti was only saying this morning how pleased she was to have you come to tea. Weren't you Beti?'

Several tea plates dropped from Beti's hand in an effort to control her temper and she was grateful that they landed on the edge of the table.

After all, they belonged to the set her mother had given her!

She had not forgiven Wil for his sudden invitation to his cousin and her family. Martha was a relative, but Beti would have liked at least a week's notice of her coming. She wanted everything at Cefn Glas to be perfect, as she knew Martha would enjoy telling everyone what sort of welcome she'd had. Once, on a previous visit, she'd caught Cousin Martha running her fingers across the dark oak sideboard to see if she could find any dust visible there! Such was the woman's nerve!

One good point that had come from Wil's invitation, however, was that Beti would have a chance to meet with Iestyn Roberts, Martha's son-in-law. She would then be able to decide for herself if this man held any interest for her daughter.

A few moments later, Marged arrived on the scene.

'Where's Morgan and John? Are they not with you?' asked her father, who was concerned that they would not be here to listen to him sing later on in the evening.

'Morgan has taken John to Bryn Cethin,' she said. ' Do you remember, I told you it's Mrs Thomas' birthday Da? John had to call to see her, but he'll be here in plenty of time for Chapel. He wouldn't miss his Grandpa Wil singing, would he now?' she asked as she smiled at her father.

Then she began to notice the person sitting on a chair nearby.

Wil spoke up,

'You remember our daughter Marged?' he said to Cousin Martha.

Martha hesitated for a moment. So this was the one all the talk had been about she thought. Then she smiled at the girl.

Marged nodded and smiled back, however she began to feel uneasy in the older woman's company.

Wil sensed the feeling between the two women and so he said,

'You'll meet the others later, Martha. Our John is a grand lad that he is, and it's only fair that he visits his other grandmother on her birthday.'

Martha noticed that Wil, her cousin was making every effort to explain about the boy and so she muttered,

'Ah! Yes, I see!'

'Well I certainly hope you do Cousin Martha,' was his reply.

However, Martha found herself staring at the girl once more. A lot of nasty things had been said about her at the time. Fancy her allowing the boy to go to the Big House she heard of? Whatever next she asked herself? And the Thomas family? Well they had money and land! Maybe Wil was playing safe, advising his daughter to let the boy get a foot into some of the wealth due to him one day, she thought.

Marged, aware of Cousin Martha's stares, removed herself to the kitchen where she began to fill the large iron kettle in readiness to make the tea.

Then she heard the children's voices as they played in the garden. She prepared to join them, but as she looked out of the window she saw Anna talking with a strange man. He must have arrived with cousin Martha, and from the look in her sister's eyes it was plain to see that Anna was listening intently to his every word.

Marged felt sure that Anna had been withholding something from her for sometime now. Could it be this! Was she interested in him, surely not? She dismissed it from her mind and decided to return to the parlour, Cousin Martha or not!

Anna walked down the narrow path, all the while pretending to watch the children as they played at the bottom of the garden. Iestyn followed her closely behind wanting all the time to reach out and touch her, to hold her gently in his arms.

Why did she feel so cool toward him, it wasn't just his imagination? Was it? They reached an iron gate shaded by a large lilac tree and its heady perfume began to make Anna feel slightly giddy. She clung to the gate for support, and for a second his arms reached out to grasp her.

'I'm alright!' she said quickly.

Iestyn placed his arms at his side, the looking around the garden at the colourful plants and flowers, he remarked politely,

'Cefn Glas is a lovely place Anna. It was kind of your father to invite us here. It also gave me the chance to speak with you again.'

Anna did not reply.

Iestyn looked toward the swing where the two little girls played happily together.

'Becky is obviously enjoying herself. She and Kate are becoming firm friends,' he said as he tried to draw her into conversation with him once more.

Anna looked at the children then turned to open the gate. As she walked through she allowed it to stay open for Iestyn to follow her.

'What's wrong Anna?' he asked sincerely. 'If it's about yesterday, then let me explain.'

'There's nothing to explain. Why should you think otherwise?' she asked politely. 'I am pleased you could come at my father's invitation. After today, I doubt whether we shall see each other again. Now, can't we leave it there and enjoy each other's company while you are here?'

'This is all about Sarah Madoc, isn't it?' he asked. ' You think that she and I!'

Before he could continue further, Anna turned sharply around to face him and with her dark eyes flashing said,

'It has nothing to do with Sarah Madoc. I am not interested in the woman or what she may mean to you!'

How dare the man presume she had been upset by either of them.

Iestyn looked at this gentle woman who held an unknown fiery temper, and took hold of his chance, a chance he might regret forever.

Then he said,

'You are jealous, Anna! Admit it. You do care a little for me.'

'I certainly do not!' she declared. 'It's a pity my father had not invited Sarah Madoc as well. This conversation would not be taking place. You presume too much Iestyn Roberts!'

She saw the look on his face and immediately began to regret the words she had said to him and she turned away quickly so that he would not see the guilt she felt.

Iestyn caught her arm and swung her around to face him.

Angrily he said,

'I don't know what insane idea you had of myself and Sarah Madoc, but you are wrong Anna! Sarah is a friend, nothing more. When Morwenna died, I was heartbroken. I had no will to live and felt nothing for my children or my home. I cannot expect you to believe it. You on the other hand, made a new life for yourself and your children here while I threw myself into my work giving nothing to no-one. I had no love left in me to give.'

Sarah Madoc and Martha held my family together during that time, or I would have lost it all. For that, I shall always be grateful to both of them. As for any other feelings towards Sarah, I have none. I have never led her to believe otherwise. I want you to know this.'

As she listened to his words Anna knew he was speaking the truth and she felt ashamed that she had doubted him.

Had she not felt the same heartache and loneliness? Who was she to judge this man?

Softly she spoke,

'I'm sorry, Iestyn. Last night I thought that you and she.' But before she could continue, he touched her lips gently with his fingers saying,

'You thought wrong. Sarah may have her own ideas where I am concerned, and needless to say that Martha encourages her. I do not love her, I never could. I can see now that I shall have to try harder to get her to understand this. She will never be other than a friend. The love I had for Morwenna was a special one. She was special to me but I hoped that one day I could learn to love again. Do you know what I'm trying to say Anna?'

Tears filled her eyes. Anna knew all too well. No-one would ever take the place of her beloved Peter. But would she ever fall in love again?

Seeing her tears, Iestyn added,

'I'm sorry if I've upset you. I feel I can talk to you because you understand what I've been through. May be it would have been better had I not come here today.'

Wiping away a tear from her cheek Iestyn said,

'Can we at least be friends Anna?'

She knew the situation was hopeless, but before she could give him an answer, they heard Marged's voice calling from the house that tea was prepared.

The children came running past them, eager to sample the food.

Anna wiped the tears from her eyes and followed the children into the house, leaving Iestyn Roberts to stand alone in the garden.

o o o

Later that evening, after Chapel, they all remained behind to say farewell.

Iestyn thanked Wil once more for his hospitality as Wil shook hands with him. Then Iestyn made his way through the crowd to where Anna stood with the other women.

'Have you seen Becky?' he asked. 'It's time to leave and I can't seem to find her.'

'She was in the vestry with Elizabeth and Kate a moment ago,' said Beti. 'Wait here, I'll go and find them.'

Marged noticed the look on Anna's face as the man had approached them. Her sister had remained quiet all through tea. Even as John had begun to tell them all that had happened at Bryn Cethin. This was not like Anna who loved to hear about everything her nephew had said. Iestyn Roberts had remained quiet also, although Marged had found him gazing with interest at Anna more than once.

'I'll go after her,' said Marged as she saw Beti disappearing inside the Chapel. If there was anything between Anna and Iestyn Roberts then they were best left alone. Anna would tell her sooner or later.

Iestyn took hold of Anna's hand as if to shake it in farewell, but he held it for a moment or two longer.

Anna looked around to see if anyone had noticed him. She blushed as he held her hand and said,

'I cannot leave without saying this to you Anna. I asked if we could be friends and you did not reply, but I cannot go without saying what is in my heart. I would like us to be friends, good friends. You have to know that you have lit a spark in this lonely life I have.'

'Please Iestyn,' she implored looking around once more. 'You have no right to talk this way. I promise our friendship will remain, but as for anything else. It can never be. Our lives are separate ones and they must continue to be so.'

Her heart beat quickly as she pulled her hand from his, wishing she had not said those fateful words.

He took her hand in his once more and drew her over into the shadows where they could not be seen. Then kissing her lightly on the lips he asked,

'Can I at least hope that you will think of me?'

Anna knew then what her heart had been trying to tell her all along - she cared for Iestyn Roberts more than she wanted to admit.

She whispered softly to him,

'As each day dawns, I shall think of you.'

'That is all I can ask for,' was his reply.

The tender words they had said to each other were interrupted as Marged, Beti and the children arrived to join them and soon they continued with normal conversation until it was time to part.

Unknown to Anna and Iestyn, however, their tender farewell had been witnessed by a shadowy figure hidden in the Chapel doorway.

It was Sarah Madoc who heard their words of tenderness, but the poignant scene between them meant nothing to her. She would not be beaten. Iestyn Roberts was hers and hers alone. She had worked and schemed for far too long and she was now more determined than ever to win his love. There would be little chance of his meeting with Anna Malone. He would soon come to his senses.

With that thought in mind she had withdrawn back into the shadows, a satisfied smile now beginning to form on her recently distorted face.

Sarah Madoc had proved herself right. There had been little if no chance for Iestyn to meet with Anna Malone again.

Sarah made sure she was a regular visitor to Iestyn's farm, fussing over the children, bringing them gifts and taking time to help Martha with the daily chores. Never once did she give Iestyn the opportunity to be on his own with her as she knew he would try to dissuade her from spending so much time there. Sooner or later she intended to win him over.

Iestyn would sit of an evening, thinking about Anna and wishing he could find a way to solve the problem for them to meet again.

Anna on the other hand kept her promise to him. Not one single day went by without she thought of him. She tried to remember the words he had said. The way he had kissed her lips. Unlike him, she was fortunate to have Marged to confide in. Her sister had understood how she felt, but even Marged had tried to tell her how hopeless is would be for them to meet.

Try as she may, she could not forget him. Soon, however, she began to realise that their declaration to each other was all in vain. Her children were her life now and she must make the most of it no matter how lonely it had become.

Many times she would go to the Chapel and kneel at Peter's grave. There she would ask his forgiveness, and try to tell him of her loneliness without him.

Her life with him had been so real, so special. But her feelings for Iestyn could not be overcome, however hard she tried.

CHAPTER 23

Time passed quickly for Anna who was always busy with the children. Elizabeth helped all she could especially now that Peter John was walking and running everywhere.

That particular morning, Beti and Wil had taken a ride to market while Anna decided to bake a few loaves of bread. She stood in the kitchen kneading the dough backwards and forwards in the large earthenware bowl.

David came running through the door just as she was about to take the first few loaves out of the oven.

'Mam, they're putting notices up everywhere,' he shouted, full of excitement. 'Can we go, Mam!' The boy was almost out of breath as he slumped down in a nearby chair.

'Now what have you been up to again?' his mother asked, 'and what notices have you seen?'

'It's coming in two weeks and it'll be held behind Llew Morgans' barn in the top field. The notice says there'll be stalls and carousels, swing boats and a boxing booth. And there'll be dancing ladies on a stage as well,' panted the boy.

Anna wiped the flour from her hands on to her apron and fetched the boy a cup of cool water saying,

'Here, drink this!'

The boy took the cup and gulped the water greedily, then asked again.

'Mam, can we go, please? I've never been to a real fair!'

'Two weeks is a long time David. You'll just have to wait and see. Now run along with you, I'm busy here this morning,' said Anna.

The sullen boy left the kitchen. It would do no good to argue with his mother. At least, she had not refused outright he thought.

Anna smiled to herself. David looked so disappointed. Well why not go she thought. It would do the children some good and she would have something to look forward to as well.

David Malone was not the only boy to run home with news of the forthcoming fair as the posters had been circulated for miles around.

Daniel, Iestyn Roberts' son had also arrived home with the same exciting news.

Sarah Madoc sat at the table drinking tea with her friend Martha. She had been a regular visitor for months but try as she may, she could not get Iestyn Roberts to return her favours and she had become very bitter over this.

Iestyn walked into the room just as Daniel began to tell the others about the fair.

'Can we go Dada?' asked Becky, while her two brothers joined in the chorus.

Iestyn began to laugh as he saw how excited his children had become.

'Let's go Dada. Perhaps I'll see my friend Kate there.' Sarah immediately stopped drinking from her cup. She'd had enough of this and she smugly said,

'Yes, why not take them Iestyn. It would be another opportunity for you to meet your friend. After all, you've just been waiting for a chance to meet Anna Malone again!'

Iestyn could not believe his ears, but the spite shown in Sarah's face only convinced him further.

In a stern voice he ordered the children to leave the room and they knew by the tone of his voice that he would not be disobeyed.

They each left quietly.

'Explain yourself, Sarah,' he said. While all the time Martha sat there in bewilderment as she listened to the younger woman's accusation.

'Don't come the innocent one with me,' Sarah replied.

'I'm sure I don't know what you're talking about,' he said trying hard to control his temper. 'However, if you have anything on your mind, then out with it now,' he said.

Sarah stood her ground. He would not get the better of her. She looked him directly in the eye, now would be her chance to say what she thought.

'I thought we had an understanding, you and I, Iestyn. I've stood by you, helped you and, yes, even loved you in my own way. Surely you knew this. Anna Malone can mean nothing to you. Open your eyes, for God's sake. Everything you need is here. Only I can give it to you, if you will let me!' she cried out.

Before Iestyn could reply, it was Martha's turn to be heard.

'What is going on here, will someone tell me? What is she saying? Is there something going on with you and Anna? If so, why am I the last to know?' she asked Iestyn.

All these questions! Before Iestyn could reply to any of them, Sarah again cried out.

'Of course there's something going on Martha. They so good as told each other on the day of the Gymanfa. Why do you think you were invited to Wil Lewis' home? It was so that they could meet again, and I saw them kissing outside the Chapel before we left. Ask him to deny that if he can.'

Iestyn gasped. Sarah had spied on them. God forgive him. What had he done to this woman that she hated him so much?

'Ask him what they promised each other Martha?' said Sarah again.

This time Sarah had gone too far!

'You have a wicked tongue Sarah Madoc and it has made me see you for what you really are. You could have only known this through you eavesdropping. How could you stoop so low?' he asked.

Sarah looked defiantly at him but said nothing.
'Have I ever led you to believe I care for you in that way Sarah?'
She remained silent.
'Answer me!' he bellowed.
Sarah knew she had gone too far, there was no going back now.
'Well not exactly Iestyn,' she replied meekly. 'I just thought it was understood that you and I.'
'Well you thought wrong,' he interrupted her. Then turning to the other woman, his dead wife's mother he said,
'As for you Martha. You have to believe me. There is nothing to tell.'
Martha shook her head in disgust after witnessing the scene before her.
'You must believe what you wish,' said Iestyn. 'There has been nothing underhand between Anna Malone and myself but if you want the truth then you can have it. Given half a chance I would like to know Anna better but this can never be.'
'There you are,' said Sarah, 'by his own admission!'
Then he turned to Sarah,
'You Sarah, have fabricated a story and blackened Anna's good name. I advise you to say no more.'
There was no more to be said. Sarah picked up her bonnet, placed it on her head and throwing her shawl over her shoulders she said,
'Don't worry Iestyn. This is the last you'll see or hear of me.'
Then turning to Martha she added,
'I'm sorry, but you see how it is. This makes it impossible for me to help you with the children any longer. If it's Anna Malone he wants, then he can have her!'
With those words, Sarah Madoc stormed out of the house.
'Now look what you've done,' cried Martha. 'How am I to manage without her. Sarah's been good to us. She's a kind woman and you Iestyn, are a fool!'
'You don't understand, do you?' he asked.
'Quietly he said,
'I do not love her!'
'Love,' said Martha. ' What has love got to do with it? You lost Morwenna and you said your love died with her. Sara could make you happy again. Surely you can settle for that?'
Iestyn knew it was hopeless. He would never make her understand. Martha was right in one thing however. He had lost his love but at last he had found another kind of love.
Martha left the room, but she had vowed to herself that she would take matters into her own hand. Her mind was made up.
Come next market day she would go to see Cousin Wil and confront him with this news. Wil would know what to do about Anna. As for Iestyn, he

would come to see that it was for his own good. Then Sarah could return and everything would be the same again.

o o o

'I didn't know that you planned to go to market today,' said Iestyn as he watched Martha preparing to take certain things along with her.

Since the row involving Sarah Madoc they had spoken very little to each other.

'I need a few things at the market,' she answered curtly, 'so if you don't mind, I'll be getting an early start.'

'Then you'll not mind taking Becky with you. The boys can help me in the bottom field,' replied Iestyn.

'Very well' said Martha.

She hoped to go on her own but if she refused to take the child with her it might make him suspicious. It would be no hardship to take Becky along for company.

Soon Martha and the little girl were on their way. She'd arranged a lift in Edwin's cart. Their neighbour travelled every week to Market where he sold eggs by the dozen, he was pleased to offer his assistance.

As they reached their destination, Martha lost no time in seeking out her cousin Wil Lewis. She found him unloading a cart full of vegetables, and she called out to him.

'How are you Wil? I'm surprised to see you here. How is Beti and the family?'

Wil put down a sack of turnips he had just lifted from the cart.

'What are you doing here so early Martha?' he asked.

'I needed some things and as Iestyn in busy, I came early. I have Becky with me as well,' she replied.

Becky wandered off for a second to see what was being sold on a nearby stall. Martha called for her to come back.

Wil continued once more to unload the cart.

'Are you planning to be here long, Wil?' Martha asked.

'No merchi, I hope to return home by noon. Why do you ask? Is there anything I can do for you?' he asked in return.

Martha decided to make her move.

'No thank you Wil, but I think there is something I may be able to do for you. When you are free, I'd like to have a word with you,' she said.

'Very well, as soon as I've finished here I'll meet you,' he replied, wondering why she appeared to be so mysterious.

'I'll be at Bronwen's stall, over there,' Martha pointed to where Bronwen Owen stood setting up her ribbons and lace stall.

Wil carried on working but still wondered what she wanted with him.

Half and hour later he was free to join her.

'Now then Martha. What's all the secrecy?' he asked.

Martha sent Becky away with a few coppers to buy herself some taffy, then she began to choose her words carefully as she told Wil the tale of Sarah Madoc and how the quarrel with Iestyn had developed.

Wil listened to her every word as each one cut his heart like a knife. Finally she ended,

'And so I thought it only fair to tell you Wil. If any talk should get about your Anna, it would only be a repeat of what you and Beti went through with your Marged. Awful it was, the way people gossiped you know!'

'Now Martha,' said Wil sternly. 'Our Marged is not the issue here. Carry on with what you have to say.'

'I only want what is best for the children. My poor Morwenna would turn in her grave if she knew the half of it. I took it for granted that Iestyn's intentions were none other than honourable toward Sarah Madoc, but it seems I was wrong. We should never have come to tea at Cefn Glas that day. It only gave chance for Iestyn and Anna to meet each other again,' said Martha.

'I am as much to blame, but I did not know of this deceit when I invited the man to my home. Are you sure of all this Martha? I cannot believe Anna is involved. She has given us no reason to suspect her in any way,' said Wil. Then he added quietly, 'But she has been very quiet of late. It seems something has been bothering her.'

'Well, there you are, then Wil!' said Martha. 'It is obvious it has to be this reason. Sorry I am to be the one to break this to you,' she said meekly.

Martha felt elated as she looked at Wil's troubled face. The seeds had now been sown and it was time for her to leave.

'You won't say any of this to Iestyn if you meet him, will you? If he found out I was the one who interfered, then I don't know what he'd do.'

She took a lace handkerchief from her pocket and pretended to wipe her eyes.

'Now then Martha,' said Wil, softening to her. 'Don't distress yourself. Leave it to me. I am grateful that you decided to bring it to my attention. I will deal with the situation in my own way.'

Martha put the handkerchief away and smiled gratefully to Wil. Then she bade him farewell and went in search of Becky.

She had done the right thing. Hadn't Wil said so himself? It would only be a matter of time before everything would once again return to normal. Martha was well pleased with herself.

As for Wil Lewis, he had already begun to reload his cart for the journey to Cefn Glas.

Was it true about Anna? His anger overcame him when he thought how good he and Beti had been toward her. How could she do this to the children? It would be food for the gossipmongers yet once more!

As for Iestyn Roberts! Wil had liked the man. Even, felt for him when he lost his wife. And it could not have been easy for him having to rely on

Cousin Martha. She'd always been a difficult woman to live with. However, this time she had done the right thing. The man was a scoundrel and the sooner Anna knew of it the better.

Wil's heart was sad as he journeyed home. He dreaded the confrontation that would take place between himself and the daughter he had loved. Anna would have to see reason. Before he decided to say anything to her he would have to discuss it with Beti. The childrens' livelihood was at stake also. Yes, he would hold his temper, talk it over with Beti then they would both decide what to do.

Anna was busy pegging out the washing on the line when she heard the cart trundling into the farmyard.

She thought it odd that her father had returned home so early. He must have completed his trading earlier than usual.

Wiping her hands in her apron she called out,

'You need a hand to empty the cart Da?'

Wil did not reply.

Anna called out again thinking he had not heard her.

'No, I can manage,' he answered gruffly.

'I'll be there in a minute, I've nearly finished out here. Ill put the kettle on and we'll have a cup of tea,' she shouted to him.

'Don't bother, I've work to do in the barn. Where's your mother, is she around somewhere?' Wil asked.

'She's over at Nesta Hughes' place. One of the children has taken poorly and she's gone to see if there's anything she can do to help poor Nesta,' said Anna as he heard his footsteps disappear in the direction of the barn. She thought no more of his untimely return.

During supper Wil could hardly contain himself. There had been little opportunity during the day to speak with Beti about the matter, which had troubled him greatly.

Beti noticed her husband's strange mood but knew better than to comment on it. If there was something troubling him, he would tell her sooner or later.

Anna took the children up to bed, they were always eager to listen to one of her stories before they went to sleep.

Beti sat by the fire, darning David's socks yet again.

'I don't know how the boy manages to get so many holes in his socks,' she muttered to herself.

Wil sat in silence. How was he to bring up the subject of Anna and Iestyn Roberts? The words he longed to say just would not come to him.

Beti could stand the silence no longer, and so she asked,

'What's the matter, Wil? You seemed so quiet at supper. What on earth is troubling you?'

'Be thankful it's quiet I am,' he said. 'My temper is raging inside of me. One push and out it will come merchi!'

'Stop talking in riddles, man. Out with it for goodness sake,' said Beti becoming quite irritated with her husband's behaviour.

Wil then began to tell her the tale of deceit and his disappointment in Anna. Beti interrupted him several times and it became obvious that she did not believe one word he said about their daughter.

Finally, Beti said,

'And you think that old fool did you a favour by telling you? She did it for her own ends. I will not believe that Anna is to blame!'

'Hush woman,' said Wil sternly. 'There's no smoke without fire. Martha came to me out of the goodness of her heart. What has hurt me the most is that Anna has lived here and tried to hide her involvement in the matter. How could she do it to both of us and to Peter's memory as well?

'We must give her a chance to explain, Wil,' argued Beti. 'Because if there is anything between Anna and Iestyn Roberts, we could not only lose her, but the children as well.'

Beti was right of course, she was always right in these matters. But if he were not satisfied with Anna's explanation, then he would be the one to make the final decision. Wil was certain of that!

'At last they are asleep,' said Anna sitting down on a stool near the fire. 'I'll carry on with the mending, Mam,' she said holding out her hands to Beti.

Her mother began to put the darning needle and wool back into the box she held on her lap.

'Never mind this,' said Beti. ' I have something important to say to you.'

Anna glanced at her father who had begun to light his clay pipe. A cloud of smoke filled the air as he began to puff gently on its stem. How serious he looked she thought to herself.

'What has happened Mam?' she asked Beti

'You tell us Anna,' was her mother's reply.

Anna looked bewildered, she did not know what was expected of her. So she sat there not able to utter a word.

Then Beti continued,

'Your father returned from market after meeting Cousin Martha there. She has told him that you and Iestyn Roberts have become far more than friends, and that certain things have gone on between you involving his break-up of friendship with that woman Sarah Madoc. If this is true then you have betrayed both of us. We feel however that it is only fair to give you a chance to speak for yourself.'

Beti did not say that she herself believed the story, but she waited for Anna to reply, praying all the while that her faith in her daughter was true.

Anna looked at her father and asked,

'Do you believe what she told you Da?'

Her question was answered by his silence.

Then quietly she spoke,

'Perhaps you'd better tell me all that you heard, then I can give you an honest answer.'

So for a second time that evening Wil related Martha's story to her. Anna remained silent until he had finished speaking.

'What have you to say for yourself?' asked Beti desperately wanting to believe in her daughter's innocence.

Anna took a deep breath, her heart pounding within her.

'Not all of it is true. Iestyn Roberts did make his feelings known to me,' she whispered.

'There, what did I say!' said Wil shaking his head.

'Be quiet, Wil,' said Beti, ' let Anna continue. 'Iestyn's intentions have been none other than honourable. His loneliness is equal to mine, there is no shame in that. We came together in friendship, nothing more.'

Wil stopped her,

'How can you be lonely? I don't understand you at all girl. You have the children and what is more, your mother and I have supported you all that we can.'

'Let me finish, Da!' she pleaded. ' How can you understand the meaning of loneliness? You and Mam still have each other. Have you ever stopped to think how life would be if this were not so?

Iestyn and I have never been alone with each other until that day he came here and we walked in the garden. We told each other then how lonely both of our lives had become. I made it clear that there could never be anything between us and he has accepted this.'

It was now Wil's turn to speak.

'Fool that I was to ask him to come here. I showed him my hospitality, and if I had known his intentions I would have asked him to leave. As for Sarah Madoc, his wife's friend at that! He has not played fair by her. Cousin Martha was right after all!'

Anna leaped to Iestyn's defence.

'How can you say that? Iestyn has never promised anything to Sarah. She was just a friend to him - that is all. Surely he has a right to live his own life, to make his own decisions?' she asked.

There!' said Beti. ' I knew Anna was innocent. Didn't I say so Wil? The fault had to lie with Iestyn Roberts. Why doesn't he leave Anna alone? Tomorrow you'll go to see him, he has to get this nonsense out of his mind and leave Anna to get on with her life!'

'Wait, I've not finished,' urged Anna. ' I did tell him we would be nothing more than friends, because I knew in my heart you could never accept him. You would be against us from the start. And I was right wasn't I? Until tonight I had not realised how much more he could have meant to me. You needn't worry however, I knew then as I know now, he and I could never be.'

Wil could stand this no longer, his temper began to explode,

'Are you mad,' he said. 'To even allow yourself to think of another. This family has seen enough trouble. Where would you go? We couldn't allow the children to leave here. Not after all they mean to us, it would break our hearts and God knows what it would do to them!'

'Calm down!' she said to her father. 'Iestyn wanted more than friendship, I agree, but any talk of marriage certainly hadn't arisen between us.'

'You have been underhanded and deceitful Anna. I could not have believed it of you,' said Wil

'Listen to her Wil' begged Beti. 'I believe her. Anna is telling the truth. I'm sure she has made it plain to Iestyn Roberts. Nothing will come of this.'

Wil looked at his daughter,

'Then let me tell you this, my girl. I am the one who makes the decisions in this house. If it ever came to be that you and that man will have notions about each other, there will be no room for you under my roof!'

Anna gasped at her father's statement as she cast her eyes toward the floor.

'You will never have a man as good as Peter Malone, and it is to your shame that you can even think of belonging to another,' he said sadly to her.

Wil stormed out of the room leaving the two women speechless. Then Anna began to cry.

'Believe me Mam, there has been no deceit. I live for my children and would do nothing to harm them. I am lonely without Peter. Was it so wrong to learn that I could begin to love someone again?' she asked.

This time Beti replied, her voice was full of compassion.

'I will try to understand, but my heart is sad for you Anna. Your father is too set in his ways, so he will never give in. I'm afraid the decision he has made will be one he'll not go back on. It is up to you now. You hold the future in your hands.'

Anna nodded to her mother through her tears.

Beti went toward her and hugged her as if she were still a little child.

Anna climbed the stairs wondering what the future would hold for her. It all seemed so desolate. As she opened each bedroom door, the moon shone its light on the silhouettes of her children as they lay sleeping safely in their beds.

Something or someone moved to the right of her and she found Elizabeth standing behind the door.

'What are you doing here Elizabeth?' asked Anna. 'Can't you sleep cariad? Back to bed with you now,' she whispered to her daughter.

Elizabeth climbed beneath the bed-clothes, then she whispered back,

'Are you alright Mam? I heard voices so I came to see what was happening.'

'You heard?' asked Anna, concerned now of the daughter's reaction.

I'm sorry Mam,' said Elizabeth. 'I heard what was said. Grandpa Wil has a terrible temper, hasn't he?'

Anna suddenly felt ashamed that her daughter, still a child in many ways, had been expected to understand all that had happened.

'It is I who should be sorry,' she said, kissing the girl on her forehead.

'No,' said Elizabeth, ' you have done nothing wrong. I believe you Mam. We all loved Dada in our own way, nothing can change that. But one day when we are all grown up who will you have to share your life with? You must do what is right for you, and whatever you decide I want you to know that I shall always love you.'

Tears rushed to Anna's eyes. Her daughter had grown up all of a sudden.

'Hush now,' she said, ' it will all work out, I'm sure of it.'

Then she whispered,

'I'm so lucky to have you Elizabeth.'

Anna kissed her daughter again but as she tucked her into bed she prayed that it would be as simple as she had made it sound.

o o o

'Why won't you speak to her Wil,' asked Beti. Wil did not reply. He had no intention of discussing the subject of Iestyn Roberts with his daughter again. He had made up his mind and he was sure that Anna had also made her decision as well.

Anna knew she had no choice and so she began to accept things for what they were. The children had settled at Cefn Glas. This was their home now. She would not put their happiness at risk for the sake of her own. Se became convinced that her father would confront Iestyn at the earliest opportunity and the thought of it filled her with shame.

She needed to talk with Marged but her sister had been ill of late. When Elizabeth asked if she could go and stay with her for a few days, Anna readily agreed. It would do Elizabeth some good to get away from Cefn Glas for a while, as she had begun to worry more and more about Anna. Her Aunt Marged would look forward to her visit.

A few days had passed before Elizabeth began to confide in her aunt. She told her of the row between her mother and Grandpa Wil and Marged could see how distressed her niece had become in telling the story to her.

'It's terrible you know,' said Elizabeth. 'They don't talk to each other and it's making Mamgu sad as well.'

'Don't worry yourself,' said Marged. 'I'm sure things will turn out fine. You wait and see!'

Elizabeth stayed a few days longer, by which time Marged had decided a plan of her own. She persuaded Morgan to take her to Iestyn Roberts' farm. Pray God she would be more successful in pleading her sister's cause this time! Morgan did not agree with her plan but he knew it was hopeless to try and talk Marged out of it.

They started out early the very next day. As soon as they reached the farm Marged lost no time in telling Iestyn Roberts of the agony her sister faced from day to day.

Iestyn became furious as he realised what Martha had done.

'Martha has been very cunning,' he said, 'but I can assure you that she will not have her own way. I promise you I will do nothing to harm the relationship between your father and Anna. All I want is for her to be happy. There has been nothing underhanded between us. As soon as I am finished here I intend to see Wil and put matters right, once and for all!'

Marged believed what he said but she added,

'Then choose the right words Iestyn Roberts. I'll not see my sister hurt any more than she has been already.'

Iestyn returned to the farmhouse and quickly began pumping water into a pan to wash himself.

Martha heard the splashing of water from the yard outside and called out to him.

'Finished early then, have you? There's plenty of warm water here. I'll bring some outside for you.'

'Don't bother,' he shouted back as he sat down on the stone steps to undo his muddy boots. He removed one, then the other, and as he entered the house he called out gruffly,

'I'll not be wanting dinner. I have to go somewhere immediately.'

'Not have dinner,' said Martha. 'It must be important then?'

Iestyn could restrain himself no longer. He walked into the kitchen saying,

'If you really want to know where I'm going to woman. I'm off over to Cefn Glas to see Wil Lewis. I intend to put him straight about the rumours spread about myself and his daughter Anna. Rumours that you seem to know plenty about.'

Martha looked at his large frame as it blocked out the light in the doorway and she became aware of how angry he had become.

'You've gone too far this time Martha,' he said.

'I don't know what you mean Iestyn,' she said innocently.

'Don't give me that. How could you say such things to Wil?' he asked.

Martha began to wonder how Iestyn had found out.

'I only did it for your own good,' she stuttered. ' It was right that Wil should know what was going on. Look what happened before to Marged. People would only start to talk again and you were not being fair to Sarah.'

'Talk!' he said. ' What did people have to talk about I ask myself? Can't you accept that we were just friends? That is all it was,' Iestyn shouted at her.

Martha looked him straight in the eye.

'You expect me to believe that? If so, tell me that you do not love Anna Malone.'

Iestyn did not reply, he could not. The old lady had finally spoken the truth.

o o o

It was getting on for nightfall when Iestyn Roberts neared Cefn Glas. Lamplight shone through the farmhouse windows, lighting up the yard where he stopped to tether his horse.

He strode up to the front door and knocked on it loudly, then stood back waiting for someone to answer.

Anna opened the door, astonished to find him standing there said,

'Iestyn! Whatever are you doing here this time of night?'

'I've come to see your father. I found out what Martha has been up to, and I'll not stand by to see you humiliated. He has to know the truth. If anyone's to blame, then it has to be me,' he said earnestly.

'Please go Iestyn. It will do no good. My father will not listen to reason. Go now before it is too late,' she pleaded.

He lifted his hand and touched her cheek gently as he said,

'Trust me Anna. I have to do this, for both of us.'

She knew she could not dissuade him and so she stepped aside to let him in.

As they entered the kitchen together Wil jumped up from the chair almost knocking the lamp over at his side.

'Good God man, you've got a nerve coming here,' he said. 'Get out, before I put you out!'

Iestyn could not answer before Beti interrupted.

'Wait a minute Wil. At least hear what he has to say. After all that's been said and done, you owe Anna that much surely?'

Wil ignored his wife's pleas.

'What have you to do with this Anna?' Wil accused her. 'I might have known you'd have a trick or two up your sleeve.'

'She's had nothing to do with my coming here,' said Iestyn rising to Anna's defence. 'I've come not to quarrel but to put matters right.'

'Very well then,' said Beti. 'now the two of you go air your differences elsewhere. I'll not have the children woken up here.'

Wil crossed the room and took a lantern from the corner. He lit the candle inside saying to the two women,

'We'll be out in the barn and I do not want us to be disturbed. Understand?'

Beti nodded as she watched her husband leave the room followed by Iestyn who gave one last glance in Anna's direction.

'What will they do?' she asked her mother.

'Don't worry Anna. Your father will have his say but he's no match for Iestyn Roberts. They won't hurt each other, I'm sure of it,' said Beti.

Anna wished she had her mother's confidence in the two men.

The lantern lit up the barn as the two men faced each other.

Wil spoke first,

'What have you to say for yourself then?' he asked the younger man. I showed you my hospitality and look how you repaid it. Surely you realise you could not get away with lies and deceit. Anna does not deserve that, she's already lived through a lifetime of unhappiness. You have turned us against each other.'

Iestyn could see how bitter Wil Lewis had become. Had he really caused the man to turn against his own daughter? If so, the time had come to make him see the truth.

'Speak up man,' shouted Wil. 'Or does Martha do you talking for you?'

Iestyn hesitated, looking for the right words to convince this man of his daughter's innocence. Then he spoke,

'I came to tell you that Anna and I were united in friendship at first. A friendship shared through our loneliness, but I can see that you have already decided not to believe this. So I am prepared to tell you the truth.'

I do love your daughter but until this evening I had not realised how much I love her. It is plain to see how unhappy she's become. I have never had the chance to reveal my true feelings to her and now I realise it maybe too late.

She is innocent of all this. Now that I can see the rift between the two of you, I realise I can never approach her with my love. I had hoped one day we would find happiness together, now I can see it will never be. If it were not for Martha's meddling we might just have continued as friends.'

'Martha was right. Who knows where all this might have ended. You are no good for Anna,' said Wil defiantly. 'She has settled here with us and the children are beginning to feel secure again. I am determined that nothing and no-one will take them away from us. Surely now you can see no good could have come from your so called 'friendship'.'

Sadly Iestyn replied,

'All I want is her happiness. It's a great pity that you do not want it also. I will therefore abide by your decision, but I hope and pray Wil Lewis that one day you shall live to regret it.'

'You've said all there is to say. Before you go I must have your promise that you will not see Anna again,' said Wil

'Then I would like to say goodbye to her,' said Iestyn politely.

'I don't think it is wise. She will only upset herself further,' said Wil.

Iestyn nodded, he knew he had been defeated.

'Your promise then Iestyn Roberts. Do I have it?' Wil asked again.

'Yes, I promise you,' he said.

Anna's good name had remained intact, and if he had managed to repair the damage between Anna and her father, then Iestyn had succeeded with his plan. He knew the only loser in the game had to be himself.

He strode out of the barn, then he untethered his horse and giving one final look toward the farmhouse, Iestyn rode off into the night.

Anna ran from the house.

'Where has he gone Da?' she asked her father. ' What did you say to him?'

'Now then merchi. It's all over, he'll not bother you again,' he answered.

'What have you done?' she cried as she ran back into the house.

Wil watched her go. It was for the best, sooner or later she would get over it. As for Iestyn Roberts, he had the man's promise to stay away from her. Wil blew out the candle that lit the lantern before he himself entered the house.

Later, Anna lay in bed wondering what both men had said to each other. She knew her father would never reveal their conversation. Iestyn Roberts had gone out of her life or so it seemed.

All she had left were her dreams and from now on it seemed they would only remain troubled ones.

CHAPTER 24

From the night Iestyn Roberts had come to Cefn Glas and disappeared out of her life, Anna had little time to dwell on her troubles.

There was so much work to do on the farm, she threw herself body and soul into keeping busy. That way she had no time to think of that fateful night. She was up before dawn, helping with the milking and she was the last one to go to bed at night.

Beti became so worried about her daughter. Wil on the other hand seemed to take it for granted that all was now well with Anna.

The children were excited at the arrival of the fair, which was due to open soon. On their way home from school they had stopped several times to look at Llew's field, empty now but soon to be bustling with the fairground folk.

David had plans of his own regarding the fair. That evening, after school he sneaked off with some boys from the village to watch the arrival of some of the travellers.

It was all very strange. There they were, carts carrying planks of wood, all shapes and sizes trundling along the road followed by weird looking caravans. He had heard the people were called tinkers and came from nowhere in particular.

Painted wooden horses, coloured swing boats were all piled up on the grass in Llew's field. More caravans arrived, some of them weird in shape. Some round, some oblong, all were pulled along by horses whose halters were decorated with multi-coloured ribbons and bows. Curtains hung from the tiny windows and each of these homes on wheels was decorated with elaborate carvings on the fronts and sides of them. They were driven by people the likes of which David had never seen before.

People whose tanned faces and swarthy skins had travelled the countryside in all climates calling no place their home for long.

The boys hid themselves behind a large bush. They had been forbidden to go to Llew's field.

'My Mam says they are gypsies - travelling folk,' said Ben Mathias who was one of the bigger boys. ' And if you're a bad boy they'll steal you away and you are never heard of again!'

The boys looked at him in awe. Was this true? Suddenly a man caught sight of them and shouted out in a loud gruff voice,

'Hey there! What are you boys up to? Come to spy on us is it? Well then, come and lend us a hand if you dare!'

On hearing his voice, the terrified boys took flight in all directions, falling headlong over each other as they fled.

David was the first to make his escape. He ran as if the devil, himself, was after him and he did not stop until he reached the safety of Cefn Glas. He dared not tell his mother where he'd been, as he knew only too well that it would spoil his chances to go to the fair on Saturday, where he would be in the safety of his family.

The day finally came. Kate and Elizabeth had dressed themselves early for their trip to the fair. They were so excited as they ran to their grandfather's side.

They were filled with disappointment as they saw him standing dressed in his working clothes.

'Aren't you coming then?' asked Elizabeth.

'No merchi, I've still lots to do here. You can tell me all about it when you return,' said Wil putting his hand in his pocket and taking out several coppers which he handed to the girl.

'There now, treat yourself and the others to some taffy, I'm sure you'll find a stall there.'

'You are coming with us, aren't you Mamgu?' asked Kate as she watched Beti place a shawl over her shoulders.

As they walked away from the farm Beti looked back to where Wil stood waving to them. She knew he worshipped the children and however stern he seemed on times he was kindness itself toward them.

The children ran ahead of Beti and Anna. All except little Peter John who toddled by the side of his mother. His steps were so short that it would seem like an age before they would reach Llew's field, which was only a short distance away.

'Go ahead Mam,' said Anna. 'Catch up with the children. We'll see you when we get there.'

Beti quickened her step and hurried after the others, so excited they were to be going to the fair at last.

Anna walked behind clutching the child's tiny hand until he began to tire, then she picked him up and carried him the remainder of the way.

She reached the entrance gate where she saw the crowd of people as they surged forward into the field. They all seemed to be going in the same direction, so she followed them.

Peter John again walked by her side. A colourful scene met their eyes. Caravans, stalls and stands were arranged here and there. Fairground people sold fruits, lace and trinkets. Some of them stood high on platforms, turning cartwheels and performing tricks. A man took hold of a burning stick and held it high above his face. Then slowly he lowered the firebrand and began to swallow it inch by inch until its bright red flame went out leaving only a puff of smoke behind.

There were gasps from the crowd! Anna passed by the boxing booth where a small untidy man called out to passers by, inviting them inside to witness the boxing match between his own champion and one of the village lads. People queued up to pay the entrance fee while the man greedily pocketed the money inside his shabby coat.

She heard music, which came from a nearby stage and there they were. The dancing girls her son had told her about. She hurried past picking Peter John up in her arms. There were so many more interesting sights to see but she had to find her mother and the children first, then she could enjoy herself.

Anna walked a few yards further when she hears her mother's cry. What was happening? She hurried forward to find Beti looking anxiously upward to the sky. There sitting in a large red swinging boat was David. Opposite him sat Kate and Elizabeth scared out of their wits. The boat swung higher and higher with every tug David gave to the thick plaited rope. The two girls began to cry as they spied their mother below them on the ground. David however, shouted with glee.

Anna handed the small child to her mother who had now become frozen to the spot. Beti kept apologising to her again and again saying,

'I'm so sorry Anna. I never would have allowed them to go on it, if I realised it could swing so high!'

'Don't worry Mam, I'll handle this,' said Anna as she shouted and urged her son to let go of the rope.

The boy continued to ignore her.

'David, listen to me!' she yelled again. Suddenly Anna felt a strong hand touch her shoulder.

'Can I help?' he said. ' Perhaps he'll listen to me.'

She turned around to find Iestyn standing there.

He called out to the boy,

'Look David, the beam is loose!'

David looked up above him nervously, and as he did so he accidentally dropped the rope he held in his hands, causing it to swing loosely in the air.

As the swingboat began to slow down a fairground man darted forward. He picked up the large plank of wood situated at the base of the boat and lifted it high above him causing the swingboat to come to a sudden stop with a huge thud.

The two girls almost fell out, they were so full of gratitude to reach safe ground. Then they ran crying to their mother who immediately began to comfort them. David climbed out assisted by the man who scolded him for being so reckless. He looked shaken but no tears were to be seen.

Beti also scolded the naughty boy while, Anna warned him he would be dealt with when they reached home.

The boy kicked at the earth beneath his feet and said,

'Sorry Mam, but it was so exciting. It was almost like flying!'

'One of these days David, you'll find yourself in real trouble,' said his mother.

As she turned around to thank Iestyn Roberts for his help Anna found he had disappeared into the crowd.

'He went in that direction,' said Beti quietly, knowing that there were things her daughter had to say to this man.

'I'll walk on with the children, you can catch up with us later. Go after him Anna!'

Anna hesitated for a moment then realised her mother's offer was a genuine one.

'What are you waiting for?' said Beti with a smile on her face.

'Thank you Mam. I'll not be long,' she said knowing now that her mother had become her greatest friend.

She ran, quickly, in the direction her mother had told her. Then she saw him a few yards ahead.

'Iestyn, please wait,' she called out, hoping he would hear her voice in the noise of the crowd. He turned and a smile covered his lips as he waited for her, then he led her to a secluded spot hidden away from prying eyes. He wanted to reach out and take her in his arms but he held back.

'Why did you leave?' she asked. 'I wanted to thank you for your help. David can be so wilful, it's hard to reason with him sometimes.'

'There's no need to thank me Anna,' he replied

'Then why did you leave so suddenly?' she asked again. 'Surely we have things to say to each other?'

Iestyn hesitated for a moment, then he said,

'I met Morgan at the market, he said you'd be here at the fair today. I wanted to see you, to tell you why I left Cefn Glas so suddenly but when I saw you just now I knew it was not fair to involve you again.'

'Then it is goodbye that you wanted to say to me?' she asked sadly.

He did not answer her question but said,

I made a promise to your father that I would not see you again. He made it clear what he expects of you. I realise now how much he loves you and the children, and I will not be the one to come between you. Before I carry out the promise I made, I wanted you to know that I cannot hide my love for you any longer and wherever I am I shall always love you.'

He took her hand in his and gently kissed her fingertips.

'Anna, I have to know if you care for me also, and if the answer is yes, then it will make it so much easier for me to bear.'

She gazed into his dark brown eyes and whispered,

'God only knows I have tried not to love you Iestyn Roberts. At first I told myself it was impossible. My love for Peter will always remain in my heart, but my love for you is here and now if you will take it.'

Iestyn wanted to take her in his arms and kiss her at that very moment but he hesitated as he said,

'I can offer you nothing but my love Anna. The promise I made to your father cannot be broken for your sake. I would not expect you to leave Cefn Glas. Martha would make your life hell if you came with me and I will not allow that either. So I shall bide my time and however long it takes I know now that our love will survive. One day we shall be together I promise you.'

Anna trembled as he said these words to her.

'I wish I could be certain of it Iestyn. All I can see are empty years ahead of us,' she said sadly.

He tilted her chin and kissed her tenderly on the lips. This gave way to their emotions, as he crushed her body to his kissing her again and again until she was breathless from his embrace.

She broke away from him saying,

'I must go Iestyn.'

Reluctantly he released her body.

'Think of me often,' she whispered as she slowly turned away leaving him standing there.

As he watched her disappear into the crowd he called after her,

'One day Anna, you will be mine!'

She kept on walking, desperately wanting to look back to find him still standing there. Her heart almost leaped from her body. He had declared his love for her at last!

The crowd jostled her along as she searched for her mother and the children. She knew that Beti would never tell her husband what had happened at the fair today. Nothing could prevent the joy Anna felt in her heart as she walked along.

A hand pulled at the sleeve of her dress causing her to stop suddenly.

'Buy some heather for luck, my dear. Only a few coppers, that's all I ask. Picked it myself this morning I did,' said a voice.

The hand, which was wrinkled with age, belonged to an old gypsy woman who appeared to belong to the fairground people.

Anna looked at her and there was something in her eyes that compelled her to stop.

'I only have a few coppers,' said Anna, delving into her purse.

The old woman took the money, which Anna held out to her, but as she withdrew her hand the gypsy took hold of it. She opened the palm wide and began to run her gnarled fingers up and down each line of Anna's outstretched hand.

Anna immediately tried to pull it away but the woman held on tightly.

Then looking up at Anna she said,

'There has been much sadness in your life, the loss of a loved one and the parting of another, the love of your family has sustained you through it all. Don't be afraid of the future, your dear one is happy for you. Be patient, accept your destiny, for a greater love awaits you and once again you shall find your true self.'

Anna pulled her hand away but not before the gypsy said again,
'One thing more. Beware of murky waters. I hear screaming!'
At this point Anna broke free from her grasp and ran as fast as her feet could carry her. The old woman's voice called out to her,
'You've forgotten your heather, deerie!'
But Anna continued to run, oblivious of the old woman's cries, until she saw her mother and knew she was safe at last.

CHAPTER 25

Morgan Harries surveyed the surrounding pastures of Bryn Cethin Farm. He knew that it was by sheer grit and determination Owen had finally restored this land to what it once was.

He lifted his hand to shade his eyes from the sun's rays as he looked beyond the pasture to where the fields lay full of golden wheat and corn.

'We can expect a good harvest this year Mog,' said Owen walking up behind him.

'All credit to you,' Morgan replied. You've worked hard Owen and now it's time to reap the benefits. Just remember John and I are here if you need our help.'

'It's not been easy I can tell you, though Mrs Thomas gave me a free hand to do as I liked. Sometimes I wonder if my place really is here at Bryn Cethin,' said Owen.

'Surely you don't regret it? What would have happened if Rhys Thomas had stayed?' asked Morgan.

'There would have been no Bryn Cethin by now,' replied Owen.

The two men leaned against the old wooden gate as they talked. Owen's eyes scanned the countryside around.

'It's times like this that I think of our Huw. It seems only yesterday when we planned the harvesting at Cefn Glas. What with Peter gone as well, I wonder what the two of them would think of me now,' he asked.

'Peter was a good man, that he was. And Anna has to be admired for the way she loves the children. It must be very lonely for her,' said Morgan.

'For the life of me I cannot agree that Iestyn Roberts is the answer for her,' replied Owen.

'You heard about the row then?' said Morgan.

Owen nodded.

'I went over to Cefn Glas but it was no good. My father is a strict man, he will not go back on his word to her.'

'Marged worries about her also. She looks so unhappy and we have offered her and the children a place with us but you know how proud she is. Anna will never leave Cefn Glas,' said Morgan.

'I know my sister too well,' said Owen, ' but I also know my father. He became like an empty shell after Huw died. Now Anna and the children are his hope for the future and he cannot see that he is the cause of her unhappiness.'

Their conversation came abruptly to an end as they heard John calling from the stables.

'I'm going down through the pasture to the pond,' he shouted to his father.

A brown and white pony trotted toward them carrying young John on its back.

'Be careful,' called Morgan but the boy only laughed as he rode past.

'I'm glad you came today,' said Owen. 'The old lady certainly looks forward to his visits. She's not been able to get around as she used to.'

'What will happen after her days,' asked Morgan. 'Will Rhys return to claim everything you've worked for?' he asked Owen.

'I haven't an answer to that question. She has no contact with him and doesn't mention his name. She has told Medi and I that we shall be provided for. As for Rhys, I cannot think what his intentions would be it anything happened to her. God forbid it should happen for a long time yet as I am not confident of the future. I know he is capable of anything,' said Owen.

'He's a clever man, and he'll want what is rightly his,' said Morgan waving to John once more as he rode past.

'Why not leave John here this evening?' asked Owen.

'He'd like that,' replied Morgan. 'I'll tell him now,' he said as he walked to the stables.

The boy was delighted to accept his uncle's offer and ran off to tell his grandmother the good news.

Leah Thomas sat in her favourite chair by the fire. Even though the day was hot and sunny she found it necessary to have a fire lit in the grate. She had become quite frail and relied now on Medi to run the household.

The sun's rays poured through the glass windows and with the heat from the fire warming her, Leah Thomas had drifted off to sleep.

She dreamt of better days filled with memories of her beloved Carwyn. Rowena her daughter had been so like her and her son Rhys. What had become of him now? Her eyes opened slowly as he she heard the handle of the door being gently turned.

'I thought you were sleeping,' said John entering the room.

'Come in John, let me see you,' said his grandmother.

'I've come to tell you that I'm to stay the night,' he said.

'I'm pleased to hear that. We shall have breakfast together,' she said. 'I think you've come to love this place,' she added. 'Come nearer, there's a good lad,' Leah said holding out her hand to him.

John pulled a green velvet footstool in front of her feet and sat down on it. She stroked the damp hair back from his forehead and asked,

'What have you been doing young man? You seem all hot and bothered.'

'I've ridden Gelert down to the pond and back again,' he said as he unbuttoned the collar on his shirt. Why did she need a fire on such a warm day as this he wondered?

'Are you cold, grandmother?' he asked her.

'It's my old bones John. They just won't warm any longer.'

She coughed and moved about slightly in the chair. The boy stood up and arranged the cushions behind her back.

She nodded that it felt better and he sat back down again.

John looked at his grandmother closely. Her silver grey hair was fashioned into a chignon, held at the back of the head with a large pearl comb. Her long, black silk dress was buttoned to her throat and she wore a beautiful cameo brooch at her neck. In her hand she held a fine lace handkerchief and on her finger she wore a ring, its stone was a blood red ruby. Her hands though wrinkled with age, showed no signs of her ever having to do any hard work.

How different she was in comparison to his Mamgu at Cefn Glas. Her hair was always neat but strands of it fell here and there from her brow and the nape of her neck. Her dresses were cotton, one of them always set aside as Sunday best to go to Chapel. She owned no jewellery, none that he was aware of. And her hands were red and rough from the toil of the land.

They were two entirely different women but in his heart he loved them both equally.

Leah was aware of his gaze and asked,

'Is something wrong John?'

'No, Grandmother,' he replied.

'You're getting quite tall,' she remarked, 'so like the men in our family.'

The boy smiled at her.

'Stir the logs on the fire will you Rhys?' she asked feeling the cold once more.

'It's not Rhys I am Grandmother,' he said as he leaned forward with the poker in his hand.

'There's silly I am John,' she said, 'you looked so like him for a second.'

The room became silent, then he asked,

'What was he like, my father?'

The old lady hesitated. The boy had a right to know that his father was not always so difficult. There had been happier times in this house and she was saddened to think her son had missed so much. If only he had accepted his responsibilities then it would have been he sitting here with his son today.

So Leah Thomas began to tell her grandson all he wanted to know.

The afternoon passed by quickly as John listened to her talking, interrupting her only now and then to ask a few questions of her.

'And so as the years passed by,' she said ' Rhys became very jealous of your Aunt Rowena. Perhaps your grandfather and I were to blame after all. We never intended to make more of one that the other and now I look back there are many things I regret. Maybe I should have taken more notice of him. I should have been a better mother to him,' she sighed.

The boy sprang to her defence saying,

'No, Grandmother! I cannot believe that! He had everything he ever wanted and he valued nothing!'

Leah Thomas smiled, the boy had an old head on his young shoulders she thought.

'Now then, that's enough of my ramblings for one afternoon. Go and ask Bethan to make us some tea, I'm thirsty after our long talk,' she said.

As Leah Thomas watched her grandson leave the room she knew it was time to put her affairs and those of Bryn Cethin Farm in order. She had journeyed back over the years that afternoon and now it was time for decisions to be made.

She would ask Owen to contact Mr Harvard the solicitor from Carmarthen. James Harvard would advise her what to do.

Soon her eyes began to close once more, she felt so tired.

By the time John returned carrying a tray of tea things she was soundly asleep. He looked at her sitting there in her favourite chair, and was thankful that he had spent the last few hours talking with her.

He had been curious to learn about his father, but the more he knew about Rhys Thomas the less he liked him.

He had made up his mind never to be like him, no matter what!

o o o

It was not James Harvard the Solicitor who arrived at Bryn Cethin the following week but his young partner Simon Penley.

He was shown to the sitting room where Leah Thomas waited. Immediately he began to apologise for the senior partner's absence, which it appeared was due to a prior engagement.

'I hope you have no objection to my advising you on any matter ma'am?' he said politely.

Sit down young man and we'll see what transpires,' she said.

Simon Penley pulled up a chair and sat beside her.

'I've had plenty of time to think things over the last few days and I have already decided what I want to do, so let us begin,' she said smiling to the nervous young man.

He did as he was told and opened a small black leather case, then he took out several sheets of paper and began to write.

An hour later they had concluded the business. Leah Thomas was well pleased with the way the young solicitor had conducted himself.

'You've been very helpful, Mr Penley,' she said. ' Now I can rest in peace when the time comes knowing that my wishes will be carried out to the letter.'

'Then I hope that it will be a long time before either myself or Mr Harvard's services are required ma'am. I wish you the best of health for a good while yet,' he said as he put away the copy of her will and testament.

'You are too kind, Mr Penley, but one never knows does one?' she smiled as she shook his hand. Then she said,

'I want to thank you for your honesty.'

Simon Penley nodded to her, it had been his pleasure to advise her.

Leah Thomas watched him leave and in her heart she knew she had made all the right decisions.

A month later, Simon Penley unexpectedly found himself again on the long journey to Bryn Cethin Farm. This time he was accompanied by James Harvard his partner.

Leah Thomas, that grand old lady he had liked so much had died peacefully in her sleep, and the two men were now required to attend to the legal matters of her estate.

Her death had come as a great shock to both Medi and Owen even though they had begun to realise how frail she had become.

It came as a greater shock to John who had come to love and respect his grandmother. He had wanted to believe she would live forever, they'd had such little time together.

' I should have been there with her,' he cried when Marged broke the sad news to him.

'You must be grateful for the happy times you spent together, John. I believe she loved you very much,' she said as she tried to comfort him.

'I shall miss her,' said the boy. 'Bryn Cethin will never be the same without Grandmother.'

Morgan looked at his son and immediately the boy's words made him think out loud.

'What will happen now?' he asked. 'Will Rhys Thomas come home like a bad penny to claim his inheritance? Owen and Medi may have to leave Bryn Cethin if this is so!'

'He's sure to come back,' said Marged, 'especially if he knows of all the hard work Owen has put into the estate.'

John looked at them solemnly and said,

'If that is so, one thing is for certain, I'll not go to Bryn Cethin again!'

John, however, had no choice in the matter. Shortly after the funeral was over and Leah Thomas was buried with her beloved Carwyn, John was summoned to Bryn Cethin for the reading of his grandmother's will.

At the boy's wish his mother and father were to accompany him as he did not understand why his presence was expected. As they arrived at Bryn Cethin, John noticed a grand horse and carriage with its driver waiting at the entrance to the house.

'Rhys Thomas, I expect,' said Morgan gruffly.

'Now then, no trouble I beg of you,' said Marged to her husband. We are here today for John's sake, not to dig up old wounds.'

They went inside the house where they met Owen waiting for them. Immediately she saw her brother Marged asked,

'Why does John have to be here today? Do you know anything Owen?'

'I have no idea what is about to happen,' replied Owen. 'I can only guess Grandmother Thomas has left something for him in her will. Surely you realised how close she and John had become?' he said as he saw the look of surprise on his sister's face.

'Is that Rhys' carriage outside?' asked Morgan.

'Yes,' replied Owen, 'he's in the sitting room and already he's taken charge issuing orders to the servants. Medi is quite upset by his actions. As for myself I intend to ignore the man.'

At that precise moment Simon Penley appeared at the doorway. He called out to Owen in a reverent tone,

'Is everyone present? We should like to begin.' Then he saw the young boy standing with his parents and he said,

'You must be young master John. I'm pleased to meet you. Now follow me will you?'

Morgan stepped forward and politely said,

'Excuse me sir, anything that affects out son affects us also. Could we ask your permission for us to be present? We shall sit in the back of the room and be a bother to no-one.'

'I shall see to it that there are no objections,' said the young solicitor showing them the way into the sitting room.

The room was in semi-darkness and Morgan failed to see the man standing by the large ornate fireplace.

Rhys Thomas immediately began to assume the role of a newly founded landowner. He crossed the room and threw open the curtains which had been closed as a mark of respect for his dead mother.

'That's better,' he said. 'Let's have some light in this dreary room. Now you can get on with the business!'

Marged could now see Medi sitting near her father Ryland Preece. Goronwy Evans, the minister, sat next to them. Several servants sat around, and finally the woman she knew to be Rhys Thomas' wife sat in a chair near the fireplace. Owen stood at the back of the room facing the two solicitors. She went to join him followed by Morgan and John.

Mr Harvard and Mr Penley sat at a large oak desk, which had obviously belonged to the late Carwyn Thomas.

'Is everyone present?' asked Mr Harvard, looking around the room. 'Then I shall begin' he said.

'First I should like to say how sorry I am for the passing of such a gentle lady as Mrs Leah Thomas. Our condolences are extended to you the family.'

Before the solicitor could continue, Rhys Thomas began to rudely interrupt him saying,

'Get on with it man, you are wasting valuable time. There's no need for all this sentiment!'

James Harvard paused a second and with a look of disgust he ignored the foolish man. Then he continued,

'For many years it has been my privilege to act on behalf of both Carwyn and Leah Thomas in matters of this estate. However, it was my partner Mr Penley who last saw Mrs Thomas, and he will now read her last will and testament as it was given to him only a short few weeks ago.'

Simon Penley lifted the parchment, took a breath and began to read.

'This being my last will and testament, I Leah Thomas of Bryn Cethin Farm, bequeath the house known as Bryn Cethin to my granddaughter Medi Lewis.

The surrounding lands and estate and all that remained on it I leave equally to my granddaughter Medi Lewis and my grandson John Harries, on the understanding that Owen Lewis will continue to manage the said estate and therefore ensure that all proceeds shall equally by divided between the said persons stated above.'

At the back of the room Marged gasped out loud. Morgan touched her arm to silence her.

The solicitor continued,

'As for my only son Rhys Thomas, I bequeath any two of the finest horses in the stable along with one hundred guineas to take him away from Bryn Cethin, never to return.'

Suddenly Rhys Thomas who had remained silent up to that moment, shouted out,

'This is an outrage! You'll never get away with it. The old woman must have been out of her mind!'

Mr Harvard tried to silence him and for a moment or two he succeeded. He instructed Mr Penley to continue. Several small bequests were made to her faithful servants which left Bethan Jones wiping the tears from her eyes. While Goronwy Evans thanked God for Leah Thomas' kindness in leaving her beloved Elim Chapel a small but generous amount of money.

Simon Penley had hardly uttered the final wishes of Leah Thomas' will when there came another outburst from Rhys her son.

'She's cheated me out of my inheritance. How could she do it? When my father died she told me everything would be mine after her days. Who or what changed her mind? I want to know.'

He gave an accusing glance in the direction of James Harvard.

It was Simon Penley who stood up to reply to him.

'I may have the answer to your question,' he said to the arrogant man. 'The day your mother wrote her will she enquired if I knew of your whereabouts. Or if you had been in touch with the firm for any reason. Naturally I told her the truth. That you had recently enquired into the profits being made out of Bryn Cethin. I can only assume that she took your sudden interest into consideration before she decided what she wanted. Then she finalised her wishes.'

James Harvard looked at his young partner. Should he have divulged this information to Leah Thomas? It was too late now, what had been done was done. It appeared Rhys Thomas had brought this disaster on himself.

Rhys showed no remorse and angrily shouted again,

'I'll not stand for this! The land is mine!'

Suddenly a voice from the back of the room cut through him like a knife.

'You are wrong! The land and all it stands for shall never be yours. I'll see to that!'

Rhys did not have to turn around to see where the challenge had come from. He knew it was the voice of his son who spoke.

John walked toward the father he had never been allowed to know and he said,

'She told me all about you. You were the son she loved, how dare you say these things about my grandmother. You robbed me of a family and a grandfather I never knew but you could not take away the love she had for me. You caused her so much heartache and she began to regret having sent you away. Then she found out that you were waiting and watching while Uncle Owen made this farm a success once more and she knew you schemed to take it all when she had gone. You cared for no-one but yourself, that is the reason why she turned her back on you. You deserve what you've got!'

Immediately Rhys could see he had lost his case, then his mind began to devise a plan. Would it work he wondered?

'Wait boy,' he cried. 'Perhaps we could come to an agreement? You are my son after all, and I could be of great help to you. I could manage your affairs until you come of age. And I will make sure that Owen will play fair by you.'

Owen sprang forward but it was Medi who stood up and faced her uncle to speak,

'How dare you! If it were not for Owen there would be no Bryn Cethin. He worked hard for grandmother and he will continue to do so for John and myself. You could have asked her forgiveness but you chose to let her end her days in sadness. Because of us, she was happy here. John also made that possible. You reap what you sow and now you must realise what a fool you have been!'

'She speaks the truth Rhys,' said Ryland Preece his partner, proud that his daughter had spoken in defence of her husband.

Before Rhys could reply, someone else began to speak. It was Eleri, his wife.

'Enough of this bickering. I'll not be silent any longer. The boy is right in what he says. He gave your mother the love you so readily denied her and she in return loved him. Your life would be so much richer if you learned to give instead of take. I could never give you the child you so badly wanted and you never allowed me to forget it. Gradually, you stopped loving me also. Now you have to pay the price. Your mother knew what she had to do and I admire her for it.'

Rhys was stunned. Even his own wife was against him.

'I think it's time for us to leave,' she said as she walked over to where Medi sat nearby.

Then she turned to John and said,

'I am truly sorry.'

As Eleri left the room, the only sound to be heard was that of the rustle of silk from her long black dress as it swept along the floor.

Rhys looked at the jubilant faces around him and was stunned beyond belief.

His wife's voice then called out to him,

'Rhys! I'm ready to leave. Are you coming or not?'

He walked solemnly toward the door and with one last determined look said,

'Go to hell all of you. You can keep the bloody farm and as for the money and the horses, you can keep them as well.'

As he stormed out of the room Marged broke down and began to weep. It had all been too much for her.

John comforted her,

'Don't cry Mam. He's gone now and I doubt he'll ever be back.'

Marged clung to her son.

'I've waited a long time for this day to come. I'm so proud of you John,' she cried.

Both Mr Harvard and Mr Penley were relieved to be returning home. It had been a nasty experience especially as the old lady was not yet cold in her grave.

Morgan Harries still reeled from the shock of his son's new inheritance as he began to comfort Marged who was still upset.

John walked to his grandmother's favourite chair near the fire and as he sat down on it he quietly whispered,

'Thank you Grandmother, I'll not let you down.'

Owen stood at his side, he had heard the boy's promise to the dead woman.

'She was a clever old lady, may she rest in peace,' he said.

'I know she will,' was the boy's reply.

'We will work this land and make her proud of us,' said Owen. 'Can I count on you?' he asked John.

The boy took his uncle by the hand and shook it.

They were watched by Marged and Morgan.

'It's time for us to go,' she said to her husband. 'It looks as if we've lost our son at last.'

They could see how excited John had become at the prospect of his newly found wealth so they left quietly telling Medi that he could stay the night if he wished.

'Your grandmother was a woman of her word,' said Marged. 'She once told me that John would be provided for but I never expected this.'

Medi kissed her, then she left.

Marged climbed up into the buggy beside her husband and just as they were about to drive away, John came running out of the house and climbed aboard beside them.

'Where are you going without me?' he panted.

'We thought you might want to stay' said his mother.

'You thought wrong Mam,' replied the boy. 'Now can we go to tell them the news at Cefn Glas?' he asked. 'Then the three of us can all go home.'

Marged and Morgan smiled at each other. Despite his inheritance their son was still their son.

o o o

News of Leah Thomas' bequests and the fate of Bryn Cethin spread like wildfire throughout the village. Many people agreed that Owen Lewis deserved the old lady's recognition. He had worked hard to keep the farm together.

Others said it was a shame to think Rhys Thomas had lost his inheritance.

But the biggest shock of all was that Marged Harries' son John was to benefit greatly from the estate.

This became the topic of conversation at almost every meeting place.

Wil and Beti received the news of their grandson's legacy with trepidation. They knew Leah Thomas had done right by John but they hoped and prayed that it would not alter him in any way. Only the future would tell.

Wil predicted that once more the old story of Marged's involvement with Rhys Thomas would be brought to light and the gossip would start again.

He was right!

When asked how they felt, Marged and Morgan stated they would stand by their son and try to guide him in his future. They knew Owen would make the right decisions for him.

'All we can hope for is that John will learn to accept things for himself,' said Morgan one evening.

'The lad has a strong character,' replied Wil, and with your support, he'll do just fine.'

'I hope you are right,' said Morgan, 'as I'll not stand by to see his mother hurt again.'

CHAPTER 26

The keen wind whistled through the trees and specks of rain began to sting at John's face as he ran down the lane to the cottage.

He was almost out of breath as he reached the garden gate. His tightly clenched fists was the only sign of the temper that raged within him.

What had that boy called him? A rich bastard! That was it!

Well, he had shown him a thing or two, but John had paid the price for his success.

His nose was bloodied and a large purple swelling had begun to appear around his left eye, which had almost become closed.

His coat was ripped and muddied where he had fallen to the ground in a fight which had taken place at the back of the schoolhouse. The other boys had laughed and poked fun at him, but though he was shaken and bruised he'd made them regret it.

Wiping the blood from his nose he staggered through the back door to the kitchen. He intended to go to his room before his mother could see him. John had been ashamed of the things those boys had said about her but he felt more ashamed of himself, believing some of them to be true.

Luck was not on his side, however, as he turned the corner to sneak up the stairs he came face to face with her.

Marged gasped,

'Dear Lord in Heaven. What has happened to you John?'

She reached out to touch his face but he pushed her hand away saying,

'Don't touch me, leave me alone!'

'Are you hurt,' she asked again. 'Let me bathe your eye at least.'

This time John did not reply.

'You've been fighting, haven't you?' asked Marged.

Still he did not reply.

'Very well then, I'll call your father from the garden. perhaps you'll tell him what is wrong.'

Marged turned away.

Suddenly the boy's eyes filled with tears,

'My father you said? I know who my real father was, but you never told me how he became my father. A long time ago I said it didn't matter but now I'm not so sure. My friends call me a rich bastard. Is that what I am? Did Grandmother Thomas only feel a duty or pity for me? Did she not love me? If not, I want nothing from her whatsoever.'

Marged could see her son had been deeply hurt but she said,

'Stop it John. This is all nonsense, you don't know what you're saying.'

'How could you Mam? Why did you let that man even touch you. Have you no shame!'

Marged could not believe her ears. She dare not try to reason with him, and she broke down into tears.

The commotion brought Morgan running through the door.

'What the hell's going on here?' he asked as he saw the scene before him. John scowled at him and refused to answer. Marged stood there crying, afraid to say one word.

Morgan took her in his arms and she clung tightly to him.

Then he looked directly at John and said,

'I am waiting for an answer!'

Seeing Morgan in such a temper, both Marged and John began to speak at the same time.

Morgan advised each of them to sit down where they could all discuss the problem rationally.

John walked to the table, Marged sat on a chair nearby while Morgan stood towering over them.

'Now then lad, been fighting have you? Well it had better be for a good reason. What was it all about?' he asked.

'She'll tell you!' was the boy's arrogant reply as he pointed in the direction of his mother.

Morgan raised his voice slightly,

'No John. I want to hear it from you,' he said.

John then began to tell of the taunts and gibes he'd had at school. All the while, Marged continued to sob quietly.

Morgan remained silent until the boy had finished his story.

Then he spoke,

'We decided a long time ago never to hide the truth from you John, and we were proud of you and the way you handled it. Maybe we took you too much for granted. We thought you had finally grown up. However, I can see we were wrong. Your mother owes you no explanation and if you believe all those boys have said about her then you will have allowed them to win. I have tried to be a good father to you. Let's hope I've not failed. As for your mother, I think you owe her an apology.'

John looked at him in defiance, refusing to utter a word.

Then Marged began to speak.

'I think I knew in my heart that sooner or later the legacy would affect our lives but I never realised how it would turn you against me. Morgan is the only father you have known, he worships you. I shall not forgive all the things you have said here today.'

John looked at both of them but the words those boys had said to him were still ringing in his ears. It was no good, he would not apologise under any circumstances.

'Well John. It's up to you now boy,' said his father. John turned on his heel and ran upstairs. Within a few minutes he came back into the room as if nothing had happened.

'I'm going out,' he said. ' I'll be over at Cefn Glas, I want to talk to Grandpa Wil.'

'Is that all you have to say?' asked his father.

The boy nodded, then left.

Morgan attempted to follow him outside, but Marged pleaded with him to let John go.

'Very well,' he said angrily, ' but be sure, this isn't the end of it!'

o o o

John rode his pony as fast as he could and as he reached Cefn Glas he went in search of his grandfather. There were things he desperately needed to ask him.

However, the only person he could find was his Aunt Anna.

She was sitting on a small stool near the back door shelling peas into a large earthenware bowl which she held in her lap.

She looked up as she heard him approach.

'John bach. What are you doing here? I wasn't expecting you.'

The boy stooped to pick up a large green pod out of a basket that lay at her feet. Then splitting its side it revealed several succulent green peas which he popped into his mouth before answering her.

'I thought I'd ride over to see the old folks. Where are they?' he said as he looked around.

Anna continued to shell the peas saying,

'They've gone to see Twm Shenkin. He's not been well of late.'

She noticed his swollen eye, but made no reference to it. John would tell her soon enough if there was something troubling him.

'You look hot and bothered after your ride. Come inside and I'll get you a cool drink,' she said. Anna handed him a cup of water, then she began to ask him how his parents were.

John replied that they were well but she knew by the look on his face that something was very wrong.

'Trouble at home is it John? Come now you can tell me. Let's sit outside then we can talk,' she said.

He followed her outside and before he knew, he had begun to tell her what had happened. When he finished Anna said,

'Boys can be cruel John. One minute they are your friends, and the next your enemies. They don't know how to handle this situation, and they see you not as the boy they grew up with but the person who has now become rich. You must not punish your mother or father for that. They love you and cannot bear to see you hurt in any way.'

He could see the sense in her words but he said,

'I am so confused. I want to believe my mother wasn't at fault, but why doesn't anyone tell me what actually happened?'

Anna saw now the time had come to tell the boy the truth of his birth. He was old enough to understand what had happened to his mother all those years ago.

As they sat together in the yard, she began to tell him Marged's story and the long and difficult road she had decided to take to rear her son on her own.

'So my mother was innocent then?' he asked as Anna finished the tale.

'Yes,' she said. ' You are so very special to her John. She has endured so very much for you and as for Morgan, he stood by her all the way. He is a good father to you and you could not have wished for a finer man to have shared your mother's life. Think hard on what has happened today. Where is the boy who stood in the chapel with his head held high for all the gossipmongers to see?' she asked.

'It's your mother who gave you this life John. Don't waste it in hatred, I beg of you!'

The boy sobbed as Anna took him in her arms.

'What will I say to them?' he asked knowing now how right she was.

'I don't have to tell you what to say John. Look into your heart and the words will soon come to you,' she answered.

He kissed her farewell.

She watched him untie his pony and as he began to ride away she was reminded of her two brothers when they too had been the same age as John. Owen, now grown to manhood, and dear Huw who was now just a lovely memory.

John suddenly looked back over his shoulder and shouted to her.

The words she heard were 'Thank You.'

Anna smiled as she waved farewell to him.

o o o

Marged looked anxiously out of the window wondering how and when her son would return. Then she heard him ride up on his pony.

The plate she held in her hand fell and smashed on the floor, she was so nervous.

As she carried on washing the dishes she hoped and prayed that tempers would not be set alight again. Morgan had been determined to confront his son as soon as he set foot in the house again.

John entered the room but neither mother or son spoke to each other.

Then in a subdued voice he finally spoke,

'I'm sorry Mam, I've behaved so badly and I don't expect you to forgive me. I'm ashamed of all the things I've said and done. All I want is a chance to try again. I want you to be proud of me once more.'

'What changed you mind?' asked Marged not knowing if she was able to forgive her son for all that had happened.

'I've spoken with Aunt Anna and she told me everything. Rhys took advantage of you and you were innocent all the time.'

Marged gasped, so he knew the truth at last!

'I know now how difficult it must have been for you having to rear me on your own, and everything you did you did it all for me. Before I go to ask my father's forgiveness will you forgive me Mam?' he asked.

Marged held her arms out to her son and said,

'There's nothing to forgive.'

Morgan stood hidden in the shadow of the doorway, and as he watched the tender scene between mother and son, he knew at last that all would be well again.

CHAPTER 27

Anna began to set the table for tea. Soon the children would be running in from school as hungry as ever.

Peter John played at her feet as she hurried to and fro. She was glad the little child had slept while John was there as they were able to talk with each other without interruption.

The time they had spent together however, had now caused her to fall behind with all the things she had left to do. Anna did not mind as she knew that John would make the right decision. A great deal of apologies would have to be made but she also knew the love both her sister and Morgan had for their son.

She felt in the heart that all would be well between them.

She looked at the old grandfather clock as it ticked away in the hall. It was getting late, Mam and Da should have been home by now. Anna feared that they may have found Twm Shenkin to be worse than they thought. She hoped she was wrong. Twm had been a good friend to all of them and now it was their turn to look after him.

Ever since that night he had returned bringing home Peter who had been so desperately ill, he had become like one of the family, and with his only sister living several miles away, Twm had been welcomed at Cefn Glas as if it were his own home.

She heard her mother and father as they approached the back door to the kitchen. Beti took her bonnet and shawl off as she entered the room and placed them on the back of the chair. Without looking toward her daughter she sat down, dreading to hear the words her husband had to say, as she knew what her daughter's reaction would be.

Anna noticed how serious the look on her mother's face had become and so she immediately asked how they had found Twm Shenkin to be.

'The news is not good Anna,' said Wil trying to be gentle with her. 'Your mother and I found a big difference in him. His breathing is so very much worse. It's no wonder after all the years of chaffing corn and threshing wheat in the fields. His lungs are filled with the dust from both. Your mother tried hard to persuade him to come home with us but he's too stubborn to give in.'

Anna tried to be strong but her eyes had begun to fill with tears. She was so fond of their old friend that she could not bear to see him suffering.

'There is more,' said Wil.

'Doctor Pugh came to see him while we were there. He advised Twm not to be left on his own any longer. We've talked it over with him and Twm had decided to sell the cottage and move to Login where his sister Catrin will look after him.'

'He can't do that, Da!' cried Anna. 'He loves that little cottage, it's always been home to him. I can look after him, I'll go to see him in the morning. When he hears what I have to say, he'll change his mind,' she said.

'No merchi,' said her father kindly. Wil reached out to touch her arm knowing how distressed she felt. 'Twm has made up his mind, there is nothing more we can do. Everything is to be sold. Furniture, livestock and such. He'll be better off with Catrin. She's got plenty of room there and they've always got on so well together. It's all for the best, you'll see.' Wil said as he tried to convince her.

I shall miss him, Anna sadly.

'Now then, we have to do what's best for him Anna,' said her mother. 'We shall all miss him, especially the children. 'But we'll be able to visit him and I know he will look forward to that.'

Anna nodded, she had to agree with them but it would not be the same without old Twm around them.

'When does he plan to go to Catrin's?' she asked.

'As soon as possible,' she said. 'Your father had to arrange the auction in the next day or so.'

'Then I'll go to see him in the morning to offer my help,' said Anna.

'He'll appreciate that,' replied Wil, not venturing to tell his daughter the worse possible news he and Beti had received from Doctor Pugh.

Twm Shenkin was desperately ill and there were only a few months left of his life to live.

It would be time enough to break this news to his daughter as the words had failed him at this very moment.

o o o

Anna walked down the leafy lane towards Twm's cottage. The trees full of leaves would soon begin to fall as autumn approached. It had been a hot summer but today there seemed to be a cool breeze in the air.

Her thoughts turned to Twm. What was she going to do now that he had decided to move away? So many times he had come to her aid and she felt he had become one of the very few links she'd had left with Peter. She'd accepted that she would not be able to visit him so often but she knew he had decided for the best. His sister Catrin would look after him until he was well again.

Twm had come to see her at Cefn Glas after he'd heard of the row between Iestyn and her father. What was it he had said?

'Live your life to the full Anna. Be answerable only to yourself or you may live to regret it. You above all people deserve a measure of happiness, Peter would not want you to grieve.'

Why had he chosen to say those words to her? Was it because of something which he had experienced during his life?

How easy it had all begun to sound, but how hard it had become for her to live a life of her own. The longer time passed the harder it had become. Her father had not relented over Iestyn Roberts. And although she had the love of all her family, Anna knew in her heart she was being denied the one love she longed for.

As she caught sight of the grey smoke rising from the chimney before her Anna quickened her step. She decided to put on a brave face in spite of all she felt for her old friend, it would do no good for Twm to feel sad as well.

She walked through the little wooden gate and closed it quietly behind her. Then turning along a small path, past the pigsty and the wired chickens' coop she found herself at the back door to the cottage.

She knocked and then opened the door and walked through a dark, narrow passageway into the kitchen.

There she found him sitting motionless in the rocking chair near the fire, a woollen rug pulled over his knees.

From where she stood, she could hear his laboured breathing.

He looked up and smiled as she entered the room

'Anna, it's good to see you. I wondered if you would come,' his voice rasped within him.

Immediately she saw his features had changed since the last time she saw him. His skin had become a yellowy-grey colour. This was not the man she knew.

Twm always looked so sturdy, with a ruddy outdoor complexion. He now looked much more ill than her mother and father had conveyed to her.

She took a loaf of bread and some cheese from her basket and placed them on the table. These were followed by a freshly baked loaf cake, rich with sultanas and raisins.

'I've brought a few things for you Twm,' she said, trying all the while not to look at him for fear she would fail to hold the feelings of sadness within her.

'How are you today?' she asked.

'Not so good merchi,' he replied 'and I'm not very hungry but I could do with a nice cup of tea.'

Anna filled the kettle with water and put it on to boil.

'The cups are in the dresser there,' said Twm pointing to where all the best dishes were stored in his mother's sideboard.

The old man watched her closely as she continued to fuss with what she was doing.

Suddenly their eyes met. Anna stopped what she was doing, walked toward him and finally knelt at Twm's feet.

'So you've decided to leave this old place at last then? Best thing too! You'll have Catrin to look after you. We'll miss you, of course, but the children and I can come and visit you often. Everything will be alright Twm. Just you wait and see!' she said trying to convince herself as well as her old friend.

Twm looked at her with a great sadness in his eyes and with difficulty in breathing said,

'The day will come soon merchi, when this old door will finally close behind me. It has always been my home and wherever I am I shall always feel I am still here.'

Anna nodded, as she could not find the right words to say to him.

She went back to making the tea and when it was ready she poured the two cups and they sat together talking of old times.

The afternoon passed by, time was of little importance until Anna finally glanced at the clock.

'I came to see if I could be of use to you Twm. Was there any sorting or packing to be done? All we've done is talk together. I'll have to come another day,' she said.

'Don't worry yourself merchi,' said Twm. 'Maldwyn, our Catrin's boy, intends to come for me on Saturday. Sian his wife will sort everything then. You know that there are many things that will have to go under the hammer don't you?' he asked sadly.

'Do you have to go that soon Twm?' asked Anna, shocked that arrangements for him to leave had already been made.

Twm nodded.

'But I've done nothing to help you,' she said.

'You've helped me far more than you realise merchi. Our little talk has done me a power of good. Let us remember this afternoon shall we?' he asked.

'Then I shall be here on Saturday to see you leave,' said Anna.

'No,' the old man replied and taking her by the hand said, 'I want no sad farewells Anna.'

She could see how very ill he was and knew it would only distress him further if she tried to reason with him.

'Very well then Twm, but I'll come over to see you in your new home as soon as it is possible,' she said.

'I'll look forward to it,' Twm smiled at her.

Anna stood up and placed her shawl around her shoulders. Despite the warm fire in the grate she suddenly felt a chill run down her spine. She bent to kiss him gently on the forehead, and as she did so Twm began to reach inside his waistcoat. From the pocket inside he took out a white handkerchief. He unfolded it to reveal a small silver brooch, delicately shaped like a lace fan, its marquisette setting shone from the light of the fire.

Holding his hand out to her he whispered,

'This is for you Anna.'

'It's beautiful,' she gasped 'but I couldn't accept it Twm.'

'I want you to have it to remember me by,' he said kindly. 'It was intended for someone I knew a long time ago but her heart belonged to another. She was as lovely as yourself Anna, but she and I were never meant to be. I could not part with it until now. Please take it, for my sake.'

Anna took the brooch and pinned it to her dress, which was far too modest for such a fine gift.

'I shall always treasure it,' she said as she kissed him gently on the forehead again.

Twm nodded, then closed his eyes which had become very tired.

As she left the room his eyes stirred again and he opened them. Then he smiled to himself as he knew that finally the brooch would be worn by the only woman he had dared to love.

Anna had slipped quietly through the back door leaving Twm sleeping in his chair. As she walked back to Cefn Glas she touched the delicate gift now and then to reassure herself that if was still safely pinned to her dress.

She wondered to herself what sort of woman had Twm Shenkin loved, and she felt sad that there had been no-one to share his life with him.

He had been her good friend, and in her heart she felt they had already said goodbye. She desperately hoped however that she was wrong.

CHAPTER 28

Iestyn Roberts knew that however hard he'd try he would not be able to erase Anna Malone from his mind despite all the promises he had made. Since the day of the fair it had proved twice as difficult to forget her.

Anna had declared her love for him and he could not forget that, but the future seemed so desolate. There were so many things to consider if she left Cefn Glas one day.

Would all the children get on with each other and what is more, would Martha ever accept her after all that had been said?

The problem presented itself over and over again in his mind until it nearly drove him crazy. There was no answer to it. Iestyn became moody and irritable until after many attempts to throw Sarah Madoc and he together again, Martha finally packed her bags and left.

It was rumoured she had set up home with her daughter's friend Sarah Madoc. Two of a kind people said they were. It was not until she'd gone that Iestyn realised how much better he began to cope with the children who never asked about their grandmother.

A good neighbour Polly Wilkins on hearing of the rift soon came to offer her services. There had been no love lost between her and Martha and with an understanding husband like Emrys she soon fell into the role of housekeeper, coming and going on a daily basis. Things had not been so good in Iestyn's household for many a year.

Iestyn travelled to market at least once a week and during those visits he tried to avoid contact with Wil Lewis at all cost. It seemed as if there would be no further opportunity to meet with any other of Anna's family and therefore he would not know if the feeling between her and Wil had improved.

Then he heard about Twm Shenkin. It appeared the man was very ill and his place was to be put up for auction. He knew Twm was a close friend of the Lewis family and they were almost certain to be at the auction.

He decided there and then that he would be present but he would remain in the background. If only he could see her again her thought.

o o o

'Come now! Who'll bid for this fine piece of furniture?' shouted the auctioneer as he stood on a large wooden box in the middle of the yard in front of Twm Shenkin's cottage. He pointed to a large highly polished

Welsh dresser, which stood alongside several other interesting pieces of furniture for sale.

Anna stood in the crowd listening to the man who would try his best to auction everything there today.

Poor Twm, she thought. Thank God he wasn't there to see all his lovely possessions go under the auctioneer's hammer. She lifted her hand to shade her eyes from the sunlight as she looked toward the dresser. In her mind she could still picture it standing in the kitchen of Twm's cottage with all the beautiful jugs and fine china plates displayed on it.

Everything had belonged to Twm's mother but he had treasured every piece of it since she'd gone which had been many years ago.

Now the dresser stood bare, but even in its nakedness it still stood proud and tall.

An elderly man standing nearby raised his hand and bid for the dresser.

Several other bids were made raising the price much higher each time. Finally, the auctioneer brought his hammer down on a large piece of wood with a thud as he shouted,

'Sold, to the gentleman in the far corner!'

Anna was saddened to see so many things already sold. Quite a crowd had gathered. Some came out of curiosity but others came genuinely to help Twm who was a respected member of the community. They had said it was a shame that he had to move to his sister Catrin's home but Anna knew that few of them realised how ill Twm really was.

She had taken the children to visit him several times but his health had become far worse.

Beti and Wil had been at the auction earlier on but it had upset Beti to see the old home disappearing in front of them. She had asked Wil to take her home while Anna decided to stay a while longer. Even Owen and Medi had turned up and bought several small items, although there was nothing that they didn't already have at the Big House. Anna was grateful to both of them.

The auctioneer raised his voice once more and shouted out loud to draw the attention of the crowd.

This time a beautifully carved settle was to be put under the hammer.

Anna remembered where it had stood in the hallway. The bench with its highly polished back and arms engraved with intricate flowers and leaves had been Twm's mother's pride and joy. Twm said a relative of theirs had carved out the patterns and they were very proud that they had kept it in the family.

It was obvious that Catrin his sister could find no room for this piece of furniture as there was no other way Twm would have parted with it.

'This is not only a decorative piece, ladies and gentlemen. It is a useful one as well,' he said as he lifted the seat to reveal a large empty compartment hidden beneath.

Seeing this, Anna immediately remembered Twm telling her that his mother always stored her heavy winter woollen blankets inside.

'What am I bid here?' shouted the man again.

Suddenly, Anna became aware of someone moving closely behind her and her heart skipped a beat as she heard his voice. She could not bear to turn around and so she looked straight ahead of her and whispered,

'What brings you here Iestyn?'

'I came for the auction, nothing more,' he whispered in her ear.

He stood so close to her she could almost feel his breath on the back of the neck and a shiver ran up and down her spine.

As the bidding continued Anna became oblivious to those around her. All she could think of was that he was here, near her at last.

Iestyn looked around, then asked,

'Are you here on your own?'

Anna nodded, then said,

'Mam and Da have left some time ago.'

Then their attention turned for a moment to the auctioneer who now pleaded with the crowd,

'Come now, it's worth far more than this,' he said pointing to the settle again. 'Will someone make a final offer?'

'Do you like it Anna?' asked Iestyn quickly.

Before she realised what she was doing she said eagerly,

'Oh! Yes, I always admired it!'

To her surprise, Iestyn raised his had high in the air and the auctioneer's hammer thundered down once more.

'Sold to the gentleman and his lovely lady over there!' he shouted.

By then Anna had quickly disappeared to the back of the crowd for fear she and Iestyn be recognised together. She saw Iestyn dart forward to settle the account with the auctioneer's assistant then he came in search of her.

As she waited, Anna knew she should return to Cefn Glas but she wanted so much to stay and be with him if only for a little while.

'We have to talk Anna,' he said as he took her to one side.

'It's too risky Iestyn. What if someone noticed us, they'll be sure to tell my father and the trouble will start all over again,' she said anxiously.

A man's voice called out in their direction. It was to let Iestyn know that his cart had been loaded with the precious settle.

'I bought it for you Anna. Maybe one day when we will be together,' he said.

Anna shook her head.

'I must go,' said Iestyn, 'but if you change your mind, I'll wait for you at the end of the lane. We may never have another chance to talk together.'

Then he hurried away.

Anna began to ask herself whether she should join him or not. It would only be for a little while. Suddenly, she knew her heart had overruled her mind and she slowly made her way to the back of the cottage that she knew so well. There she waited for a moment so that Iestyn would reach the lane before her.

When she thought it was time she ran as fast as she could. The breeze sent her bonnet tumbling from her head to where it hung by its ribbons around her pale neck. Her long black tresses sprung to life as she continued to run.

She saw the gate in front of her and hurried through it. There she saw him waiting for her and as he heard the sound of her footsteps running toward him he leapt down off the cart and ran to meet her with open arms. They laughed together as he covered her face with kisses.

Then he lifted her up beside him saying,

'There's a place I know, not too far from here where we can be alone.'

He jerked the horses' reins and they pulled away.

They sat with their bodies leaning against an old oak tree. Iestyn put his arm around her and Anna leaned back to rest her head on it. Her eyes closed for a moment, she could hardly believe she was here with him.

Iestyn could not take his eyes away from her. He remembered the first time they had met at the Chapel picnic. He thought how beautiful she was, even though she was dressed in her dark clothes of mourning, with the wide black silk frill covering her delicate throat. She had excited him even then.

Today she looked so different, more beautiful than ever. Her blue linen blouse stood open at her throat and her skirt clung to the curves of her still so young body. Her dark hair fell in curls down over her shoulders, he took it in his hand and gently kissed it.

Anna opened her eyes as Iestyn bent to kiss her throat again and again. He knew this time he could not stop himself as his hands began to caress her body. Anna felt herself quiver and she began to moan softly as his hand found her breast and touched it ever so lightly.

He began to undo the buttons at her bodice kissing her all the while. Then quickly he slipped his hand inside caressing her gently. Anna did not attempt to remove it but as their pleasure mounted and he pushed her down on the ground she suddenly realised that this was not how she wanted it to be.

She pushed him away as she came to her senses and she sat up with a start. Then she quickly began to button her blouse. As she stood up she smoothed her long grey skirt over her hips saying,

'I'm sorry Iestyn, forgive me. I can't do this!'

'It's alright Anna,' he said taking her in his arms. 'It's I who am to blame. I was carried away, I had no right to touch you.'

'It will never be right for us Iestyn,' she cried.

'It can be Anna, if only you would leave Cefn Glas. You could come to me with the children and we could be married,' he pleaded.

What was he saying! It could never be possible.

'I mean it Anna. Say you'll marry me,' he said.

'And what of Martha?' she asked not even allowing herself to think of her own difficulties at home.

'Martha has left us. She's set up home with Sarah Madoc and I have a housekeeper to look after the children. I didn't want to tell you this way for fear you would think I only wanted a mother for my children. I love you Anna, you are in my thoughts day and night and I cannot live without you,' he said.

She turned away shaking her head.

Iestyn pulled her toward him, crushing her in his arms.

'Please don't say anything just yet, think on what I've said. You know I speak the truth and I have to know that you feel the same as I,' he said.

Anna looked up at him.

What was she to do? How could she make him understand that although his life had changed for the better hers had remained the same.

She would always owe her mother and father a debt of gratitude. They in turn would never accept Iestyn into the family no matter what happened.

As they had very little time left to be together, Anna promised that she would think carefully about his proposal.

It was enough to satisfy Iestyn for the time being so he took her hand in his and led her back to where the horse stood waiting.

'When shall we meet again Anna?' he asked hopefully.

'My father plans for us to go to the County Fair,' she said. 'We could meet there.'

'You'll have your answer for me then?' he asked again.

'Yes, Iestyn,' she replied.

Anna desperately wanted to believe in miracles but it would take more than a miracle for them to share a life together at last.

She knew then that her answer to him had to be 'No!'

o o o

The next time Anna and Iestyn met was not at the County Fair.

It was a much sadder occasion which brought them together at Elim Chapel.

Twm Shenkin had finally given up his struggle for life. He had passed away just a few short weeks after leaving his beloved home.

His wish was to be buried in the tiny chapel graveyard alongside his friend Peter Malone.

The rain beat down on a sea of black umbrellas sheltering the mourners as they huddled together at the graveside. There was a sigh of relief as Goronwy Evans brought the burial service to an end.

Iestyn stood several yards away from Wil Lewis and his family, and as he caught a glimpse of Anna through the crowd he nodded to her in recognition.

She saw him standing there, the rain pouring down over his face but sadly she turned away to follow her father back to the carriage that waited for them.

Since the day of the auction she had found no answer to the solution. There was nothing she could say to Iestyn, no promises to be made to him. Now with the sadness she felt from Twm's untimely death she had begun to resign herself to her fate. She would remain at Cefn Glas.

Anna had finally taken both her brother and sister into her confidence and told them of Iestyn's proposal.

Marged was saddened to admit she had no solution to offer her sister. She knew their father could be a hard man when he stuck to his principles.

Owen on the other hand stood firm in the belief that Anna should now be given the chance to live her own life, and it surprised her to find he was on her side.

He's become selfish in his old age Anna,' he said of Wil. 'You shouldn't allow him to control you. At least let me have it out with him. I'm sure I can get him to see reason.'

Anna was grateful to her brother for his concern but it was of no use and so she said,

'Thank you Owen, I realise you mean well but it will not work out. He's helped to rear my children and given us a roof over our heads. He supports us financially and he's made it perfectly clear that if ever I decide to leave Cefn Glas he will have nothing further to do with any of us. The children love him and so do I but however will I be able to explain it to them? No I can't risk that happening,' he said sadly.

'I understand all that you are trying to say Anna,' replied her brother. 'But for how long do you go on repaying the debt? Forever?'

Anna knew that nothing she could say or do would alter the fact that sooner or later she would have to come face to face with Iestyn, and he would have to be told that she could never marry him.

CHAPTER 29

'Hurry along Anna, we're ready to leave,' called her mother.

Anna threw her red and black shawl over her shoulders and hurried outside to where the others waited for her.

Lifting her long skirt she climbed on to the buggy and joined her mother sitting with Elizabeth and Kate. She lifted Peter John and sat him on her knee.

'Are we all ready now?' said David sitting up front with his grandfather.

Wil flicked the horses' reins and off they went. It had rained heavily for several days before and although the sky was still overcast the weather had improved slightly for the County Fair. there would be many things there for the children to see and do and they were filled with excitement as they chatted on the journey.

Anna seemed very quiet, or so Beti thought.

'Is everything alright Anna?' she asked. 'You don't seem to have much to say merchi.'

Anna's thoughts were troubled ones and so she made some excuse by saying,

'I'm alright Mam, I just wondered if Marged and Morgan would be at the fair today.'

Wil looked straight ahead of him as he held on to the reins but he joined in the conversation at that point.

'Young John won't be there for sure. Some horses are being sold at Bryn Cethin today and Owen thought it would be good experience if John stayed to watch the bargaining,' he said full of pride.

Wil was delighted to see his grandson beginning to take a rightful part in the running of Bryn Cethin Farm. Owen had become a good teacher and John was more than willing to learn the ropes.

'They have a good relationship, our Owen and John,' said Beti, equally proud of her son as well as her grandson. ' Thank God all is working out well for them' she added.

'Yes,' replied Wil, ' they are certainly shaping a future for themselves, that they are!'

Anna remained silent.

As she listened to her mother and father praising the others she began to wonder what exactly would it take to convince them that she too would give anything to be able to have a rosy future ahead of her.

Soon it would be time to tell Iestyn her decision. That is if he would be there today, and if she would find chance to slip away from her family.

For the remainder of the journey Anna put her thoughts behind her and concentrated on her children and their happy laughter.

They soon reached the ground where the County Fair was being held. David ran to where a man sat whittling a piece of wood with a sharp knife. Soon the wooden piece took the shape of an animal. The boy watched, fascinated at the speed of the man's hand. Several small shapes were already displayed at his feet. David picked up a small horse. Wil could see the delight in the little boy's eyes as he played with the model. And as Wil paid the man, David ran off to show his mother his new toy.

The grass felt damp under their feet as they wandered from stall to stall. It had not dried from the previous day's rain but it did not hinder them however.

They walked to where the farm animals were being penned. A huge black bull with a large brass ring through its nose snorted at them as they ventured near it.

Kate took her mother's hand pulling her away from the bull in fright. Anna laughed at her. Strains of music, from a harp, was heard in the distance, then they came upon a group of dancers. Some in Welsh costume, the ladies in their tall black hats and check skirts and the men in white shirts and leather breeches holding fast to broomsticks which they jumped over again and again to the music being played.

A young man accompanied the harp with a fiddle as the crowd stood around clapping their hands to the beat of the music.

Further along, they came to some women again dressed in their native costume as they sat at their spinning wheels their feet working the treadles while they spun the yarn.

Beti stopped to watch a man selling pots and pans while Wil wandered off in the direction of a large tent which had farming tools on show. Anna stopped at a stall nearby to look at the beautiful pieces of crocheted lace on display. There were so many to choose from that she could not make up her mind and it was several minutes later she heard Elizabeth say,

'Look who's here Mam. It's Becky Roberts.'

Anna turned her attention away from the stall to see the little girl clutching Elizabeth's hand tightly. Kate stood alongside them.

She looked around half expecting to find Iestyn standing there but the child was alone.

'Hello Becky,' she said. ' You've grown since I last saw you.'

The little girl smiled at Anna while Elizabeth continued,

'Becky's father has gone in search of her two brothers. It seems they've wandered off. Mamgu told him Becky can stay with us for a while. She also told me to tell you that he went off in that direction.'

Anna knew then that her mother had once more become her ally. Beti had wanted her to know that Iestyn Roberts was here today.

'Take the girls back to Mamgu. Tell her I'll see her in a short while,' said Anna.

Elizabeth did as she was told and walked back to her grandmother with the two little girls in tow.

Then Anna called after her daughter,

'By the way, have you seen David lately?'

'He's with Grandpa, I think!' Elizabeth called back.

Anna was aware she had to avoid her father at all cost.

Then she went in search of Iestyn who she now knew could not be very far away.

o o o

David Malone had not followed his grandfather into the large tent as he had decided to wander off on his own. There were so many sights to see for a boy of his age and he looked forward to maybe even having an adventure ahead of him.

As he walked along, he became aware of people shouting at two naughty boys who chased each other in and around several stalls.

Finally they collapsed on the grass, too breathless to talk to each other. From where David stood, he recognised them as the two boys he had beaten in the races the day of the Chapel Picnic which had taken place some months back.

A man ran over to them scolding each boy in turn. It had to be their father from the row he was giving them.

Yes, he could see him now. It was the man who had come to Cefn Glas for tea. It was Mr Roberts.

David walked over to them and stood on one side until Iestyn recognised him saying,

'Well, if it isn't David Malone. Are you on your own boy?'

David replied that his Grandpa Wil was last seen heading for the tent at the other end of the ground. But his mother and grandmother were following behind.

Iestyn realised his chance had now come to find Anna, and so with a word of warning to the boys to behave themselves, he took a few coppers from his pocket and told them to wait by the barn for his return.

Jethro waited until his father had gone, then shared the coppers with his brother Daniel.

David stood looking on while the two boys planned what to do next.

'He'll be gone for a while,' said Jethro after his father had departed, 'so he'll not expect us to be by the barn for at least half and hour. I've seen enough of animals, let's go and buy some taffy, then we'll go down by the river.'

'Great!' shouted Daniel who would have followed his older brother to kingdom come, if he'd asked him. 'The river's bound to be swollen after yesterday's rain. Perhaps we'll see some fish jumping there.'

This was the adventure David had been hoping for. Would they let him go as well? Plucking up courage he asked the older boy who seemed to be in command.

'Very well,' said Jethro. 'But you must do as I say.' He knew the Malone boy was younger than either his brother or himself but be had remembered how agile this boy had been when he'd beaten them all at the Chapel games.

The three boys set off through the crowd telling no-one of their plans.

Meanwhile, Iestyn had begun to walk in the opposite direction thanking God his luck was with him. So far he had not caught sight of Wil Lewis.

His eyes searched the crowd for Anna. There she was, standing only a few yards away from him, her eyes seemed to be searching also.

He hurried toward her and took her arm saying,

'At last! I've been looking for you everywhere. Let's get away from here shall we?'

Anna looked back over her shoulder to make sure all was clear but suddenly she saw her father talking with someone he obviously knew.

He had not seen them. Thank God!

Wait a minute! Where was David she thought? There was no sign of him alongside her father.

'Come Anna, before he has sight of us,' said Iestyn urgently.

'Wait!' she replied, ' I have to find David I thought he was with him!'

'Don't worry Anna. He's alright, I left him with my two boys. They are waiting for me down near the barn,' said Iestyn.

As they hurried away he began to explain how he had come across David and Anna was satisfied that her son was safe.

'We'll go down to the river,' he said. 'It's unlikely we shall be seen together by anyone there.'

He led her by the hand toward the riverbank. The grass was still damp and slippery in places.

As they began to leave the sounds of the County Fair behind them, Iestyn could hardly wait to take her in his arms.

They walked a little further then he stopped. His eyes began to search her face, waiting for the answer he longed to hear.

When he saw the sadness it held he knew she had made her decision.

Anna spoke softly as she tried to choose the words she knew would hurt him deeply.

'It has to be 'no' Iestyn. I have thought long and hard and there is no way that I can leave Cefn Glas.'

'Please Anna, I beg of you to think again,' he pleaded with her. 'Surely we deserve some measure of happiness?' he asked as he held her tightly.

'It's not that I don't love you,' she cried. ' But I have to put my children first, and I cannot uproot them from the home that they've come to accept. Please say you understand Iestyn?'

Before he could reply, they heard several shouts coming from the direction of the river, and the sound of someone running toward them.

Suddenly, Jethro came bounding along the path and as he saw his father he could not believe his good luck.

'Come quickly!' the boy shouted. 'It's Daniel, he and David are in trouble. They won't listen to me!'

Anna ran toward him and caught him roughly by his arm,

'David, you said. Where is he?' she asked.

The boy was almost out of breath but managed to say.

'They are balancing on the bridge over the river. I told them it was dangerous as the stones are loose. I'm afraid one of them will fall.'

Jethro deliberately failed to say it was he who had dared the younger boys to climb on the dangerous parapet.

Iestyn tried to calm his son but the boy broke free of his grasp and began to run back to where he had come from. He shouted for his father to follow him. Anna had already began to run in his direction but Iestyn soon overtook her and she lost sight of him in just a few seconds.

A piercing scream filled the air, followed by an almighty splash.

My God! They're in the river Iestyn thought, as he began to run faster.

He reached the bridge to see that a large stone had been dislodged and had fallen over the top into the river below.

Then he saw Jethro and Daniel as they peered anxiously over the edge of the bridge.

Jethro was shouting,

'Hold on the David! Help is on the way!'

Iestyn peered over the top to find David hanging dangerously on to a huge branch of a nearby tree. His feet almost dangled into the swirling muddy waters of the river below.

'Go quickly, get help!' Iestyn shouted to his two boys. 'I'll try to reach him if I can.'

The boys ran off, terrified they were of the consequences should their father fail.

Anna arrived on the scene just in time to see Iestyn tearing off his coat and trying to unbuckle his leather boots.

She began to scream as she saw her son clinging to the branch below her.

David heard his mother's voice and he began to cry. His body then began to shake with fright which caused the branch to bend beneath his weight.

'Hold on there boy,' shouted Iestyn as he balanced on the parapet. He climbed the narrow wall and descended on the other side, his feet barely touching two stones which had also become loose.

He reached out to grasp a stout branch nearby in the hope it would help him to reach the boy's arm and pull him to safety.

'Be careful!' called Anna, feeling so helpless at not being able to do anything to save her son.

Iestyn climbed on to the branch and leaned forward but he was unable to reach him.

'Look up at me David,' he said firmly.

But the boy's eyes were fixed to the swirling waters below.

'Give me your hand. You're nearly there!' he said as he tried to instil the boy with confidence.

At that precise moment several men arrived on the scene followed by the two young boys. Among them was Wil Lewis.

'What is God's name are you doing here?' he shouted at Anna.

Before she could reply, they heard a loud crack, which caused everyone to run to the side of the bridge. The branch, which had borne David's weight, had finally snapped in two sending the boy hurling down into the river below.

Anna screamed,

'Oh, my God! David! No!'

Wil stood there petrified, unable to move as he witnessed what was happening to his grandson. Iestyn still clung to the branch above. He heard Anna's screams and without a thought to himself he jumped into the swirling waters which were by then carrying the boy downstream. What seemed a lifetime had taken place in just a few minutes.

The onlookers ran from the bridge, scurrying along the riverbank as they constantly yelled to Iestyn, urging him onward in his attempt to save the boy.

Wil Lewis ran faster than any man there. His heart pounded at the threat of losing his beloved grandson.

Anna's long skirts dragged in the muddy grass preventing her from catching up with the men who ran ahead of her. As she ran, she prayed constantly for the safety of both her son and the man she loved.

Iestyn, however, could do little other than allow the river to carry him forward until finally he thought he saw David's head as it lifted and sank in the waters ahead of him.

The boy had somehow managed to keep afloat by threshing his arms and legs as the water carried him onward.

With great difficulty Iestyn reached out to grab him taking huge gulps of air before he too sank again in the water.

Luck was on his side as he caught around the boy and began to swim against the current of the river. He swam to the river bank where many pairs of hands waited in turn to haul the boy to safety.

Iestyn felt David's weight lifted above him and knew the boy was safe at last!

Unnoticed to everyone, a large piece of driftwood floated nearby. It was taken up in the swell of the river and before Iestyn could also be helped out of the water it struck him on the forehead. His body became engulfed once more into the swirling waters, which again carried him downstream.

He almost lost consciousness, but in one final effort to save himself he grabbed at the driftwood and clung to it for his life.

The crowd on the riverbank stood there helpless at the scene before them.

Then someone shouted,

'He's heading for the weir. God help him!'

Iestyn forced his head above the water as he was carried along until he heard a noise like thunder in his ears. And it was the last sound he heard as his body was dragged over the tumbling white waters of the weir.

Seconds later, as if by some miracle he opened his eyes. He was lying in calmer waters now and as he heard the sound of voices approach him he knew he was safe.

Several men waded into the deep water and he was conscious of his body being lifted into the air, and taken to safety on the embankment.

Blood ran down his face from a large gash on his forehead. He felt dazed and every limb in his body ached. He shivered with cold as some young men began to take off their coats to cover him. Others praised his bravery as they marvelled at the two lives, which had been spared.

Jethro and Daniel pushed their way through the crowd and ran to their father's side crying with relief to find him alive.

Moments later Anna arrived, determined to find the man who had saved her son from drowning. The man she now loved more than life itself.

As she knelt beside him, she began to cry. He reached out to touch her and whispered,

'Don't cry, I'm alright, Anna.'

'I thought I'd lost you forever Iestyn,' she said.

'And David?' he asked. 'What of him? Is he injured?'

'My father is arranging to take him home and we will send for the doctor as soon as we can. Thanks to you he is alive.'

She took a lace handkerchief from her pocket and held it over the wound on his head.

'I don't want to leave you Iestyn,' she said, her eyes filling with tears.

He caught her hand and held it tightly.

'You must go Anna, your son needs you now.'

'Iestyn,' she began again as she tried so hard to tell him how much she loved him. Words failed her as sadness overtook the feeling she held in her heart.

He lifted his fingers to his lips and kissed them softly, oblivious to the crowd around them.

Then he whispered in her ear.

'Go now Anna, but always remember - I love you!'

She nodded to him sadly, then turning away from the man she loved she disappeared into the crowd.

CHAPTER 30

In the days that followed the accident Anna had little time to think of herself or Iestyn Roberts.

She grew sick with worry over her son whose condition had begun to worsen from day to day. David had survived but he still remained in a state of shock.

Neither food nor drink had hardly passed his lips as he lay there motionless in his bed.

Anna sent for Doctor Pugh again but the news was not good.

'It can go either way, Anna,' he'd said. 'Taking the length of time he was in the water, added to the shock that followed, it's a wonder it hasn't killed him already,' he told her.

From then on Anna hardly left her son's side. In his delirium he began to mutter several words as he thrashed his arms in the air.

He seemed to be struggling once more in the icy waters of the river, tossing and turning in a bed now damp with perspiration.

Doctor Pugh had called again and this time Anna's greatest fear had become a stark reality with the news that David was now suffering from pneumonia.

The house had become silent, and as Anna sat at the bedside she prayed the doctor had been wrong in his diagnosis.

She wrung a wet flannel and held it to her son's fevered brow. Slowly she began to feel that he was about to slip away from her. She had already had to part with her beloved Peter. Surely God would not take her child from her as well?

He had become quiet now; his body was quite still. She could hardly hear him breathe. Not a sound could be heard as Marged had offered to take Kate and little Peter John home with her.

Elizabeth, however, stayed to be at her mother's side, for fear she would be needed.

Beti busied herself around the house as she silently prayed for David to get well again. Other sad thoughts she quickly erased from her mind.

As for Wil, his heart ached for his grandson and he too prayed for his recovery. However, he was so consumed with anger, he continued to lay blame at his daughter's side. What had she been doing with Iestyn Roberts at the time of David's accident? There were times Wil despised her for what had actually happened.

Not a word had passed between father and daughter since that dreadful night when they had returned home, and feelings had become very bitter between them.

As for Iestyn Roberts, Wil had not cared if the man lived or died.

He would have been horrified to learn that both Owen and Morgan had decided to visit Iestyn's farm. They had wanted to show him their gratitude for the child's safety and to offer him their assistance until he got back on his feet again after his injury to his head.

At least they were able to put Anna's mind at rest and she was grateful to know that Iestyn was much improved. Owen was ready to admit that his father had been a fool!

Wil remained unforgiving, blind to the fact that without Iestyn Roberts' immediate reaction, David could well have been drowned that fateful day.

It was early in the afternoon that Elizabeth peered through the bedroom door to find her mother dozing in a chair by the side of the bed.

Her brother David, his face now drained of any colour, looked so serene as he lay there in what they now knew to be a state of semi-consciousness.

She shook her mother's arm gently as she whispered to her.

'This is not good for you Mam. Please go and lie down to rest awhile.'

'I'll just stay a little longer,' said Anna not wanting to leave her son.

Elizabeth could see the dark circles, which had begun to form beneath her mother's tired eyes and so she pleaded again with her.

'I'll call you if you are needed. Trust me,' said the girl again.

Anna knew she should listen to her daughter. Her body ached from sitting for hours in the chair. It would be good to lie down again, even for a little while.

She kissed Elizabeth and as she slowly left the room she thanked God for the extra strength the girl had given her.

As she lay on the bed Anna gathered her strength in an attempt to pray, but her body was exhausted and her mind as empty as a shell. She could fight it no longer and within minutes she fell fast asleep.

It was not long after that she was awakened by the sound of raised voices which when she opened her eyes she realised they came from downstairs.

She jumped from the bed and ran to the landing where she peered down over the stairs. She could see nothing, then she ran back to the bedroom and asked Elizabeth if there was anything wrong.

'There's no change Mam. David is very quiet but I don't know what has happened downstairs. I think Mamgu and Grandpa Wil are having an argument. I didn't want to leave David to find out what it was all about,' said the girl.

'Stay here,' said Anna, 'I'll go and see for myself.'

She went to the top of the stairs where she could hear her mother and father. They were still arguing with each other but this time it was with more subdued tones.

She tip-toed own the stairs feeling guilty as she overheard her father say,

'Damn it all Beti! Am I master in my own house or not? Of course I realise how ill David is. He's my own flesh and blood and God knows we may even lose him yet. I've never forgotten how we lost our Huw.'

All I'm saying is that none of this would have happened if it was not for Anna. She should have kept an eye open for David not attempt to go off with that scoundrel.'

Anna tried to prevent a sob as it escaped from her lips. Her father's accusations had pierced her heart like and arrow.

Then she heard her mother plead with him.

'For God's sake Wil, keep your voice down. Do you want her to hear you?'

Raising his voice slightly again her father replied,

'I don't care if the whole village hears me. She should be ashamed of herself, to put another man's feelings before the lives of her children!'

Through the gap in the doorway Anna could see her father as he banged his fist on the table in anger.

Wil walked toward the door where his daughter had remained hidden and Anna shrank back into the shadows praying that she would not be seen. But it was her mother who took him by the arm and halted him.

'Sit down Wil. Now it's my turn to have my say. I've listened to you long enough,' said Beti.

Anna held her breath, what was her mother about to say? She could see her father as he sat down near the table. His face was serious as he had never heard his wife use such a commanding tone to him before.

For a second there was silence then Beti began.

'Now then Wil Lewis.

The master you may well be in your own home, but I have a right to say my piece also. I've remained silent for far too long, and now the time has come to put you straight on a few matters. If you are looking for someone to blame then it has to be yourself!'

Wil jumped up from where he sat and turned on his wife saying,

'What do you mean Beti? You can't be serious. How am I to blame?'

Beti ignored him and continued,

'It's many a night that I've lain awake, hoping and praying you would come to your senses Wil. Can't you see what you are doing to this family?'

Wil began to interrupt his wife once more but Beti quickly began to silence him.

'You won't be satisfied until you drive Anna away from here with your anger and bitterness. What will you do with the children gone? You'll become a selfish old man with no-one left to love you but me!

Can't you see she loves Iestyn Roberts and it's plain to see he returns her love?'

Wil shook his head in defiance, wanting to shut out the words his wife wanted him to hear.

But Beti continued once more,

'What is more, the man nearly lost his own life trying to save our David. What of his children? Did he think of them when he jumped into the water, and would you have cared if he had left them orphaned? You have been against Anna and Iestyn from the very beginning, and all because you believed that old witch, Martha! Surely Anna deserves some happiness? A happiness you and I can no longer give her?'

Wil looked at his wife and said,

'And what of Peter? She has betrayed his memory!'

In a calm voice Beti began to choose her words carefully,

'I loved Peter Malone as if he were my own son and I miss him now more than ever. But he has gone Wil, and I know in my heart that he would not wish for Anna to grieve for him for the remainder of her life.'

Anna's eyes filled with tears as she heard her mother's words from where she remained hidden. She could not bear to listen to any more and so she turned on her heel and began to climb the stairs slowly.

All at once she began to feel and urge to be near Peter. To hear his voice and see his face. She entered the bedroom and whispered to Elizabeth,

'Is there any change? Has he opened his eyes?'

Her daughter shook her head.

Anna calmed her daughter's fears as to what had taken place downstairs. Then she asked,

'Could you manage here awhile, Elizabeth?'

The girl nodded.

Anna placed a shawl over her shoulders and as she reached the doorway she looked back saying,

'I shan't be long, cariad, but if I'm needed, you'll find me down in the Chapel. There's something I have to do there.'

Elizabeth did not question her mother, knowing that she would have good reason for wanting to go there.

Beti and Wil did not hear their daughter slip quietly through the back door as they were still deep in conversation together.

Rarely had his wife spoken to him in this manner and her aggressiveness had cut Wil to the core.

Could she be right he asked himself?

Beti could see the doubt in her husband's mind and so she said,

'If you are not prepared to see reason then I'm afraid you will have lost all. No-one can help you Wil, least of all me. You have to decide to come to terms with yourself, then maybe you'll know how to finally keep this family joined together.'

Wil placed his head in his hands. There was no turning back now. He lifted his eyes to her and quietly said,

'What you have said is the truth. I realise now how wrong I've been. But it was for love of Anna and the children that I have become the way I am. I have been selfish for my own ends. Can it be too late to make amends Beti? Will she forgive me?' he asked.

'Go to her Wil. Tell her how you feel, then you shall know,' said Beti as she gently kissed him on his forehead.

Silently, she began to thank God for finally showing her the way to her husband's heart.

CHAPTER 31

Anna knelt by the graveside and as she brushed away a few fallen leaves she whispered,

'If only you had lived, Peter, we could have been so happy together, you and I. My love for you will never fade but can you understand how lonely life has become for me? Could you forgive me if I came to love another, and have I done so wrong that God will take our little boy away from me? Am I to lose him as well as you?'

Her only answer was the sound of the wind as it brushed through the trees which surrounded her.

Suddenly, the sun appeared from behind a cloud, adding its warmth to the chilly autumn air. She lifted herself up and felt compelled to walk toward the Chapel door which had always remained locked.

Anna grasped the large cast iron handle and turned it. The door opened and she stepped inside the porch. Cold air surrounded her causing her body to shiver and she began to clutch her shawl tightly around her shoulders.

She went inside the Chapel and walked to the pew she had always shared with Peter. There she sat down.

If only these walls could speak she thought to herself as she gazed around in silence. She lifted her eyes to the pulpit where she knew the large black leather bible lay in its place. Then she knelt down and bowed her head in prayer saying,

'Dear Lord, if I have sinned I beg you to forgive me. Please let my son live and show me the way forward so that I may believe in myself again.'

A shaft of light suddenly burst through the window and came to rest directly on the seat beside her. Immediately Anna began to feel an inner peace as if all her cares and worries were about to disappear.

Tears fell from her eyes as she began to weep. When at last she could cry no more, she sat in the silence of the Chapel. She had become exhausted but at last her body and soul felt free from all their anxieties.

Then she heard someone calling to her. It sounded like Elizabeth's voice.

'Are you in there, Mam?' she called.

'Yes, I'm here, cariad,' answered Anna.

Elizabeth entered the Chapel and ran down the aisle to her mother's side.

Anna's eyes began to scan her daughter's face. What had brought her here? Had David's condition worsened she thought?

Immediately she began to regret having left her son's side.

Elizabeth saw her mother's anxious look and dispelled her fears saying,

'Don't worry Mam. David is fine! It's a miracle! He's opened his eyes and he's asking for you. What's more, he says he's hungry. Mamgu has already fed him with a little soup. Hurry now, he's waiting for you!'

Anna hugged her daughter tightly. She knew her prayers had finally been answered. Her little boy's life had been spared.

As she followed Elizabeth out into the sunlight, Anna knew at last where her destiny lay. And as she walked away from Elim Chapel she did not look back.

It was time now to find Iestyn and begin their new life together.